Phoenix

IRISH SHORT STORIES 1997

Phoenix IRISH SHORT STORIES 1997

edited by David Marcus

PHOENIX HOUSE
London

First published in Great Britain in 1997 by
Phoenix House, Orion House
5 Upper St Martin's Lane
London WC2H 9EA

A CIP catalogue record for this book is available from the British Library

Typeset at The Spartan Press Ltd, Lymington, Hants

Printed and bound in Great Britain by Clays Ltd, St Ives plc

ACKNOWLEDGEMENTS

'The Walking Saint', Copyright © Michael Collins, 1996, first appeared in *The Feminists Go Swimming*, published by Phoenix House, and is reprinted by permission of the author and A. P. Watt Ltd.

'Eel', Copyright © John Dunne, 1996, first appeared in *The Sunday Tribune*, 'New Irish Writing', and is reprinted by permission of the author.

'The Angel of Ruin', Copyright © Mike McCormack, 1996, first appeared in *Getting It in the Head*, published by Jonathan Cape, and is reprinted by permission of the author.

The following stories have not previously been published: 'Fortune-Teller', Copyright © Sheila Barrett, 1996; 'Writing Cookbooks', Copyright © Maxim Crowley, 1996; 'Tierra del Fuego', Copyright © Leo Cullen, 1996; 'Transplants', Copyright © Anthony Glavin, 1996; 'Boat', Copyright © Sheila Gorman, 1996; 'The Ginger Rogers Sermon', Copyright © Claire Keegan, 1996; 'The Jack Darcy', Copyright © Bryan MacMahon, 1996, is published by permission of the author and A. P. Watt Ltd; 'Heaven Lies About Us', Copyright © Eugene McCabe, 1996, is published by permission of the author and A. P. Watt Ltd; 'As Kingfishers Catch Fire', Copyright © Colum McCann, 1996; 'Peddling Air', Copyright © Peter McNiff, 1996; 'A Door in Holborn', Copyright © Padraig Rooney, 1996, is published by permission of the author and A. M. Heath and Company Ltd; 'The Last Laugh', Copyright © Dermot Ryan, 1996; 'The Letter', Copyright © Una Woods, 1996.

CONTENTS

INTRODUCTION

How long is a piece of string? Or, to put the question in context, how long is a short story? The opening chapter of most how-to books on writing short stories can usually be relied on to air this topic, but I ask the question only to highlight the fact that the stories in the following pages run from under two thousand words to over ten thousand.

It is true that even in the heyday of the genre's popularity, a story of the latter length would have had little or no chance – in these islands anyway – of finding a home outside the pages of a collection by a single author or of an anthology. That is hardly surprising and cannot fairly give rise to complaint, but what has happened at the other end of the scale is a major worry.

In recent decades there has been inexorable pressure on the length of those stories for which editors in the print media are willing to provide any platform at all, and that only very occasionally. Most of the time the short story is treated merely as a once-a-year guest, provided it is wearing traditional Christmas attire. Radio, in both Ireland and Britain, is a consistent and valued supporter, but one could wish that producers would more often increase the iron ration of the fifteen-minute time slot, which only allows approximately a meagre 2,200 words. If a listener is sufficiently interested for that long, why should it be supposed that he or she will switch off if presented with something longer? After all, the thirty-minute play is a regular and popular feature, so why not a regular thirty-minute story? And precious though space is to print editors, it is surely worth finding out whether, within reason as to frequency and length, a good short story wouldn't be at least as welcome to readers as many of the repetitive, played-out theme articles diurnally favoured. The short story has served Irish literature well. It deserves the air and space to take more than just a few short breaths.

Which brings me back to the question, how long is a short story? The answer, as far as *Phoenix: Irish Short Stories* is concerned, is: as long, within reason, as it needs.

DAVID MARCUS

ANTHONY GLAVIN

Transplants

I knew Fintan was a piece of work the day I hired him. 'There's no bowling team?' he jokes as I hand him a pair of coveralls off a nail in the garage. Maybe it was a case of one spider knows another – both of us Irish. Only compared to Fintan, I'm definitely more the garden variety kind. 'No team unless you start one,' I tell him. 'You start meantime at seven tomorrow.'

He shows up at seven too, which itself is unusual for Irish. Not that anybody, Italian or Portuguese, is much better these days. The Greek kid I fired was always late, but Evangelis was probably on Chinese time anyhow, crazy about karate. It so happens the coloured guy Fintan had me hire shows up on time, but Lionel comes later in the story.

It's slow that first morning, even at the pumps, and by noon I lose sight of Fintan. Just when I'm figuring him for a half-day wonder, I spy him in a corner of the lot, picking up trash from the overgrown grass. Now I garden myself at home, but that patch of weeds and dog shit is so hopeless I don't even police it. 'Any money is mine,' I say when he finishes, only to hear him ask have I a grass hook?

He was the same way about the rest room, as I shortly discover. 'What are you using on the toilet bowl?' I enquire, barely recognizing it. 'Coca-Cola,' he tells me. 'I'll buy some Ajax,' I say, 'so you won't be out of pocket.' 'Not to worry, Mickey,' he says. 'I was buying them out of the till.'

Mention of the till makes me worry, but I get some Ajax

anyhow, and pretty soon Fintan has the place so you can eat off the floor. Which leads to our first tug-of-war. 'If I leave it unlocked,' I explain, 'every bum off the street'll be in there.'

'Bums need a toilet too, Mickey,' he laughs. 'And if it's clean, they keep it so.' The door stays locked, but Fintan opens it for any derelict, most of whom, I admit, admire its tidiness. 'I could clean my razor in the urinal,' one guy marvels, making me wonder if I'm running a garage or a hotel.

Our location in Central Square, five blocks down from City Hospital, and midway between O'Brien's and the Shamrock Inn, ensures a certain class of foot traffic at all hours. Winos, junkies and loony tunes, we get them all. Meanwhile Maggie and I still live the other side of Mass Ave, down in Cambridge-port, and I still walk to work each morning. The Square has run down of late, which usually means the developers can't be far behind, only this time I think they've gone bust too. Anyhow, the Port is still lovely in spring: the odd magnolia in bloom, forsythia coming on, tiny maple seedlings where the sidewalk has cracked. There are even elms yet along Western Ave, great lofty trees under which these three tall, skinny, coloured guys sit in lawn chairs each morning early. 'Rice farmers from Haiti,' Fintan informs me when I remark on them. 'One of them now runs the numbers for the Haitians,' he says, however he knows this stuff.

Fintan himself is about ten years in America. From Donegal, he worked a few years in a garage there before emigrating. I left Dublin myself around that age, though at nearly sixty I must have thirty years on him. There weren't many cars in places like Donegal when I departed Ireland, but it happens Fintan is an ace mechanic, even trouble-shoots the electronic stuff in the newer models which I don't touch. 'People nowadays are driving appliances,' I tell Fintan. 'Toasters, not cars.'

It's nice having another Irish around, somebody who understands just how different the States are. 'You could live on what's thrown out over here,' Fintan says, and he's right, of course. Forty years here and I'm still amazed at what people discard. Trash day is the best, with seventy-dollar shoes or freshly ironed trousers in rubbish bins at the kerb. Fintan has fairly furnished his rented room that way, and I ask him to look out for storm windows for the small greenhouse I'm building at home.

'What drives me mad,' he says another day, 'is how people here insist on happiness.'

'Have a nice day!' I jeer, but he has the bit in his mouth by now.

'Happiness is only the premature profit on imminent pain,' he quotes some Irish poet, whatever that fellow was smoking.

'You should garden,' I tell him, but Fintan says he coped enough spuds growing up in Donegal to last a lifetime.

Anyhow, he's good with customers as well as cars, especially, like I said, the non-paying kind. A couple of older dipsos en route to the City Hospital detox floor now occasionally stop by to sing 'Danny Boy' or 'Kevin Barry' for us. 'St Mary's is two blocks down,' I tell him, 'you want to lead a choir.' Fintan tells me his mother used to write, 'Do you ever miss Mass, son?' 'Truth is,' he laughs, 'I don't miss it a bit!'

Word travels of course, and soon we're a port of call for any number of tramp steamers. Before long Fintan has names for most: the Philosopher is this skinny alkie who's always staring into space, while Mario Andretti has a wheelchair he moves by shuffling his feet along the road. My favourite is Father Flanagan with the stubble and dirty collar who pretends to be collecting for some charity. Fintan gives him a buck and the next day he's back, mumbling the same pitch. 'Father, I gave yesterday!' Fintan laughs. 'Oh yes, thanks very much, God bless,' the padre mutters, moving off.

'They're like stray cats,' I tell him. 'Feed 'em, and twenty-four hours later they're back.'

'Cats eat too,' responds Fintan. Yet it beats television all to hell, like the afternoon this floozy and her boyfriend stagger past the garage, thumbing a lift. Amazingly a car stops, only to have your woman pass out spread-eagled on the hood, her pal doing a drunken stumble dance beside her. The driver blows his horn, then shouts out the window, 'If you want a ride, get off the fucking hood!' Another time Mario Andretti overturns his wheelchair out front. 'Hold on.' Fintan stops Lionel from going to his rescue. 'He'll get attention now,' Fintan says, 'plus money.' Sure enough, a couple of pedestrians give him both.

I wouldn't wonder Fintan takes an occasional dollar from the till for a hand-out, but I don't bother much with Mass any more, so I figure it's only what I'd be putting in the collection basket. I draw the line, however, at leaving our loaner unlocked in case one of his Apostles needs a place to kip at night. It seems in Donegal they often found somebody asleep in their loaner, who couldn't quite make it home from the pub. 'At least they *had* homes to go to,' I point out to Fintan.

As it is, we do an occasional tune-up for this guy with some kind of muscular ailment who actually lives in his 1969 Plymouth. The car is a rat's nest of tins, newspapers and blankets, and reeks of piss besides. I can't get near it, but it doesn't take a feather out of Fintan. 'I don't have an address,' the guy says when Fintan goes to write up a bill. 'How about Plymouth Inn?' Fintan cracks, causing Lionel to just shake his head.

Lionel, as I said, got hired thanks to Fintan. A few coloured have always come in, but not many, which I'll admit suited me just fine. Most usually show up first thing mornings, after cruising all night. They don't get out during a tune-up either, just sit in the car sharing a beer or a joint. Anyhow, one week Fintan mentions this coloured mechanic he knows, and how hiring him would be good for business. It happens we're short-handed, Evangelis having left for a career in kung fu, but I couldn't see hiring a coloured. Or 'black', as Fintan, who'd teach his grandmother to suck eggs, keeps informing me. He keeps at me too, until I finally agree to take the fellow on part-time. Lionel looks like an ageing middleweight, shaved head and all, but it turns out he's good under the hood, and honest far as I can gauge. What's more, we begin to pump some gas for those neighbourhood brothers who drive to work instead of cruising Mass Ave all night.

To be honest, Lionel is easier to figure than Fintan, who I sometimes think has some furniture missing. 'Imagine being a pond skater,' he says one morning. 'Surface tension, not gravity, would rule your life!'

'What's a pond skater when it's at home?' I enquire, struggling with the rusted water pump on a '77 Nova.

'A bug that walks on water.' Fintan hands me the proper wrench. Later that afternoon I'm admiring this classy MG pulled up at the pumps. 'Nice as it is,' Fintan tells me, 'it's hardly a substitute for coming to know yourself.'

'Piss off!' I reply, in case he's taking the mickey out of me. In fact it's hard to draw a bead on him at all. Some days he's in foul humour, a real antichrist, the next morning all sunshine, dispensing alms to the poor. I doubt he sleeps much, judging from the yarns about the whores and hustlers in the Hayes Bickford on Boylston Street, where he often sits up half the night drinking coffee. Sometimes I get the feeling he's perpetually ahead of himself, leaning against the garage on a slow afternoon like he was waiting to become a mechanic again.

July comes, and if there's a smell of ripe garbage in the alleys, at least there's sun in summer, unlike bloody Ireland. The sumac trees throw their saw-toothed shadows, and at home the cat crouches on a chair by the kitchen window, waiting for a breeze. One morning at the garage I arrive to find all hell has broken loose. 'Mrs Kelly is waiting for you,' Fintan warns me as I pass the pumps. 'She finally caught on?' I ask, spying husband Paddy slumped in the passenger seat of their Ford. 'Aye, she caught on all right,' Fintan laughs.

I don't know how long we'd run that scam, all in aid of providing her poor husband with a little beer money. 'Charge her for a quart of oil whenever we fill up,' Paddy had requested, 'and I'll collect the money off you inside.'

'You son of a bitch,' Mrs Kelly shouts at me in the office. 'Charging me two dollars every week,' her face flushed, 'for an empty can of oil.' I hadn't the heart to tell her different, though it cost me a steady customer. Afterwards Fintan tells of an uncle in Donegal who ate only brown eggs. It proved no bother to his aunt, until the day the uncle found her boiling a white egg in a pan of tea.

'Marriage is like a military campaign,' I explain.

'You and Maggie aren't so bad,' Fintan says.

'When you're gardening, you're not fighting.'

'You can't garden in winter.'

'So I do a few chores Saturdays. Sundays I go down the basement where I've an easy chair and have a couple of drinks. When the wife comes home from Mass, I bang on the pipes with a hammer once or twice so she thinks I'm working. When I come up for the dinner, she looks at me and says, "You've had a couple?" "I had a couple," I tell her. "Just enough to keep the rust off." '

Fintan had a girlfriend when he started at the garage, but I gather she gave up on him. A nice girl from Mayo, she came by once for a fill-up. 'She said I was a high-maintenance boyfriend,' Fintan tells me with a puzzled laugh. I noticed Maggie took to him quick when he came over for a Sunday dinner, but that's kind of her way, given we never managed to have any kids. Yet there's something about Fintan that makes women want to do for him, because Mrs Lynch, his landlady, is the same, wanting to fix him bag lunches and such. What they miss, I think, is Fintan's at heart a man's man – as most of us are. Which is not to say he was particularly crude or anything. 'I couldn't get fucked with a fistful of fifties,' I heard him tell Lionel after he started drinking on the job, but that was the booze, not Fintan, talking.

It began then in August to go wrong for him. Fintan always kept a bottle in the back room for any Apostle in a bad way, but now he begins to hit it himself. 'You're going to end up in O'Brien's,' I warn him, 'watching *Candlepins for Cash*.'

'Just enough to keep the rust off,' he replies. Later, two kids come by looking for used spark plugs – to make hash pipes, would you believe. 'Fuck off,' Fintan tells them, which is – while not bad advice – not his usual style. I notice the toilet isn't so clean any more either.

Even days now when he's cheery, there's an edge to it – as if his engine were racing or something. 'They're going to bury you in that Caddy,' he tells this customer so fat he can hardly walk, and both Lionel and I hold our breath until the guy decides to laugh. Something is clearly out of whack, but people, unlike cars, don't have timing belts you can adjust, or little red lights like a washing machine, indicating an overload.

One afternoon, pumping gas, I hear this bellowing in the

garage bay. Inside I find Mario Andretti seven feet up on the lift, cursing a blue streak, while Fintan pokes a grease gun underneath his wheelchair. 'Get him the Christ down,' I yell, 'before he falls and breaks his goddamn neck.'

'Not to worry, Mickey,' Fintan says. 'I locked his wheels before I took him up.'

'You're pushing it,' I reply, as Fintan hits the air handle which lowers Mario, wheelchair and all. Mario is shook up, whatever about the bottle in his lap, his tongue moving back and forth like a windshield wiper.

'No drinking and driving,' Fintan admonishes as Mario wheels off, but it doesn't strike anybody as funny. Watering my tomatoes that night, however, I concede a stunt like that at least differs from the indifference most of us feel for the Marios we encounter.

A month later Fintan disappears. It's early October, and a few bums sit mornings in the laundromat on Prospect Street, soaking up the heat from the dryers. One Monday I arrive to find a note from Fintan in the till, saying he'll be back in a few weeks. There's also some forty dollars missing, but I owe him that much easy for overtime; besides, money is definitely not what Fintan's about.

That afternoon Lionel tells me of some credit card scam Fintan was on to. It seems you pay this party in the billing office fifty bucks, who then tears up your charge slip. 'Fintan was going to fly to Bermuda that way,' Lionel explains. I say nothing, though I doubt Fintan owns any plastic to begin with.

Over the next weeks I wonder if he'll be there as I walk to work. There's a real sting in the air now, too sharp for the Haitians, who have deserted their elms. I puzzle that displacement – from rice fields to city streets is even more of a stretch than from Dublin or Donegal to here. Transplanting is tricky, which is maybe why I was always trying to get Fintan to garden. As if by putting in a few vegetables, he might also put down a few roots. Whenever I pull weeds at home, I hear my father cursing the slugs in our tiny Dublin garden.

Lionel still believes Fintan's basking on a Bermuda beach, but I worry he's more likely sleeping rough over a hot air vent. Not many Apostles call in any more, though Mario Andretti drove by yesterday on metal rims, the tyres gone off his wheelchair. He looked even grubbier than usual, unshaven, with a threaded lump on his brow. From what Fintan told me, Mario lives in a plywood box between two tenements down in Riverside, however he manages in the dead of winter. It's a funny thing, but I'm now actually noticing the derelicts throughout Central Square, like these two winos slumped yesterday against Libby's Liquors on Mass Ave, as if beached by a receding tide. I'm also seeing the other transplants I've taken for granted over forty years, stopping today to stare at three Chinese on a bench by Magazine Street, the eldest cutting the others' hair.

The other funny thing is Lionel and me. He's full-time now, and working me hard to take on his cousin too. Of course Fintan had a cock-eyed theory here, also. 'There's a nod you give in Donegal,' he explained, 'just a wee twist of the head to whoever you meet. I've done it for years here, Mickey, and blacks are the only ones who ever read it.'

'Soul brothers,' I mock, but Fintan insisted there was something to it. 'Secret signals, Mickey. One spider knows another.'

Anyhow, Lionel and I sometimes have a beer after work in this bar on River Street, where there's maybe one or two other white guys besides myself. It's there I finally learn about the bowling team thing.

'Fintan was living someplace like Arizona,' Lionel says, the coloured barlights reflecting off his shaved head. 'He had a job with this huge diesel outfit, lived in an apartment complex with a pool and closetful of clothes.'

'How'd he mess that up?' I ask. 'Boozing?'

'Hell, no,' Lionel laughs. 'Crazy dude thought it *was* messed up!'

'I don't follow,' I say.

'Fintan said the whole set-up just freaked him out. So one day he pushes his car off a cliff, throws his clothes after it, plus a brand-new bowling ball.'

'Puzzle me that?' I say.

'Go figure,' says Lionel.

Walking home through the slush on Pearl Street, I wonder might Fintan return come spring? At heart, however, I know he was more likely an annual than a perennial. Or, better yet, a garden escape – like the fuchsia, first planted at Irish big houses, that now grows wild everywhere.

SHEILA GORMAN

Boat

The solitary woman in the small boat doesn't know how far she is from land or even if there is land. The sky is hidden by heavy grey cloud which seems to touch the top of her head. Cloud and water seem to merge and seal the space around the boat.

A clear sky will reveal infinite space over the boat. Then, in still air, the flat expanse of water, stretching in every direction, is too much to bear. Nothing can be seen.

Feeling it is important to know the depth of the water, she lowers one of the oars over the side to see if she can touch the bottom with the tip of its blade. No luck. Later she lowers a lead weight. After paying out over a thousand yards of fishing line the weight is still sinking. She rewinds the line carefully, regretting her knowledge of the depth.

'Never go out in a boat on your own.'

No land is visible. Is it hidden by fog or mist? Perhaps it is too distant to be seen. No land maybe. The fog could lift.

'Never stand up in a boat.'

The oars creak as she dips them heavily in and out of the water on either side of the boat. Her hands struggle to grip the shafts of the oars. Her hands ache. The space between her thumb and her fingers isn't wide enough.

'Never go out in a boat alone.'

Occasionally in calm weather sounds would carry across the water. Laughter, a dog's bark or even the quiet chat of distant people might be heard. Could that be the chink of bottles or ice in a glass? The voices could be reassuring as they might signal land. Or imagination.

Closing her eyes, she stops rowing, too exhausted to go any further. She drifts. There is only the possibility of hearing the voices when she isn't rowing. The sound of the oars masks the voices. Or does the talk stop when she rows?

She remembers other voices. The muffled rumblings heard under the bedclothes while reading by torchlight. Supposed to be asleep. A gap in the sound might mean one of them was coming upstairs to see if she was asleep. Straining to be sure to catch the sounds of a door closing downstairs or steps on the landing. She might be caught. Reading under the sheets by the round beam of the torch. Supposed to be asleep.

The sound of indistinct conversation downstairs was a regular event. Laughter, the clink of glasses and ice. The nightly ritual of blue-tinged gin. The spirit swirling around the ice. Sounds of safety and comfort.

On holiday, in the small caravan, the sounds had been louder. Only a curtain had divided the sleeping children from their parents. Even the sight of an occasional earwig on the roof above her head couldn't disturb the comfort of the voices. Talk of the day's fishing, the trout or salmon caught or almost caught. What pools might be tried tomorrow. The sounds of gin being poured, the fizz of the tonic. The clink of the ice if there was any. The warmth of the green sleeping bag. The ritual of the voices.

'Never swim towards the shore if you capsize, always stay with the boat.'

Pulling hard on the oars, she begins to row again, trying to maintain a rhythm.

When she was too small to reach both oars she just used one. Her father took the other. They sat comfortably side by side and rowed slowly. With two hands she tried to lift the heavy oar out of the water, to lean forward and turn the oar so that the blade dropped cleanly into the passing water. Often she would drop it too soon and cause an ugly splash or be pulled by the moving oar. Her father rowed gently to match her strength.

Being out in the middle of the lake with her father was a special treat. He might row. She might troll a line behind the boat with little chance of catching a fish but plenty of hope. It was so quiet out there at the end of the day, especially when they drifted. The water lapped against the sides of the grey boat, the gentle swish-swash swish-swash of his dryfly line cast in the direction of a rising trout. The quiet mechanical screech as more line was pulled from the reel to try to reach the growing circle of ripples which marked the fish's jump. Tired after playing all day, she watched and listened, often glimpsing the bottom as it seemed to move beneath the ribbed boat.

The voices which came across the grey water from the distant shore then were familiar. Her cousins. Her brother and sister. Her mother. All getting ready to go home. The voices louder than the distance.

Other times, other boats. Other boats rowing through the past. Other voices drifting across in the gap between mist and grey water. Laughter and the clink of glasses. But maybe no ice. Probably slices of lemon in a fluted screw-topped jar.

Coming back towards the land, her father rowed. Gauging the decreasing depth before jumping to shore, she leaped, not wanting to get her feet wet. They pulled the boat up above the water line.

All the children were sent off collecting twigs for the volcano kettle. Her father made the fire to boil water for the tea. Tea leaves in another jar with a fluted top. Heat the aluminium teapot first. Old pink and yellow hand-knitted tea cosy with brown stains at the spout end. Familiar voices. Familiar faces. Every childhood summer Sunday. Every comfort for a secure summer ritual.

Not so now. She pulls fiercely on the oars. Alone in a boat. No land visible. Maybe no land. Limitless space above, beneath and around. There is only the lapping of the water against the side of the wooden boat.

Are there mountains? Does the water end at the foot of huge cliffs? Surrounding the water and confirming its depth. Defining the boundary between water and land. Is there a sloping shore? If she could only see into the distance she might know.

'Never stand up in a boat.'

If she could see into the distance she might know which direction to aim for. What is the point of knowing how to navigate if she doesn't know which shore she wants or even if there is a shore?

At first she had heard the sounds of distant voices carrying over the water. Now no voice sounds. No sound. Nothing.

She can see no land. No shore. An occasional seagull can be heard when the clouds are low. Once she thought she could hear their wings. Even when the cloud lifts, she sees no birds. When the mist comes down very low and hangs parallel to the surface of the water she thinks she can hear splashes. Perhaps birds are diving for fish or fish are jumping. She doesn't see anything. She never sees anything. Do the birds exist? Are they hidden? Is she imagining them? Is the sound a trick of some sort? A test to be passed or failed. Would failure mean death? Would success mean land? She hears the birds again. Crying. Invisible. Unseen.

'Never swim from a boat, you'll overturn it getting back in.'

More voices. The sound travels in between the lines of mist and calm water. One soft line. One hard line. The voices laugh.

Are they laughing at her alone in the boat? Does she look ridiculous adrift, unknowingly close to land?

A ship could appear on the distant horizon, could pass without noticing – but she never sees one. Solitary. Rowing. Quiet. Drifting. Sometimes following a current. Alone in the mist.

'Never stand up in a boat.'

She stands up in the boat and gives a great shout which spreads itself over the water, filling the gap. She throws off her clothes and feels the misty air against her skin. She perches for a second on the side of the boat to overturn it, and falls into the water as it capsizes. The water feels good against her skin.

She swims away from the boat.

DERMOT RYAN

The Last Laugh

The last days of my father were like something out of a horror film. He didn't die bawling, and they tell me for that at least I should be grateful; and they may have a point. But I think myself that it would have been better for him by far to go with a big human roar, like the big man that he was, rather than to slip away into the dark with his brain stewed in painkillers.

He lived in the house where he and Mam had brought me up, down near the Park, and though I had moved away years ago to live with Miriam, and Mam was dead, I used to see him almost every Tuesday. I used to drive around in the van during my lunch break.

He was always a man for the bottle, and what harm was there in that I'd normally say, but it was getting bad by then. He was depressed, you see, despite all my efforts to cheer him up. He didn't whinge or carp. His was a silent sadness, and he faced it alone. I never tried to stop him drinking; I never allowed him to be treated as the child or myself to be the father over him. He was Dad, and while I mightn't believe any more that he always knew best, I still was sure that I didn't know any better than he did how to make him happy, or how to stop him going mad.

On that, my last visit, he gave me the first drink out of the bottle, as usual. He must have known that I couldn't drink that and then in good conscience get back behind the wheel and go to work, but I didn't ever say anything. He didn't need me lecturing him, and it would be awkward to have him drinking on his own, so I sat there wetting my lips with his hooch, but never as much as taking a sip. When he turned to watch the telly, which was always on, I would pour it into the pot of his asparagus fern. It may have been my imagination, but I could swear that fern was starting to turn amber. He might look at the telly – or through it – for fifteen minutes at a time and then return to have a chat with me. And around an hour after I'd arrived, I'd go upstairs to the toilet before returning to work, and, under cover of the noise of the flushing, I'd go over to the hot press and slip a tenner into a pair of his trousers. He can't have thought for a minute that he absent-mindedly left exactly ten quid in exactly the same pocket of a pair of trousers every week, but we kept up the pretence and we never mentioned it. That's how it was.

On this visit, we were saying nothing for a lot of the time. Sometimes he was all gaiety and light, and we would have a grand chat, and we would laugh, but other times it was more like this. I wish we had talked about Mam, and Rachel and Aisling, my sisters in America and London, and what we were like as kids, and how it was going to be great to have them back home at Christmas, and the time we all went on the ferry to Holyhead (we never thought about you coming back on the same boat to see Dad die, did we, Aisling?), and how I broke the front window once and got no pocket money for over three months, and how he gave Rachel a few wallops for ratting on me, and anything else, anything at all, anything that might have brought us back over forty years for one last look together. But we said nothing much, and let the telly fill the silence.

He looked grand that day, I suppose – well enough anyway for his age (and he was a good bit older than you'd expect, considering I was the eldest at thirty-three; he had married at forty-four). Even so, he was bald and wore a big thick set of glasses that made his eyes ogle around inside them. The years had made him thick-set and hunched, and he had a big paunch we all used to twit him about, but he looked as if he was resigned to it all. I swear I never heard him complain about being old, even though his breath was short and he had to use an inhaler, and his hip was fucked and he had to walk with a stick, and he had a weal on his leg that the nurse had to come round for. I wish I'd never slagged him about his belly.

He didn't seem happy or sad on that last visit. The days must have been getting indistinguishable for him: the hooch, the telly, and the lit fire and dinner in the evening. He always made the dinner himself. Once I offered to come round and make it for him as a treat, and he just looked at me as if I'd offered to poke him in the eye with a darning needle.

'The moment I give in and let others do the work for me,' he said, 'is the moment I open the door to the nursing home. I'll make my own dinner, thanks all the same.'

He said all that without a trace of anger, though. It was said with the airy tone of a philosophical statement. He may have drunk a lot and watched too much telly and you might think that made him a weak old pisspot, but you'd do no different, stuck inside all day with no one to talk to. He staked out his independence, and what he did inside that was his business, and not that of me or you or the nurse or anyone; and whatever compromise he reached with himself was not up for comment either. He knew as well as anyone ever does what was needed to stay sane.

There was some soap opera on that last afternoon, as we sat there with our glasses full of whiskey. It was total crap: all toothy tanned men and big-breasted tanned hysterical women having hysterical affairs. Sitting behind the telly on their shelves were all his many books – paperbacks, hardbacks, travel, adventure, comedy, how-to manuals, encyclopaedias, anything and everything. He had always been a real bookworm – I picked up the habit from him myself – but his eyes were too bad to read much now, and he was reduced to watching this muck instead.

He turned slowly from the telly and said very quietly to me: 'This is the worst hour of the day, I think. I can take the mornings and the evenings, but this time is hard. I'm glad you came round, son. Some days it's very bad now. I'm glad you came round.'

I didn't respond to this as I'd have wished. I was just on the point of tipping my whiskey into the fern pot when he spoke, and so I pretended to be inspecting the plant, like a bleeding gardener.

'Very healthy, Dad, this fern. Very hearty. Good foliage.'

He gave me the boldest roguish grin and turned back to the telly. He knew all right. I'm fairly sure of that, now I think about it. He was a smart one. I rose.

'Dad, can I make myself a *cupán tae?*'

He waved me to go ahead.

'Do you want one while I'm at it?'

'I wouldn't mind, son.'

Do you notice the way I asked did he want a cup of tea? Oh, we had our games, Dad and me, our little nods and winks. It was fine that we both knew we were playing as long as we never admitted anything, and never swapped roles. You can be very happy, play-acting. Ask any child.

As I left the room, the news had started, and Mother Teresa was on the screen. Dad was muttering something about a prune in a gabardine. He was fairly cynical about saints on Earth. He didn't like the Pope of the time that much either. I worry about that sometimes, and I wonder whether God was hard on him when he got to heaven for that one. Mind you, I can also picture God throwing a warm arm around Dad's shoulders and saying, 'Don't worry about it, Brendan. I thought he was a gobshite too.' God sees everything. He's bound to have noticed.

I never heard a thing while I was in the kitchen. I was watching the crows bullying the sparrows for crusts of bread out the back, and whistling to myself, waiting for the kettle; and when it bubbled up to the boil, I made a big pot – with leaves, since Dad hated bags – took down his favourite mug, the one Rachel had brought him back from Boston, took one for myself, picked up a packet of biscuits, put the lot on a tray, and walked back to the sitting room. I found him slumped on the floor.

I cried out and tossed the tray on to the table and spilled tea all over the place, and some of the delph smashed off the wall. Dad! I knelt over him and nudged him.

'Dad . . . Dad . . . ' I shook him firmly. 'Dad . . . Dad! Dad!' I shook him but he said nothing. His eyes were open, he was breathing in gasps and he looked horrified.

The ambulance came shortly after.

'Mr Connolly?'

I took my head out of my hands at the sound of that, and I looked up. A tall, thin young doctor with a ginger pencil moustache stood above me. 'Yes?'

'Mr Connolly, I'm Dr Sheridan. I'm looking after your father. I think we should talk.' He motioned me to follow him. We walked outside, and stood by a fountain in the middle of a little lawn. He offered me a cigarette and I took it, and we both lit up. The fountain lapped peacefully under the grey skies. I could see nothing but the fountain. I couldn't bring myself to look around, as if I was afraid of seeing my father's ghost there. The fountain was a modern-looking one, very sparely carved, with the water rising from a simple hole in the middle. It was better than the fountain one of our mad neighbours round the corner had behind the railings of his front garden. His one was in the shape of Cupid standing on a birdbath having a piss. It took up the entire tiny front garden, and it had a sign beside it saying DO NOT THROW COINS IN THE FOUNTAIN. So we usually fecked a few coins in on our way past. Maybe that's what he wanted. It was probably a little gold mine for him.

I was thinking this rubbish, and I was concentrating on that lapping sound as if my life depended on it. I felt sick and hollow inside, as if I'd woken from the worst drinking binge of my life. I heard the doctor's voice only faintly, but eventually I turned my face to him and listened to his crisp, nasal sermon.

'Mr Connolly, your father is, fortunately, in a stable condition. However, he has suffered two strokes: one at home, and the other, larger one, on his way to the hospital.'

I nodded dumbly. Yes, of course, strokes, two of them. How samply delaightful. He's alive anyway.

'He is paralysed down most of the left side of his body, and his face is partially paralysed also. He is not responding to external stimuli very much at all. When you see him, you may find it disturbing, and he may not recognize you, but I assure you he is in no pain. We have given him some drugs to relax him and make him comfortable. And I must reassure you, his condition is stable. We are keeping him under close surveillance, and we will be able to respond immediately if there is any change in his condition. He is very lucky to be alive.'

He is in his hole lucky to be alive, I thought to myself, but I didn't say that to the young doctor. At times like this, I just say the first things that come into my head, regardless of whether they are what I want to say. So I said: 'What exactly happens in a stroke?' though of course I knew the answer was: your father gets fucked up, and then he dies.

'This stroke was a cerebral—' He stopped and smiled, and began again. The ponce thought I didn't know what cerebral meant, just because I have a bit of an accent on me. 'In this case, the stroke was a brain haemorrhage. One of the vessels in or on the surface of the brain bursts, due usually to a combination of factors, such as a blood clot or high blood pressure, and this results in damage to the tissues of the brain. Often this leads to paralysis, at the very least. In your father's case, he has suffered two strokes, the first of which was probably quite minor, the second of which was very large.'

'Does he have long?' I asked quietly. I was feeling very low now, and I just wanted to go home to Miriam. I couldn't do anything for Dad. He was on his own.

The doctor was silent for a while. 'Maybe,' he said thoughtfully. 'Maybe. It's remarkable that he survived that second stroke. Even now, he has some mobility. He's an extremely strong man. I wouldn't raise my hopes, though. I doubt his condition will improve much.' He shrugged. 'I'm sorry.'

He meant it, I think. He must say I'm sorry twice a day to weeping relatives, and he still manages at least to sound as if he means it. In spite of the hollow despair that was carving its way through me, I screwed a generous smile to my face and shook hands with him.

I got home to Miriam less than an hour after that, and she was worried and sympathetic – I'd rung her from the hospital, so she knew what had befallen Dad – and she was talking and talking, but I had no heart for anything but going to bed and wrapping myself up in a deep, forgetful sleep. She was saying that we had to ring my sisters, and I agreed, but said I wouldn't do it, no, no, that I couldn't do it right now. So she did it, God bless her, and I went to bed.

Up in the room, I heard snippets of the phone conversations: 'Yes . . . all right . . . listen . . . bad news . . . after having a stroke . . . yes . . . no . . . alive . . . stable, yes, he's OK for the moment . . . ' And then the whole rigmarole all over again for Rachel. She must have got Rachel at work, because there's a time difference of . . . I didn't give a curse what time difference there was.

I shivered as I undressed, and when I looked at myself naked in the mirror, I don't think I had ever looked so frail and old. There was some emotion needed to be expressed, but I wasn't able to. When I could put a name on it, maybe I would understand, but just then, that night, I did not understand what creature of passion was plaintively calling out within me. Oh, my father.

Miriam found me curled up under the blankets, with a look as black as doom on my face.

'They're upset. Rachel was crying; she's going to come over as soon as she can get a flight. I think Aisling's already on the way to the boat.'

So my sisters were coming over. I didn't know why, but my inner creature groaned under a new weight. I didn't understand what was happening. Something was sapping me from the inside or crushing me from the outside.

Miriam got in beside me. She was cold and I flinched, but I flinched, I think, from a bit more than the cold. I felt disgusted with myself inside. I felt like an empty husk now, waiting for the wind to push me away, or for some outside pressure to screw me up into a litttle ball. I had never felt so low before. Miriam slept with her arms around me, but I didn't sleep at all that night. Despite the warmth coming off her, and even though she is as dear to me and as much part of me as my own pulse, nothing could take away my pangs of loneliness.

I was awake when the grey dawn came. As the darkness rolled back, I went to the bathroom and opened the main window, and I stood in the cold, half in the nip, taking in the cool, damp, heavy smell of morning that was rising off the grassy gardens. They spread out below, rectangular, side by side, back to back. In one a long way off, I could see a black-and-white cat prowling along a wall. The world's eyes were open by just a suspicion. I stood there for a long while, though I was cold. The sparrows had begun to sing. They were like sad buglers at the death of the heavy night. Dad . . .

I rang work the next day and explained what had happened. I went back to the hospital. I had to take the bus, because the van was to be picked up by one of the young lads, who was going to fill in for me. I arrived, and I asked to see Mr Connolly. The nurse consented, and led me down those twisting shiny corridors that echo all the way. There were some kids running about, pretending to shoot each other, and the nurse patted the head of one of them as she passed.

'They're lovely kids, aren't they?'

'Yeah. Fantastic.'

All that was said automatically; I was trying not to think too much. I was sweating buckets, and thinking rapidly but aimlessly about this and that, about Aisling coming over and staying in the house, and how I should go back to Dad's house, because the tea would have soaked into the table by now, and for Christ's sake, could they not think of a more cheerful colour scheme for the corridors than fag-filter brown, and – I was in front of the open door to his ward. I looked in nervously.

White. A television. Flowers. Beds. They're always the same.

He was sat up in the bed, propped up with pillows at his back. His glasses were on, but slightly crooked on his nose. He did not move at all when I entered. He wore a nightshirt that was as blue as bread mould. Blue for a boy, I suppose. It was hideous.

'Hello, Dad,' I said cautiously. No response. Not a suggestion of movement. He stayed still and flint-faced. It was like a joke, and any moment he'd crack and start laughing in his old way.

'How are you, Dad? OK?' Nothing. A shiver ran down my back, and my hair was half-standing on end. It was so damn weird to have Dad sitting there like a statue, as if he was in a snot with me and ignoring me.

'Can I touch him? Can I hold his hand?' I asked the nurse. She sniffed, but nodded.

'Go ahead,' she said frostily. 'But don't move suddenly or shock him.'

No, I'll jump up and hit him with a mallet, you feeble-witted bint.

'Dad . . . ' I approached slowly, great tenderness in my voice. Nothing. I slipped my hand into his. To my surprise, his hand closed around mine. I nearly jumped in the air.

'Do you see that! He's holding my hand!'

The nurse walked over to take a look. 'It could be just a reflex. Please, Mr Connolly, don't raise your hopes too much. Your father is very sick.'

I didn't listen. I sat down at the bedside and held his hand, and I was full of desperate anticipation, because I had half-convinced myself already that he was going to be all right. An hour later, I admitted to myself that the grip of his hand on mine had not even a trace of intimacy to it. It was, just as the nurse said, a reflex.

I went outside for a fag, and I was in a grim mood now.

'Do you think you could at least put him in a decent nightshirt?' I asked the nurse irritably on the way out.

Aisling came rushing up to me while I was pulling on my second cigarette and scuffing my shoes off the gravel. Miriam followed close behind. Aisling gave me a big hug and I held her very closely.

'How is he?' she said hoarsely.

I looked at Miriam for guidance. She looked away helplessly.

'Come in and see for yourself,' I said finally. 'It isn't good,' I added.

Aisling was the youngest of the three children, and the one Dad was fondest of. Her long birth had killed Mam, and I often wondered whether he loved her more because she was the last link with Mam. When she went to London, he was heartbroken. Not that you'd know by his lamenting, because there wasn't any, but during the fortnight after, whenever some small irritation should cross him, the swearing out of him would light candles. And even as I smiled at that memory, I heard another sigh of passion from the poor persecuted creature inside me. The world was heavy upon me.

'Can I hug him?' she asked the nurse.

'No,' the nurse replied, like the stupid cow she was. 'He mustn't be excited.'

Aisling sat beside him for two hours, whispering gently to him as he sat there graven-faced and unresponding. She tried so hard, God love her, but there was no getting through to him. If he heard and understood, he could not show it, for he would never play with Aisling in this way. He loved her more than anyone since Mam died, God rest her; he loved her almost as if she was the memory of her mother, and she did look like her. Aisling tried for two hours at least, chatting quietly and seriously about I don't know what. For over two hours she tried, as the nurses came and went, tending to other patients, as the two televisions passed from one news broadcast to the next (hello again, Mother Theresa), as the end of visiting hours drew near; and at the end of it, there had not been one change in the expression on his face, not one flicker of emotion or interest.

That was the end of his second day of paralysis.

When we got outside, with our coats and our serious faces on, Miriam said tearfully, 'Your one is a *pill*!'

'The nurse? Oh yeah. A total battle wagon.'

Then Aisling broke down in tears, and it was only because I was trying so hard that I did not join her. I felt a sharp twitch of pain as my passion's creature slapped his despairing hand against the wall of my heart.

The next day was as bad. The sun set without us seeing any sign that Dad was a cut above the vegetables. And we were there for his lunch, and we had to see – we should have left, we really should have – his big stupid mouth virtually being opened for him and him being spoon-fed. We were twice as depressed going home that night as the night before, and Aisling and Miriam both went to bed early and left me sitting in the kitchen until the dark night and common sense told me to go to bed.

I pulled up a chair for another unsuccessful vigil.

'Hello, Dad. Another day, another dollar.' I squeezed his hand. I nodded at the nurse. 'If your one is giving you trouble, give me the nod and I'll burst her. I'm half in the mood to do it already,' I whispered.

I sized him up. Nothing different today. I talked softly to him for fifteen minutes or so, but I gave up. It was probably enough to be here. One of the girls could do the chatting when they came in. They were better at it.

The horse chestnut outside the window was just beginning to spread its fingery leaves, and the flowery candles were coming out. The wasteground behind the hospital was dotted heavily with dandelion flowers, which were golden in the morning sun. I had seen shepherd's purse bursting through the pavement on the way in this morning, and there were a few birds returned from the winter that morning that I had not seen since last year. He loved this time of year. I hoped he was aware of it. I would have loved to take him out to the country. Put a good set of clothes on him, put him on the 65. First really sunny day of the spring. He'd love it. I don't think the Wicked Witch of the North would be on for it though. I looked in the window's reflection for her, but instead I saw a far more welcome face.

'Hello, Peter. I got here as soon as I could.'

I got up and embraced her, and pressed a kiss on her forehead. 'Hello, Rachel.'

'Hello, Dad,' she said, going over and giving him a kiss.

'Don't expect much, love,' I warned her.

'I won't, don't worry, the other two warned me.'

'Other two?'

'Aisling and Miriam. They're on their way now.'

And so they were. We all sat around the bed for a few hours. Normally if we all got together after an absence of any time at all, we'd be chatting away like ninety, but we were all kept sober by that big, silent presence in the bed. We just talked quietly among ourselves, and coaxed Dad to join in.

And it was after those few hours, and us just about to go and get lunch, that something amazing happened. Rachel was pulling her purse out of her handbag, when her handkerchief came with it, and wrapped up in the handkerchief was a spray-bottle of amber perfume, which tumbled out on to the bedspread. A wide dentureless smile opened across Dad's face. There was a barking sound as our four chairs jumped half a foot back. He was smiling! He was looking at the little bottle and smiling! And so was I, because I knew why. The old devil thought it was a bottle of whiskey!

When we went down to the canteen, all the talk was of the smile and what it meant and how Rachel was a lucky charm. Herself and Aisling did a little dance in the corridor. They couldn't hold their joy in.

'Did you see! Did you see!'

'I did! I did!'

And this frail hope had woken something in all of us. No one dared to say it, but we must all have been thinking it: he's on the mend. I was thinking it anyway, but I was trying not to, out of a childish belief that I sometimes still felt, that if you wished for something too hard or wanted it too much it wouldn't happen. It was difficult to decide what this new development meant exactly. We were too blinded by the little flicker of light in all that darkness.

In the evening, he did not smile again, and we went home a bit more sobered, but still hopeful. But the next day there was no crumb of comfort for us. Dad made not the slightest move but for the little rise and fall of his breathing chest. It was a disaster. He would not or could not smile or talk for us or do anything for us.

'Did they feed you well today, Dad?'

'Anything on the box, Daddy?'

'Do you want anything from downstairs, Dad? I'm just going down to buy the paper.'

A waste of time. Nothing. Whatever magic was there

yesterday was gone. He wouldn't have blinked if we'd waved a barrel of Jameson's finest and a straw in front of him. And when we got outside again at the end of the day, after hours of trying to sweet-talk a brick wall, and Aisling buried herself into my shoulder sobbing again, and Rachel looked off grimly into the distance, I was enraged. Was this to go on forever? I was not going to take this, Dad giving up like this, transferring all his burdens to me, slipping down the rungs of his life into a silent childhood, and ratcheting me up to replace him. I would not be the head of his household! That was his job. It was his shoulder should be wet with Aisling's tears! It always had been before. The creature shook the bars of my heart like an ape.

I knew all of a sudden what he was groaning about. The roles were being reversed, and I was going to play Dad, and he was going to play baby. I was there before Dad, like an adult before a child. Was he looking out through the windows of his dismal prison at my strength and youth and was he mourning, now that the compromise we had kept up for so long had been broken, and what we knew deep down would happen had happened? Would we pamper this helpless baby until he died? I shook quietly with a terrible anger.

'Listen, Miriam, Aisling, Rachel, go on home now.'

Aisling shook her head, but I insisted.

'Go on, please, I want to be alone with Dad for a while. Please, love, I need it.'

They went reluctantly. I waited till they boarded the bus outside the gates, and then I went back in to sort out this mess.

The nurse was still there, thumbing through the charts on the clipboard from the end of his bed.

'Mr Connolly, visitor hours are over. This isn't a private ward.'

'Please,' I coaxed her, 'just a minute, I won't be more than a minute. I just need a minute, that's all, one minute.'

She sighed and nodded stiffly. 'One minute.'

Thank you, your majesty.

When the nurse went out, I got straight to telling Dad some truths as I saw them. I kept my voice down so nobody would overhear me and stop me.

'You've had your joke, Dad. Nobody's laughing. You might as well cut it out.'

Not a stir out of him, the bastard. I poked him in the ribs with my finger, hard.

'Come on, you dosser. Snap out of it. I've got more to do than this, you baby. Just stop feeling sorry for yourself. Get yourself up now out of bed, and we'll go home. Come on!'

I gave him another poke in the ribs. He did nothing, just sagged a bit as if he was stuffed with straw. It seemed obscene all of a sudden to be talking to him like this, but I was bulling and I wasn't going to leave it at that.

I ground my teeth, and balled and unballed my fists. I caught my eye on his water jug. I picked it up. It was cool and hard and round. It would make an awful mess of his head if I swung it into it. That was unthinkable. I was looking at the jug with wide eyes and wondering did I have the guts to do it, to put him out of his misery, just as you would for a horse with a broken back.

I swung it slowly in front of his eyes. No response.

'See this, baba?'

I held it over the side of the bed and made a big show of dropping it straight on the ground.

He didn't jump at the sound. And now I could hear the nurse pattering her way back up the corridor. I gave him one last poke in the ribs.

'Steady on!' said some patient in one of the other beds.

I looked around. The other patients were gawking at me with their senile faces.

'Mr Connolly! What has happened here?'

I looked at her as if she was stupid, which she definitely was as far as I was concerned. I pointed at the glass and the water.

'I broke the jug. Of course. I know, I know, visitor hours are over. I'm going.'

She was speechless. I pressed five quid into her hand as I left. 'For the jug,' I explained.

Before I walked out, I looked back at Dad, and I swear to heaven, I was on the point of tears, because I couldn't see Dad, just that stuffed animal that looked like him. I would never see Dad again, just this vegetable. I should have broken the jug over his head, I thought, and sent him properly on his way, because it was killing me to see him like this. And if he was thinking at all straight inside that jail his body had become, he'd want me to do it.

I went home, and I hardly spoke to Miriam at all over dinner. God forgive me for being such a bastard to everyone, especially poor Dad, that day.

'It's not the end of the world, you know,' said Rachel, the voice of reason, 'and tomorrow we'll be in there again, and we'll talk to him again, and maybe we'll get a squeak out of him.'

And I nodded silently. But I did not feel any way hopeful. I went out for a walk with the dog, who had been jumping up and down like a flea in anticipation.

I nearly always cheer up when I walk the dog, because I want to laugh he looks so ridiculous. He was one of those toy dogs. I called him Hamster. Miriam, and it was her dog, called him John, which is a stupid name for a towser. Dogs are called Spot and Caesar and Spike. Presidents and labourers alike can be called John, but not dogs. He was a funny-looking little yoke. His little legs swung like the clappers of four little bells when he walked.

I walked up the green ways, and the day being warm, even as the sun set, I walked up to the hill to watch the day close. From the top, the terraces glinted in the sandy light. Hamster sat down with a miniature grunt and put its undersized head on its paws.

The kids were cycling and walking home, carrying footballs, and hurleys and tennis rackets. Some of them were clopping along on cocoa cans, with a loop of long string in their hands holding the cans to their feet. Why do we do that as kids? It definitely doesn't make you walk any faster, and I can't think of how you could believe it made you look cool.

But where do the years go? It wasn't yesterday that I was on my bike on the way home, and Aisling was tottering along on cocoa cans after me. Any of these snot-nosed kids could be me, but none of them was. This was me, this auld fella, up on the hill with his bonsai dog, and a wife waiting for him at home. And God knows, maybe a few chisellers of my own soon, for it would have to be soon or it would be never.

The sun had clipped the horizon and sunk out of view. It was dark. Hamster pawed me and whimpered. As I rose to go, I saw a big raft of clouds, very very high up in the sky, suddenly blaze with red light very vividly against the dark sky. That was it. My heart sank: the light's sudden reappearance did not mean the sun was returning, about to march over the horizon for the first western dawn of history. Dad would not recover.

Miriam found me in front of the television, picking randomly through the stations. I had sat through four hourly news round-ups (Mother Teresa must be on her world tour), and now it was four in the morning. Miriam appeared like Hamlet's ghost in the doorway, holding her dressing gown closed and squinting in the light.

'I thought it was a bunch of careful burglars.'

'Hm?'

'I thought it was a bunch of careful burglars, checking the video before robbing it.'

We both laughed. She sat on the arm of the chair and ruffled my hair with her fingers.

'What's wrong, lovie?'

'He's finished, you know that?'

She looked at the screen. 'Clinton? Oh yeah. He's fucked.'

'No, Dad.'

'Brendan? He's OK. He hasn't got any worse. There's nothing you can do, love, anyway.'

'He's going to die.'

'How do you know that?'

'Oh, I saw a sign in the sky tonight.'

'Advertising what?'

We both laughed and went to bed, but nothing could have improved my mood. I couldn't stop thinking. He hated being helpless at all. Once he'd been in bed for a week with his leg, and he'd nearly lost the head altogether. Was it like that now? Was he screaming inside his body, like a prisoner in a dungeon, begging me to send him on his way?

The next morning was overcast and blustery. The sisters and Miriam went in as usual, but I could not bear it, and so I strayed into the city centre. He was finished anyway, so there was no reason to go in and visit him. And he didn't notice when you were there, so there was no point in being there. And it didn't seem to help him at all, so there was no point in trying to help him. And he was a selfish bastard, dying on us like this, and it would do him no harm to stew in his own juice for a while, so there was no reason to feel sorry for him. And, and, and, and. So I was thinking, tramping my way around town, doing and seeing nothing much. I walked up streets and around squares and through the greens and past shops and cinemas, and I saw none of them. I was panting at the end of those hours of walking, but not loudly enough to drown the hopeless wailing of my creature inside.

I stopped off in Moore Street to buy an apple, because all that walking had given me a thirst, even though the day itself was grey and cool, and I wasn't going to drink any of that sugary gut-rot they sell in the shops. Dad never let us drink that shite when we were kids, and he was dead right.

'The weather's changeable, wouldn't you say?' said the stallkeeper.

'You said it.'

'A pity after yesterday.'

'Shocking.'

'Yesterday was probably our summer.'

'Ah, stop the lights. You're probably right.'

'Jasus, we've had it all the past few months. Rain, hail, sleet, fog. All we need to top it off now is a shower of shit.'

'Don't be talking. You're right, of course.'

A very young woman was eyeing up the oranges in the stall next door. She looked delighted with herself. Her face shone as she walked off with her purchase. It's a great gift to take joy in the simple things of life, and a gift I had lost. But it's easier when you're young. And I envied her that extra bit of youth she had over me, because it meant that so many avenues of life were still open to her, ones that had closed for me. And so many more had closed for Dad. I walked along, crunching the apple like a hated item between my teeth.

I thought of how round and smooth and cool the water jug had been before I let it fall. Could I really have done his head in? Was I capable? And would it have been an act of love or hate? It cut me up to see him helpless. But would I have done it? It would be a relief for him, wouldn't it, to be spared all the suffering of loneliness and incapacity. And it would be a relief for all of us too. We could mourn him properly when he was good and in the ground, and we could all go back to work. But if he wasn't aware of it at all? All the better; I would not be hurting him, and at the same time I would be free of all the worry. With hardly a further thought, I started off for the hospital.

So that was my plan, or at least I tried to convince myself it was. I wouldn't have done it, even had the circumstances allowed me, but brewing up this plan made me angry enough to go in and confront him again. I wasn't thinking logically. I was letting all my anger steer me, and I was giving it vent in my imagination. I wouldn't have cracked open his poor, helpless old head, and not just because they would all brand me a murderer, which would be right, but because to kill my old man would be taking away what was his, and not mine, and that would make him less than a child, and me more than a parent.

They were all there. They were seated around the bed. Dad was stock still. Big surprise. Nothing had changed. The nurse was smouldering over in the corner like damp wood.

'I hope we won't have a repeat of yesterday's ructions,' she said dourly.

'Hello, Florence. No, no. I'll behave.'

'I know you will. This time you won't be left in here on your own.'

'Thank you for saving me from myself.'

I pulled up a chair. 'Hello, girls. Hello, Dad.'

'What was she on about?' hissed Aisling.

'Oh, I was making a nuisance of myself yesterday. Anything out of Chuckles today?'

'Peter, don't talk about your father like that.'

'I bet you've hardly been able to draw breath, and him cracking jokes all over the place.'

'Peter—'

'I had a grand chat with him last night. He's such a sociable old bollocks.'

'Peter! Stop it now!' Aisling was scarlet. 'Stop it, please.'

'I love coming in here. Do you know why? I'll tell you. For the *craic*. He is such good *craic*! Mad as a bag of hammers! Sometimes I think I'm going to die of joy in here.'

Face-ache had come over.

'Mr Connolly, keep your voice down. You're upsetting the other patients.'

A flock of blue rinses stared over.

'Hello, lovies,' I trilled.

'Mr Connolly, leave the room and don't come back until you've calmed down!'

'Listen, gorgeous, I thought I asked you to change his nightshirt. He looks like a stiff in that gruesome colour,' I snarled.

'Peter, what's wrong with you? Will you quit!'

'I'll tell you what's bleeding wrong with me. Will you all stop this stupid pretence that he's all right! He's fucked, OK? He's never going to talk again! He's given up. He's going to die on us, and never another word exchanged. HE'S FUCKED!'

'Son.'

'What?' I snapped.

'Peter.'

Dead silence. Every mouth was open. The voice was tiny, but it was his!

His eyes had swum over to the edges of the lenses and stayed fixed on me, looking agonized and as sad as eyes could ever have in this world. I knew then, with sudden horror, how he had felt during the week of silence.

He leant forward a tiny bit of the way and sighed a big, loud, rusty-sounding sigh. There were words hidden there. I leant closer and bent down.

' . . . I want . . . I want a pee . . . ' was all he managed to say. I looked at him. It didn't then but it does strike me now as funny that that was the first thing he'd said in days, and not 'Son, I love you', or something that they'd say in the movies. Life is never like the movies, is it?

I appealed to the nurse. 'He wants to go to the toilet.'

She started to drag the curtains around the bed with a clatter and a shush.

'What are you doing?' I asked. She finished her circuit of the bed briskly, and put on one of those breezy voices that you use for children.

'We don't want the others looking at Mr Connolly going about his business, now do we?' she cooed. His business! Listen to her!

'What! Do you mean he's using a . . . a pan?'

'Of course he is. He's not mobile enough to—'

Right! I pulled the covers off Dad. I'd give her mobile, the wench. I put my hands under his armpits and heaved him up out of the bed. For probably the first time ever, I had some idea how to make him happy. A flicker passed over his face.

'Mr Connolly! Please! He isn't well!'

I turned on her. 'My father,' I informed her, pointing a stern finger, 'is not a baby. He can use the jacks like anyone else.' I was straining, with my shoulder propping up Dad by the armpit. That flicker went across his face again. Oh love, I had never felt stronger.

With me shored up against him, we started our slow and awkward hobble to the end of the room. Good man, Dad, good man! was all I could think, as one foot made its palsied way in front of the other. Good man, good man! The nurse was bleating something beside us, but she was just a distant irritation, like a fly in a quiet room in summer. Good man, Dad, it's not far. But it was probably a marathon for him, slow and hesitant, and dulled from the chemicals they gave him. But we were making it.

'Well done, boys, well done!' cried one of the old ladies from her bed as if she was at a Curragh race meeting. We said nothing, but grimly walked on. He was getting wet with sweat now. I thought for a moment when his clammy leg hit off mine that he'd pissed himself, like a baby, and I nearly cried, which I was nearly doing anyway. Sweat was springing off me too. He was a big man.

Ten more steps, Dad, nine more, oh good man yourself! Good man!

Two orderlies came skidding into the room and the nurse said something to them, and they made a move forward to take Dad off me, but do you think I would let them? I gave them a filthy look, and they stood there and watched, and they kept a good distance. Three, Dad, two, one, oh good man!

I heaved him into the room, and I lowered him carefully on to the seat, and he had his leak, while I panted to myself. I was a bit wet around the eyes, and the shapes through the distorted glass of the window were all grey and fat. I turned to him when he had finished. I think he managed a wink at me. I think he did. Oh Dad! The tears were pushing up under my lids now. Oh love!

I lifted him carefully and dragged him over to the wash-hand basin. The whole rigmarole, Dad, we'll leave out nothing, you're not finished yet, we know that, you're a man. We'll prove it to the lot of them.

I will remember the next moment until I come to die myself. For the first time that grim day, the knot of grey clouds that had barred the sun parted, and a warming shower of golden light fell through the hammered glass of the window and struck Dad in that pukey shirt, and illuminated the water pooled in his palms, so it looked as if he had caught the light. His eyes were never so blue as they were with that light on them. He looked at the sparkling water in his hands, and for the last time in his life he managed a tiny chuckle of quiet triumph.

And that is why now I shoulder my burdens lightly, why I took his death with fortitude, because that was all I needed: always to remember him that way, held there in his bright, trembling, momentary heaven.

PADRAIG ROONEY

A Door in Holborn

Where the Holborn underpass emerges from the bowels of the city into the light, a host of skittish little Degas dancers stood under the porch of the Church of Christ the Redeemer. They peered with anxious, excited faces at the sky. It was clouded over with great blue and black thunderheads and, just as they had begun to assemble for their Holy Communion photograph, a wind out of nowhere luffed their frocks, the late morning broke with a thunderclap and the heavens opened. The children screamed, holding down their veils and clutching new white missals, and tumbled back through the emerging congregation of parents into the rear of the church.

'Quieten down now, children, it's only a rainstorm,' the curate said. He lined them up again and looked a bit frazzled from the morning's arrangements.

They were to have their photo opportunity and then proceed in an orderly manner along the empty pavements to the primary school. The parish had organized a sherry party for the parents. Now they would have to wait out the rain.

The organ played on under the grumbling thunder and the downpour. The curate chaperoned the children and their parents back up the aisle to the front of the church where there was a passageway ending in some steps to the crypt. The crypt had been converted into a community tea-room.

'Slowly, children, no need to rush, slowly now. Don't push.'

Father Read was a slim, prematurely grey young man who fussed. His voice alternated unconvincingly between care and admonition while his choreographer's wrists flapped above the organdy and taffeta frocks and the miniature suits. He was recently ordained and his cassock was immaculate; there was none of your sloppy Joe about Father Read. Before Mass he'd directed the parents to their pews, handed them their bulletins, and had a nice word for everybody.

'Take your time, Jonathan! There's no rush.'

The congregation was bottlenecked in the aisle and at the side door of the church more waited to come back in. The narrow cobbled alley was a shiny curtain of water.

'It's rather a crush,' Father Read remarked apologetically to a man he'd just knocked against and didn't know. He made a point of getting acquainted with new parishioners. But this newcomer, who had a deep tan (it was May), contented himself with smiling at the curate and shuffled slowly forward.

He had just flown in the night before from a big, dirty Asian city, and was still jet-lagged and feeling the cold (it was the hot season out east). The people he was staying with en route to Ireland had a daughter among the communicants, and he was disconcerted – pleasantly – to find himself inside a church again and to smell, quite different from the monsoon, the heavy downpour of English rain.

He had not been home for a long time and, consequently, had been attentive at Mass. He'd observed the hats, the slinky black dresses of the young mothers, the dull silk paisley ties and lodens of the fathers, and guessed that it was an affluent parish. They were mostly London Irish and his age – early thirties. Because he had been away, and because it was a sort of rite of passage for their children, the parents appeared suddenly much older – which, of course, they were. He noted the marginal changes to the Mass, the perfumes of the women volatile in the warmth near the radiators, and the powder-grey Nikes under the red soutane of the server who had come to the altar late, his blond hair still wet from the comb. In my time, the man thought, you would never get near an altar in shoes like that.

Just as he entered the dark, tightly packed corridor leading to the crypt steps he saw this boy again. The ajar door to the sacristy was directly ahead. In the tawny space beyond, under a flickering votive light suspended from the ceiling, the boy was already halfway out of the soutane, which was up around his head in a calyx, like a giant red rose. The man saw, rapidly, framed in the doorway and with his heart beating furiously, the server's pale tummy, his dishevelled shirt tails, faded blue jeans and the ash-grey Nikes. The light, for the split second, was that of a Dutch painting. There was a spoor of perfume. The boy seemed to sway in front of him as he extricated himself, a scarlet flower with anthers for arms.

Then a marvellous thing happened – a sort of *déjà vu*. The boy quickly unzipped his jeans and tucked in his shirt, neatly and deftly, around white Y-fronts. He zipped up again, studded home, lifted his tousled head unconsciously and, through the doorway, looked straight into the man's eyes. The man and the boy held the look. The boy realized he had been watched intensely and a smile played about his lips.

The man felt himself carried along by the crush. The door, like a property, slid away to his left, and his heart boomed under his suit. Suddenly, his legs were weak under him and he thought he might faint. With the children's excitement in the house that morning and his late rising, he had had no breakfast. At the top of the steps winding down to the crypt, he saw below him the bobbing heads, shode with haircream – the little communion boys mixed in with their fathers, pushing and shoving – and the fine, gauzy veils of the laughing girls. The groined roof of the turning stairwell, like a conch, magnified their excited voices. They seemed to be tumbling, and the old smell of Brylcreem caught in his nostrils. Far off he heard the downpour and, just behind him, the voice of the curate.

'Mind your heads, now, and watch the steps, children. Hold on to the rope.'

He felt himself lifted, the steps were no longer under his feet, and the sound of the rain increased and tingled in his pores. He thought of that slight, playful smile, its familiarity, and knew that he would fall. But just as his legs buckled under him and he sank against a perfume, a fabric, the curate caught him and held him up, and all he remembered afterwards was a crowd of children parting to let them through.

When the man came to he was in the crypt and looking at the blue blur of an extractor fan set high up into the wall. For a moment he thought he was back in his apartment out east (the rustle of the bamboo grove, a gekko lizard watching him on the ceiling), but he was cool and wearing the jacket of his suit. Father Read had loosened his tie and was fanning him with a back issue of *The Far East*. Like a child waking, the man looked round him with wonder and caught the solicitous glances of other faces in the crowded room.

'You're all right now,' the priest was saying. 'You just fainted. I expect it's the crush. Would you like a cup of tea?'

A cup of tea: he still tingled, like after too much sun, and floated in a lag of time. Once, in the Scouts, he had fainted at a jamboree mass and had had to be carried in a fireman's sling. But who had carried him? His cheek was against rough khaki, he could feel a plaque of merit badges and a cold whistle on its lanyard against his bare legs. He had come to, but he played possum: to be carried, to be the carrier, to prolong that. The cool, unburnt grass under an estate tree, a spreading oak, a flotilla of pennanted tents held down by taut guys, the castle on its rise. *Are you all right, Brian?* He sat up in the folding chair and took the cup the priest held out. His hand shook deplorably, the tea slopped, and he placed it on the table. It was a homely situation: the spilled tea, the dutiful priest, the folding chair – the blond pine ones he remembered stacked in the assembly hall of his old school.

'Did you come with somebody? Is there anybody . . . ?'

Just then Lucinda Hogan, breathless with excitement, approached out of a gaggle of girls who were being rearranged and admired in their new frocks. She was followed by her mother.

'It's OK. Thank you. I came with the Hogans.'

Lucinda came skipping over and enquired in the ponderous voice of a seven-year-old:

'Did you faint? You look all white.'

'Are you all right, Brian?' her mother asked. 'Did you knock your head or anything?'

'I'm all right. I'll just have this tea.'

'You look like you've seen a ghost. I told you you should have eaten something.'

'It was the crush, Mrs Hogan,' the priest said. He laid a pale, hirsute hand on the padding of Brian's suit. The priest's solicitude had begun to irritate him and, besides, he was only spoiling Lucinda's day. He drew her to him and hugged her; the crêpe stuff of her dress rustled.

'Where's P.J.?' he asked her mother.

'He's gone for the car. Look, you can come with us if you want. They won't mind. It's only a bit of a sherry party.'

'No, I'll stay here a while and drink this tea. You go on ahead. I'll see you back at the flat – I have the key.'

When they had gone, he drank the strong tea and surveyed

the low-ceilinged room. Framed views of the Danube (Father McElvaney had got them free from Lufthansa) hung on the bare stone walls. The air had a forbidding chill which the animation of the parents and children did not dispel. The Charismatics, under Father Read's supervision, used the tea-room for their Tuesday evening meetings, the A.A. on alternate Thursdays and after ten o'clock Mass on Sunday some of the regulars – pensioners mostly – would hang on for half an hour over a cuppa and watch the altar boys play darts.

He stood to test his feet, got another cup of tea and a KitKat, and carefully negotiated his way back through the restless children to his table. Two mothers beside him were discussing Italian communion frocks.

'The quality's so much better. The Quinns had one flown in from Milan. You know the Quinns? He's with Alitalia so he got it duty-free. Two hundred pounds they spent on it – and half of London living under cardboard!'

'I've just signed up our Caroline for ballet class,' the other woman said. 'She has to get pumps. It's one thing after another.'

Then, just as he thought he might brave the rain as far as the Charing Cross Road, and the whole of London, like a drenched bird, ruffled its feathers before his mind's eye, he heard a woman call out from across the room.

'Brian! Brian Byrne!'

It was a shrill voice and his first instinct was to ignore it. But she approached through the throng and stood a yard off, surveying him with her big kohl-rimmed eyes.

'Barney Byrne?' she enquired, and then, mock-offended, rolling her eyes, 'You don't recognize me.'

'Trish.'

He said her name low and didn't say anything more. It was

enough. A whole world slid back into place, intact, as though it had never gone, and he watched it with the detachment of his thickening years, bored with his own manner – a coldness cultivated to the point of mannerism. Coming back would always be this: compensating for time and age with small histrionics in hastily chosen cafés, pubs they had outgrown, a digest of success and failure between tea and the prospect of dinner. They hugged and Brian was smothered in the ozone of all the slightly vulgar sprays and powders that he remembered her using. He held her tight, felt her sob and, relenting, his own eyes watered.

When they sat down again they were in a mess and had attracted attention.

'What are *you* doing here?' she asked accusingly. 'Don't tell me you have a . . . !' She pulled up her thought, laughed lightly – the family trait he had heard through two generations like the signature tune of an old series, revived, dusted down for a new audience – and put on her actressy voice, her career before she had got married. 'Of course not, you filthy man.' When she smiled there were new lines the kohl – her bedizened nod to the generation coming up – only accentuated.

'I came with friends.'

She was crying again, dabbing at her cheeks. She shoved him away from her and said, with the cracked smile that comes through tears:

'Oh, go away and get me something to drink. I suppose it's cocoa.' The whites of her eyes were like shelled quails' eggs and they terrified him. Their imploring look had layers of history in it. The long strand fronting the summer houses their families took at Nairn, in Donegal. *Wait for me, Barney!* In the corridor outside the *céilí* at Rannafast, over-made-up even then, the hormones zinging through them, as Justin used to say: *Dance with me, ask me out to dance the next reel.*

The children had graduated to potato crisps and were inventing games among themselves. The older ones clustered round the Space Invaders and its blips punctuated the chatter. Theirs was the newer, stronger bonding in this inner-city parish. Fathers were glancing under the cuffs of their lodens and watching the rain. Beyond the half-circle windows set into the arches of the roof it hopped off the pavement. He smelled Brylcreem again, it was to be the day's revenant, and the breath that comes off a child who has been eating crisps. He looked down at two eyes taking him in.

'My mummy says no sugar.'

'And what's your name?'

'Justin Carberry.'

'Justin.'

A thousand reflections swam about in the eyes. He had chocolate stains round the mouth and flakes of crisps on his new jacket. On the lapel a silver medal inlaid with mother-of-pearl lay in a white satin rosette. Brian touched the pleated satin and the cool dangling medal.

'Here, let me tidy you up a bit. You've got crumbs.'

Brian's gestures were talismanic, unconscious, and he was frightened at his own dexterity, at where it came from. He wet his handkerchief with his own spit and, with an index finger in the handkerchief, rubbed at the soft, yielding cheek round the mouth until it was clean. He flipped away the crumbs from the boy's jacket.

'What's *your* name?' the boy asked.

'My name's Brian.'

'Just Brian?'

'Just Brian. Or Barney. My friends call me Barney.'

'Are you a friend of Mummy's?' His forthrightness was prim; a child used to engaging adults.

'An old friend. I'm a friend of your uncle really.'

The boy considered that. The age of reason. His thin neck was strained with looking up and Brian got down on his hunkers beneath the counter.

'Uncle Tony?'

'No, your Uncle Justin. He had the same name as you. But I don't think you'd remember him.'

'He died, didn't he? He died when I was a baby and that's why I have the same name.'

And then Brian knew that he had indeed landed and that the long-haul flight was over. Often, in the previous two days, he had lifted his arms in that gesture of surrender as the metal detectors clicked over keys and coins, the static of living. He was here, in this crypt, among his generation who had all grown up, like big, wound-up dolls whose batteries are beginning to run down. The dampness of the place; the condensation seeping out of its walls; the echoing ramifications. An extractor fan hummed. He passed through the door into an old familiar self.

He sent the boy back to his mother and rose off his hunkers, taking the curate's breath away at the other side of the hatch. Father Read had removed his cassock and was in a grey lambswool cardigan. Brian wondered if he had overheard.

'You're looking much better. That tan is back. You must get a lot of sun out there in the Far East.'

His voice, when he let it go, lilted. Brian realized the priest had been enquiring.

'Yes. It's the hot season now. Way up in the nineties.'

'Oh dear! That *is* hot. No wonder you had that little turn.'

'I've met an old friend.'

'Mrs Carberry? That's always nice to meet up again with old friends. Wonderful boys she has.'

A note of disapproval had crept in. The curate turned, lifted the cosy off the dinged parish tea-pot and poured fresh water into it out of an enormous black kettle. He winced in the steam and with the weight of the kettle, returned, and placed the heavy pot on the counter.

'Two teas, is it? I'll just let that draw a minute.' They both realized that they understood each other perfectly.

While Trish talked, Barney only half-listened to her. She was so used to this that she no longer noticed. She was like a tap with air in it; it either gushed or there was nothing. They had known each other for twenty-five years, since they were her little boy's age, and it didn't matter much. He hadn't seen her since before Justin, her brother, had died – six years before, in London. He had been one of the early Aids victims.

Trish brought Brian belatedly up to date – though he had got the gist in letters – with Justin's last days in a hospice in London. From a naggin of brandy in her handbag – 'these churches are always frozen' – she discreetly topped up their teas. She proceeded to the funeral, skipping preliminaries and niceties, and Brian knew he was getting a distillation, the anecdotal something that grief had made. Trish's gusto tired him, it highlighted a shallowness youth had once excused, and made Brian aware of his own misanthropy. He was also guilty that he had not been there for Justin's last days, and she, shallow or not, had been. She had gone with her children in spring to scatter Justin's ashes in the hills overlooking Florence, Justin's favourite city.

Beside her the little boy listened with wide-open eyes.

'We'd bought a bottle of champagne and some caviare and finally got to the top of this hill overlooking Florence. And we met a couple who were on their honeymoon. Justin – this Justin' – she kissed him on the top of the head – 'was still in nappies, of course, and they were cooing and aahing and then we told them why we were there. You should have seen their faces! God, it was a scream! So Paul, our eldest, he put the urn – it was just a little thing, no bigger than a tea-pot – he put it on this rock and we opened the champagne. It just popped all over the place with the climb and the heat. We were already a bit tipsy, I must admit. And then when we went to scatter the ashes they just blew right back with the breeze into our faces. We were blinded! Paul was spitting. There we were, covered in champagne and Justin's ashes, in stitches!'

The women who had been discussing Italian communion frocks stared at a bend of the Danube with pursed lips.

Trish lowered her voice: Brian realized she had already been drinking before Mass. He remembered the few days he had spent with Justin in Florence – an autumn before college after picking grapes. The summer they were both nineteen. They had cruised the gardens of the Pitti Palace and had had fumbled sex with two runaways in a smelly Renaissance stairwell. The lights were on a timer and every few minutes Brian had pressed the switch to watch his boy, two steps higher, writhe with pleasure. At a further turning, at the edge of the light, he saw Justin spread-eagled under a child, one of the countless angels they had seen that week in frescoes and friezes. The stone steps were cold to the touch, the boy hot. It had been squalid and thoroughly enjoyable.

'Are you still with Concern?' Trish asked.

'No, that's ages ago. I'm with ODP.'

'What's that? It sounds like something to do with drugs.'

'No, it's a refugee thing; Orderly Departures Programme.'

His job was too remote to interest her, and she alluded to his sex life. Trapped by a burnt-out marriage, she wanted to think those who were single were living it up on the wilder shores. Brian disillusioned her with a reticence he had intended to mystify. It turned out that she was separated and was angry that her husband – it was a mixed marriage – had not turned up for the Holy Communion. Brian recognized the battery of self-deprecating little ironies she brought forward to shield herself from failure; he had them himself. But it was not quite failure, more a rallying optimism. Glimpsed fleetingly behind Trish's chiaroscuro (that year the girls all looked like Dracula victims), Brian saw her mother walking the dog (a red setter called Matt) on the strand, making Bloody Marys from left-over tomato juice, waiting up with a library book for her husband to come home from the golf club.

'Isn't this weather awful?'

It had wound down to the weather. They would look out at the marram dunes, under lashing rain, Trish fat in her hot pants, reading *Jackie*, the two boys still in children's summer clothes, rucked shorts, T-shirts with nothing written on them, the year before jeans. In Justin's room the boys would fight. Anything would spark it off. Winning at table football. *Byrne, you're a spa*. Sparring, fisticuffs, then a beast alternately tensed and released, collapsed on the summer coverlet. The tiny black-and-white shots with their scalloped borders, decades later, mottled in the tropics: squinting on the veranda at Nairn, with the *bean an tí* at Rannafast, leaning over the banisters at boarding school. All that time coming out like a snail, only to be crushed.

The rain had stopped and he could hear the storm drains gurgling behind the walls. Trish excused herself, edging past him.

'I'll just put on my party face. Come and have a sherry. I don't think I can face those parents on my own.'

She went to the Ladies. The altar boys had descended from the sacristy and were comparing tips by the dartboard. The boy in the ash-grey Nikes turned round on the chair, which creaked under him, and searched him out. His legs were apart on the rungs. He glanced under lowered eyelids in Brian's direction with that same knowing, familiar smile on his lips. He was pale-skinned and blond like the assembly hall chairs of long ago. The first time they had filed in to them for their pep talk they were in short trousers, and the priest, up on the rostrum, told them to stay away from 'boys who would want to touch you when you were alone':

'Any boy who asks you to do impure acts, just come along and tell any of the deans. Don't be afraid. Remember! The body is the temple of the Holy Spirit.'

Justin, two rows ahead, two decades ago, had looked round then, and smiled in the exact same way. It was the beginning of their complicity.

A draught of cold air came funnelling down the steps from street level. Far off Brian heard the sacristan bang shut the massive doors of the church and throw the bolts. Trish returned, made-up, larger than life. She'd had a last shot of brandy in the toilet.

'Are we all ready then? Where are those boys of mine?'

Justin ran over from the Space Invaders and took her hand. The boy in the Nikes ambled towards them and took the other. He'd clipped back on a small gold earring in the sacristy. For a moment they were a kind of *tondo*, a blue-and-cream bas-relief porcelain by della Robbia. Brian stared at Paul, the elder child.

'Paul's the spitting image of Justin, isn't he?' said Trish.

'Yes,' he said. 'It's uncanny.'

They climbed the steps out of the crypt. The church was dark, smelling of the extinguished candles.

'You go on with the boys,' Trish demurred. 'I'll catch you up.

I'll just say a wee prayer.' She smiled hazily and went off to the tier of candles shimmering at the altar.

They fumbled at the heavy red velvet portière which masked the door, searching for the gap which would take them outside. Behind it there was a small door set into the larger one, and in the darkness, feeling for the handle, Brian caught the closed air of the past and heard at his back the giggling voices of Trish's boys as they played with the portière. His jet lag caught up with him, and a measure of grief, and the lust that travel promotes. He was melting into him, hanging from his arms, this chunky and gangly child. Paul's breath, trapped in the velvet dark, smelled of communion wine. 'You were Uncle Justin's best friend, weren't you?' 'Yes,' Brian whispered, and they kissed once. Brian sensed, but couldn't see, the smile playing on the child's lips like new knowledge, or old knowledge coming round again. He tasted the illicit communion wine from the boy's lips on his own lips. They found the handle and pushed the small door open into the light.

He breathed the cold, scoured air of the city and heard the light Sunday traffic susurrating out of the Holborn underpass at the end of the wet alley. He was glad he was back, in these old, narrow-laned wards. Paul linked his arm, and Justin – conscious of his state of grace – held the other. The morning sun, strong after the rain, cast their shadows along the gleaming cobbles. When they reached the end of the alley, they heard the quick tapping of Trish's heels coming to join them.

Eel

My father always claimed that it was his greyhound who saw them first. He was walking her out the Green Road when – and I quote – all of a sudden she started lepping and bawling like a fecking eejit. Others maintained that it was Mrs Lalor going to Mass, or Seanie Doran coming from the night shift at the mill. Who knows? But by eight o'clock the town was hopping. Where did they come from? Did they wriggle up out of drains, fall off a lorry, get lost looking for the sea? Were they living in the sewers like them alligators in New York? Joe Doyle swore he read it in a book that one time it rained fishes in America. Millions of them.

I heard all this later, but that morning I was in no mood to be worrying about eels. I'd been twisting and turning half the night and when I got up, the kids were like dogs. Normally they're not too bad, but it was like they knew there was something on my mind and had a plan to make it worse. The kitchen was like a pigsty. Cornflakes plastered to the table, blobs of jam on the floor, cups and saucers all over the place. And the six of them racing around screaming for their clothes. She said I was mad to be bringing them at all, but I insisted, so, at exactly ten past eight, I loaded them into the back and off we went.

When I saw the crowd, my first thought was: there must've been an accident.

'Snakes!' one of the kids screamed and, sure enough, slithering across the road was a shoal or a school or whatever you call it of eels. Hundreds of them.

'God, they're horrible, turn back!'

'Will you stop.'

The Guards arrived and tried to move the traffic, but they were at nothing. Men, women and children with sacks, bags, rakes, buckets and shovels, were swarming all over the place. It was like a goldrush. I kept blowing the horn until some smartass gave me the fingers, and she told me not to be making a show of myself in public. She always does that.

A lad I knew to see rode by with a load of them squirming on the carrier. This teenager grabbed one and ran after him, swinging it like a lasso. Joe Bergin's wife was picking them up and, I swear to God, stuffing them straight into her hand-bag.

The kids were delighted, but I was like a lunatic, beating the wheel, roaring at them to shut up. She, of course, flew into me again.

'Look at those eejits running around like mice, and you tell me to control myself.'

'There's no need to shout.'

'Haven't I enough on my mind already? It's easy for you to talk,' and I shot her a look that would've broken glass.

'What do you call a Somali with buck teeth?'

'Joe, that's not nice.'

'What is it, Joe? Whisper.'

'A rake.'

'Joe!'

'Will ye shut up!'

It was half an hour before the traffic eventually got going. By the time we reached Ballybrittas, I had calmed down, but then she went and asked if I was nervous, and I was up to ninety again.

Outside Monasterevin, I began to get nostalgic:

'Do you remember the day we climbed the Rock? You said the gap in the clouds looked like Australia. I tried to lick the sweat from the gap between your breasts.'

'The kids,' she hissed from the corner of her mouth.

'Do you remember? Two virgins foostering—'

'What's a virgin, Daddy?'

'Now look!'

'A holy woman who isn't married. A saint, like Our Lady.'

'But Our Lady was married to Saint Joseph.'

'Will ye shut up!'

'A.T.H.Y. What does that say, Mammy?'

'Athy. It's a town down that way.'

'K.I.L.D.A.N.G.A.N.'

'Kildangan. Another town.'

I decided I'd better stay quiet, but the memories wouldn't go away. She whimpering my name; me trying to think of anything – Cromwell, her mother, the capital of Dubai – to hold myself back. How she laughed when I rolled over, panting, 'Thanks, thanks.' Her disgust when I threw the condom over the edge.

'Remember how you wanted me to climb into the briars after the yoke?'

'What?'

'On the Rock. When I threw the yoke, the Fren—'

'Sshh!'

The first night in Clogher Wood; clothes flying in all directions when another car pulled in behind us. The day we moved into the house and spread cushions on the floor.

Between Kildare and Newbridge, I tried to recall all the times we'd made love. I had to give up after six or seven and that made me feel guilty. You make love to someone you love God knows how many times – two or three, say, in a good week, multiplied by fifty-two multiplied by ten – and all you can remember is a blur. Then I had a vision of Archimedes counting every grain of sand in the universe, and I didn't feel too bad.

When we passed the shopping centre, the racket started up again so, just to shut them up, I promised we'd go in on the way home. I knew I'd hardly be up to traipsing around, but sometimes you'll say anything for a bit of peace and quiet.

'K.I.L.C.O.C.K.'

Jesus.

According to the Chinese philosophy of Taoism, during spring, men should limit themselves to two ejaculations per week, falling to once a week in summer and once every three weeks in autumn. In winter, ejaculation should be avoided as much as possible.

'The diplodocus was the longest.'

'How long was he, Joe?'

'His tail was fourteen metres.'

'Is he extinct?'

Suddenly it dawned on me why I had insisted on bringing them. An unconscious need to prove to myself that I had done my bit for the propagation of the species. They were living proof that I had done my duty. Look, your honour, six of them.

I was a bit shocked by how ordinary the place looked. I'm not sure what I'd expected, but it certainly wasn't a bungalow, a neat lawn with a bird-table in the centre, even a bicycle propped against the wall. Jesus, I thought, imagine having to ride home. If it wasn't for the sign outside, you'd never think it was what it was.

'Is Daddy sick, Mammy?'

'He's a friend of mine from college. I haven't seen him for ages and he invited me up for a chat.'

'Can we go in?'

'No!'

I leaned across and kissed her. They were even more surprised when I patted their heads and, one after the other, caressed their cheeks. I wanted to kiss them too, but I knew the two eldest would tell me to get lost.

Inside was even more of a shock. Seated opposite the door was an old woman clutching a straw bag. Was I in the right place at all? Beside her sat a fellow my own age with a blaze of red hair. I noticed that his knees were knocking. I took a seat next to two others who nodded gravely as I passed. I was in the right place. I knew by the way they were sitting, eyes glued to hands folded on their laps.

'Good morning.'

The chirpy voice made me jump. She beckoned me to her desk and I couldn't believe how natural she was. You'd think I had the 'flu. I suppose it must've been the nerves, but all of a sudden I was bursting for a pee. They talk about actors having perfect timing, but what happened next could never have been scripted.

RECEPTIONIST: Here are your bottles and the envelopes to return them in. It's all explained on the leaflet.

ME: Thanks very much. Where's the toilet, please?

RECEPTIONIST: No, sir, not now! One after sixteen weeks, the other two weeks later. It's all on the leaflet.

I did my best to walk casually to the bathroom. I couldn't resist the temptation, so I checked the door again and had one last look. I had to admit that I'd done a brilliant job with the razor. As I ran my fingers over the unfamiliar smoothness, I saw my mother cleaning out a turkey; heard her knife sawing through the gizzard.

Back in the waiting room, I tried to read the leaflet, but the words wouldn't lie down. I looked up and found three new faces staring back at me. One belonged to a huge bull of a man with a hairy dewlap and trousers hitched above his shanks. What was he doing in this place of subtlety and stealth? I was imagining a fearsome pizzle rampaging through the countryside, a stud-book nailed inside a cottage door, when he smiled timidly and between us passed a warm fraternal glow.

The receptionist called my name – did she have to be so loud? Could she not have given me a number? – and I followed her along the corridor. She knocked on a door and smiled. 'There's no need to be nervous.'

The room reeked of aftershave and I pictured a line of men inching forward, their hands nervous fig-leaves over organs specially manicured for the occasion.

As he gave me the anaesthetic, he chatted about the Grand National. Despite all I'd read about the *vas deferens*, nothing had prepared me for the shock that it seemed to be made of wire. Lying flat on my back, how could I see anything at all? I didn't need to. From the way he gritted his teeth, I could imagine what he was doing to me. With one foot on the couch, he was arched backwards, straining like a docker, pulling my dormant *vas*.

As I scribbled out the cheque, he said I might be sore for a few days, a week at the most. Then he led me to the door, reminded me about the bottles and wished me a safe journey.

One tablespoonful of semen contains the nutritional equivalent of two pieces of steak, ten eggs, six oranges and two lemons.

There was murder in the car. Honest to God, they were

swinging out of each other. Why didn't I have the job done years ago? She told them to be good and looked at me with a concern I hadn't noticed in years.

'How is he?'

'Grand.'

'You're as white as a sheet.'

'The house was freezing. He's lost a bit of weight, but he hasn't changed a bit.'

'You're sure he's all right?'

Why the hell did I bring them? One of the most important days of my life, and there we were gibbering in code. She turned up the radio and, while they bawled along with some pop song, I told her it was no problem, no pain at all, but I'd kill for a cup of coffee.

It took ages to park the car and find a restaurant. In we trooped like the von Trapp family, and by the time I'd finished the third cigarette, I felt, as they say, a stirring in the loins. I hadn't expected the anaesthetic to wear off so quickly, but I lit another and consoled myself by thinking of one two three four four an' a half, the middle of September. I gazed into the future and it was raining condoms – gossamer, featherlight – from the Rock of Dunamase.

We were still twenty miles from Newbridge when they started 'Better value beats them all'.

'Will ye shut up!'

I was all right as long as I could keep the legs apart, but there's only so much space between the accelerator and the clutch. I twisted this way and that, but it was no use; I had to let her drive. I experimented with every sort of posture until I felt comfortable, but Buddha himself couldn't maintain the lotus position in the front seat of a Lada.

When we got there, she wanted me to stay in the car.

'What? Sit here, locked in like an oul' wan, waiting to be brought an ice cream? I'm telling you, I'm grand.'

'But look at the way you're walking.'

I suppose I did look a bit odd, mooching along with my legs spread like a gunfighter, but people are good: they'd think I had some form of handicap. For the first time in my life, women opened doors and stood back to let me enter.

'What's wrong with Daddy?'

'He has a verucca.'

'A what?'

'The stegosaurus walks like that.'

'Will ye stop!'

Vasectomy and shopping. It's not as rare a combination as you might think, for no sooner were we inside than we discovered that I wasn't alone in killing two birds with one stone. Creeping towards us, leaning on the trolley like a walking-frame, was the hairy fellow from the surgery. I was going to offer some sign of recognition – a snip at the price, what? – but we passed each other without as much as a nod. After a few steps, I turned around to find him turned around looking straight at me. Then who came shuffling through the aisles, supported by the old woman, but your man with the red hair.

Is there, I remember wondering, some mystical bond between vasectomy and shopping? An atavistic urge to compensate for something lost by stocking up with food? Is that why eunuchs are always fat? And what about opera singers? God knows, but my abiding image of that afternoon is the three of us shuffling like arthritic Chaplins between the beans and loaves of bread.

As we turned into the Green Road, she remembered that we needed milk for the morning. Coming out of the shop, she stopped suddenly and, though I could hear nothing with the uproar in the back, I knew by the shape of her mouth that she was screaming. I struggled out and followed the direction of her outstretched arm. Draped across the kerb, cut in two by a passing car, lay the remains of a solitary eel.

BRYAN MacMAHON

The Jack Darcy

Every man has his own vision of immortality. With most visionaries it is a secret and consuming desire to be remembered after death. This urge, goad, lure or driving force assumes an intensity of incentive in view of an approaching end to life. Artists, writers, sculptors, inventors, singers, statesmen, scholars, even circus clowns, feeling in their bones and flesh the downward drag of the grave, continue with rueful compulsion to ask themselves the question, 'Will something of mine endure when my body has merged with the clay?'

Old Jack Darcy the angler was dying on his feet. And he knew it. 'I'm a spent salmon,' he would admit aloud to himself – he was half-joking but all in earnest. Each day he found it still more difficult to drag himself out of his bed in the back room of his thatched cottage which stood perched on a height above The Cot in a wide pool in the Feale River.

The old man's approaching end was reflected in the eyes of his gentle-minded granddaughter, Kate, who as the saying goes 'did for him' as best she could. Kate was neat – the gleaming dresser of delph showed her worth. Dull-witted as she was – or so it seemed – she always looked with odd steadfastness at her grandfather, as, seated at the table head, his hands trembling, he crouched over his flies and gear. The girl's eyes then reflected vague but deep concern that the old man would die without achieving whatever was troubling him. This caring concern she indicated at times in unusual ways.

Jack Darcy's goal was not as exalted as that of the soldier, the airman or the designer of a racing automobile. For, as well as being an angler of note, Old Jack claimed to be a flytier – or as he put it, a flydresser – of distinction. 'Before I die,' he kept assuring himself, 'I will tie a fly which will whiten the riverbank with spring salmon.' He was convinced that there had to be such a lure. One which would be irresistible to the running fish. This he knew was the goal of flydressers and anglers on rivers in Scotland, Norway, Sweden, Iceland, Canada and Ireland. All believed that there had to be one wonder fly that would never fail to quell the intuitive suspicion of the silver kings of the river. One which the fish would be compelled to notice and then hurrah! to snap at and be hooked, played and netted. And before God and the angling world, the old man told himself – again aloud as if convincing himself – that the name of that fly would be 'The Jack Darcy'.

To this end he had served a lifetime of apprenticeship. As a lad after World War One, he had been appointed by his father to act as gillie for an English angler on the Laune. The old man recalled that morning clearly. The visitor had caught three fine springers – all on one fly. The boy had netted all three expertly; he then asked himself how it was that this single salmon fly had succeeded, when up and down the river on that same morning all other lures had failed. There had to be a reason. Did a hatch of native insects offer a clue? Was it some type of colour harmony? The method of casting? Hour of day? Colour of the water? Temperature of the stream? Prevailing wind? The feather in a fly? But always the boy was forced to the conviction that there was or would be a single all-potent, never-failing charm which, when offered to the silver missiles that were the running fish, would compel them to pause, pounce and be hooked.

Great indeed was the lad's joy when, as the English angler was leaving, he gave his youthful gillie a book called *How To Dress Salmon Flies* by Dr T. E. Price-Tannat. 'I can get another copy in London,' he said generously.

Growing through adolescence to manhood, Jack Darcy devoured that book. He mentally analysed each illustrated fly to learn the arrangement of its constituent elements. Afterwards when, acting as gillie for other anglers, he had occasion to net a fish, he held the successful fly up to the sunlight and noted the arrangement of its materials. Quietly he asked questions and received answers. He was often the butt of jokes on the riverbank when he was seen suddenly to clap his hands to trap, and later examined, the squashed insect between his palms.

He grew to know every item of flydressing from the tag to the hackle. He queried the older anglers on traditional fly patterns. From visiting anglers he learned the names of the historians and chroniclers of the classic flies. He traced other books on the subject and read them avidly.

In his young manhood Jack dressed his first fly to his own pattern. It hooked nothing; he was ridiculed. The fly ended its days as an ornament on a lady's tweed hat. The following season he dressed his second fly; it caught two fish but that was a bumper year on the river – a year, the anglers said, when the fish would take a lighting cigarette end if it was flicked into the pool. Each successive year his 'beauties' caught erratically, just enough to keep his ambition alive, and indeed torment him further.

In manhood he could put his ambition into words, but only under breath and to himself. Year after year, even when he was too old to fish, he rose and hobbled to the gable of his cottage to eye the pool below in its hundred moods – sombre and grey in wintertime, turbulent and brown in spate, light ale in fishing season, glistening in silver in high summer. He noted the spawning fish busy in its redd and later watched the kelt as, depleted and thin as a stick, it leaped slackly from the water on its way to the sea. Until he was too old to do so he was in charge of the hatchery in the stream that formed a border to his cottage plot.

Now in his eighty-ninth year and death implicit in his bones, the old man gathered his strength for the final attempt to achieve his goal. By this time he had grown unbearably cranky, so his granddaughter, watching as was her wont, was discreet in her observance of what the old man was at. There he was with a naked hook set in the little vice (the vice was his single concession to the trembling of his fingers), his array of feathers and other materials set out before him. This was a moment the girl liked: for as he worked the old man spoke aloud as if he were alone and calling out the names of the birds and beasts from whom his materials were drawn. From the muttered clues of her grandfather the girl knew that he was dressing his final salmon fly. He growled that he was breaking new ground, and again from his broken speech the girl learned that he was recalling an insect he had caught one March in the long ago, one of a hatch of unusual flies that showed itself beside the river for two or three days, then vanished.

The old man's concentration was total – as total as a watchmaker above the works of a tiny watch or a sculptor carving the face of a Madonna. First was the tag or tinsel, then the tail of teal and ibex; the burr that was the butt was followed by ribbings and veilings and these in turn by the hackless wings and cheeks until finally he used the horns of blue macaw and the head of Berlin wool. All this with a smell of varnish in the air.

At the table end Kate's lips moved silently, repeating what her grandfather was muttering aloud. She loved it when he listed the feathers of the exotic birds from which his materials were drawn: toucan, peacock, green parrot and pheasant; bustard, florian, ibis and jungle cock; kingfisher, widgeon, partridge and mottled turkey – all the fowl as it were awaiting the call to form part of what the old fellow thought would be the last great lure.

Over the years, when the old man was out of doors angling or watching the river, Kate stole open the large drawer of the dresser. She lifted the books and stole some of the more colourful feathers. Making a posy of them, she tucked it deep into her hair, then admired herself in the cracked mirror. Once, when she heard her grandfather mutter the name of a fly called the Coch a Bonnddu, she had laughed outright. The old man's mouth fell open, a web of spittle joined his parted lips and for once a glint of gaiety appeared behind his misted glasses. Then the pair laughed together. At that moment they were closer to each other than ever before.

But the girl's face lost its gloss of humour on the realization that for her grandfather time was running out. The opening day of the new fishing season was almost upon them.

The old man finished his final morning of flydressing. He had dressed two flies; both looked identical but there were minor differences – a tippet here, a hackle there. Only an expert could tell the difference. Taking pen, ink and paper, most laboriously he began the first of two letters.

Dear Mick,
For the sake of old friendship, I ask you go get your son to mount the
enclosed fly on Opening Day. Tell him to try it at the neck of the
Kitchengarden Stream above in Denvir's place. If he gives it a fair run

I promise you that it will win. I never asked a favour before. I do so now because I'm tailing to the sea.
Your old friend,
Jack Darcy
P.S. If the fly is a winner it's to be called the 'Jack Darcy'.

That letter was for upriver; the second letter with a similar fly enclosed was addressed to an old downriver friend – all this three days before the opening day of the season. Kate posted both letters in the box at the crossroads. The girl had cycled off on her errand amid a downpour of rain. Her grandfather kept hobbling out of doors to watch the rising water in the pool.

On the morning of the opening day he was up and out at first light; for a time he was leaning on his stick and scowling at the falling spate. 'Not bad,' he muttered to himself as, breathing coarsely, he limped away. One of two anglers on the pool below looked up and called out to his companion, 'He should be in bed.'

The day passed. Feverishly from the bedroom, 'Look out, girl – anyone coming?' and again at intervals, 'Any news?' About midday Old Jack sang out, 'Cycle to the post office, phone Neeson's upriver and Hanrahan's downriver. Ask one question upriver. "Did Mick Donovan's son catch a fish?" Downriver ask, "Did Joe Foley's son get anything?" Then, if a fish is caught, in each case ask, "With what?" You have your message? Repeat it. Off with you. Hurry!'

Restlessly, the old fellow waited. The girl was back within the hour. 'A few salmon caught,' she said sluggishly. 'By whom?' 'Not by your fellahs.' 'No names? Nor flies?' 'When it wasn't what you wanted.' 'Have you any brains?' 'As many as you have.' The old fellow called her an ape. Restless, restless that afternoon. Pacing up and down. Peering out the window or lying on the bed, time passed. About four o'clock he despatched the girl again. 'Bring your message right,' he roared. 'Donovan upriver; Foley down.' In a fever of excitement he waited.

She was back and taking her time about it. 'Well?' 'Donovan killed two; Foley killed wan; lost another.' 'With what?' ''Twasn't yours.' 'With what?' he roared. 'Donovan – 'twas the "Silver . . . " something.' 'Wilkinson?' 'Yeh, and Foley – he killed and lost with . . . ' she looked up at the sky, '"Thunder and Lightning".' 'Go home with yourself. Off!' Grumpily, sulkily, 'I'll stay, Grandpa. Will you eat a soft-boiled egg?' 'Get to hell out of my sight!'

The old man went to his bedroom at the back of the cottage. The girl shut and bolted the front door. She went to her bedroom in the front. She lay on the bed looking up at the ceiling and listening to her grandfather's mutterings on the other side of the lath and plaster partition. She heard the noise of a car stopping at the mouth of the boreen below. She sprang out of bed. Pulled aside the pane curtain and looked down. Two men came out of the car. The girl sharply drew in her breath. Young Donovan and young Foley taking fish out of the boot of the car. Had they come to taunt her grandad? She flung herself on the bed and lay low.

When she heard the clack of the bolt of the little gate below the cottage she crouched lower on the bed. After the crunch of gravel she heard the sound of knuckles rapping on the door. The girl did not stir. Then came a low murmur of voices followed by the knocking of a coin on the window of her room. 'Open up, Kate,' a man's voice called out. 'We want to talk to Jack.' A pause. 'If you don't open up we'll go round the back and knock on his window. C'mon, girl.'

At last she opened the front door. The young men came in. Donovan had two salmon dangling from his hands: the other had one. The strong smell of fish was in the kitchen. 'Jack!' one of the two called out. 'Jack Darcy! We have something to say to you.' He was addressing the door of the back bedroom.

At last, his body bowed with age and illness, his diminished face as grey as the threadbare rug about his shoulders, leaning heavily on his stick, Old Jack hobbled out. With an effort, the initial look of hostility on his face was replaced by an innate gloss of hospitality. The old man raised his head and said, 'You're welcome, neighbours.'

No one answered. In the resultant silence the doorway darkened as a pair of anglers from the pool stole into the kitchen. The old man glowered at the intrusion, yet managed to preserve his dignity: he came forward a step and ran his trembling fingers over the dark head of the salmon nearest him. The fingers moved downwards and a fingernail flicked a dead sea louse off the nether fin. 'Firm, fresh and lovely,' Jack Darcy quavered. 'A true star of the sea.'

For a moment no one spoke. The young man holding the two fish smiled. His green waders seemed to make him taller than he really was. 'Aye, the "Silver Wilkinson" and the "Thunder and Lightning" – good flies both,' Jack said. The second of the two anglers laughed. Jack looked up in anger, then gathered himself. 'Well done, young Donovan and young Foley,' he muttered as he turned away. 'Thank ye kindly for showing me your fine fish!'

In the background Kate's eyes were watching every detail of the scene. Her head jerked suddenly as the taller young man said, 'We've something to tell you.'

'What more can ye tell me?' from Jack Darcy.

'That we're liars.'

'Liars?'

'Look.' Foley, holding the single fish, took one of the salmon from Donovan, his companion, who then lifted his fish and drew its jaws apart to reveal a fly deep impaled in the ridge of the mouth. 'My glasses,' the old man said and Kate hurried to take them from a ledge of the dresser. Jack peered into the mouth of the fish: old enemies, old friends meeting. Unbelievingly then, 'What fly is this? My eyesight is poor.'

'The "Jack Darcy".'

The old fellow drew back a step. Then, loudly, 'Ye planted it there to fool me. Ye said ye were liars and liars ye are.'

Foley stepped forward. Placing his hand on the old man's shoulder he said slowly, 'All three fish were taken on the "Jack Darcy". I lost a second fish and the fly he took with him.' Old Jack was not to be appeased. 'No charity,' he shouted, shaking off the detaining hand as he turned towards his bedroom door. Kate's lips quivered; her eyes glittered. The younger man again gripped Jack's shoulder at the bedroom door. 'We had it planned,' he said, reasonably. 'We met at Evans's in town on Saturday. If we have a fish on his fly,' I said, 'we'll lie to everyone and keep for ourselves the honour of breaking the true news to himself. That's God's truth for you!'

Jack Darcy's face had broken up. A choked sob escaped from the girl's throat – it was as if foreign birds were fluttering around her eyes.

'You have it now,' said one of the lucky anglers.

'That's all,' said the other. To Jack he added, 'You were the best angler ever to wet a line on our waters. Now you are also the best flytier.'

'Dresser,' the old man said with a scowl.

'Tier – dresser – have it your own way.' Turning to the others, 'From this cottage word of a great fly will go out like a fever. It will travel through the angling world and rivers of that world. Wherever there are anglers and angling the name of

Jack Darcy will be spoken with respect and pride. So we'll leave you now, Jack, as you say yourself, like a kelt tailing downwater to the sea. But remember this: when you are dead and gone and books are written on the dressin' of salmon flies, your name will be mentioned with . . . '

'With Hardy of Alnwick and Hale of the same,' one man said.

'With Fitzgibbon and Donaghue,' from another.

'With Francis Francis and Ryce Tannat.'

'With the Kelsons, father and son.'

'With the Rogans of Ballyshannon.'

'With Ould Canon Greenwell on his armchair on the riverbank.'

By this time the company was convulsed with mock heroic laughter, in which Old Jack faintly joined. 'Thank you, neighbours,' the old man said at last. He paused at the door of his bedroom as the joker present sang out, 'You should tie one last fly and call it the "Kate" for your granddaughter.'

The gentle girl came to life.

''Tis dressed already,' she shouted. 'The "Kate" for Kate Courtney of Tyne and Tweed. I read the books! And what's more . . . '

Walking to the dresseer with its gleaming delph, she took down a small china cup, and going to the angler who had lost the fly, she spilled what was in the cup into his open palm. The man held up a salmon fly to catch the meagre light. 'By hell,' he said, 'here's another "Jack Darcy".'

Old Jack snatched the lure and looked at it in astonishment. 'Who dressed this?' he called out in anger.

'Who do you think?' the girl countered in an angry tone. 'And you,' she said in a blotched voice to the old man, 'if you're tailing to the sea itself, leave me your cottage, your feathers and your gear. I've watched you, I've read the books and I know the trade.'

With a flounce of skirts and a strangled cry, the girl ran to her room and slammed the door behind her.

'That bangs Banagher,' said the angler of the two fish, 'and Banagher bangs the devil.' He walked to the table and reverently laid the first fish of the season upon it. With murmurs of farewell, all left the kitchen.

When the noise of their leaving had died away, Jack Darcy hobbled to the table and looked down on the noble fish. Pensively he ran his thumbnail down its length. Now and again he raised his head as his eyes strayed to the door of the front bedroom.

There the new flydresser could be heard stifling sobs; these were sounds mingled with the dismay of disclosure and the pride of a craftsmanship which hitherto had been a secret by-line in her blood.

COLUM McCANN

As Kingfishers Catch Fire

As kingfishers catch fire
dragonflies draw flame.
Gerard Manley Hopkins

A flock of kingfishers arrived the evening Rhianon Ryan died, in the middle of a winter so cold that other birds froze in the air. Thousands of them came on a brief and noisy migration, with a rapid gunning of wings, making it seem that the northern lights had arrived in the sky, iridescent blues and salmons and corals and emeralds and the fabulous yellows of a thousand converging beaks. They came with a marvellous bobbing action in the air, like a shoal of flying fish. It was the strangest thing – apart from Rhianon – to have ever happened to the small Roscommon town.

The kingfishers appeared from the south, low-flying and rapid, casting tenacious shadows over the farmlands. They swooped down on rivers and fed on fish found in the icy water. Farmers on tractors shaded their eyes, women at storefronts held up umbrellas to keep off the birdshit, children stood in the town square and let the birds alight on their arms, teenage boys took out rifles that they would never use. Still the birds kept coming, letting out a high sound, like a musical keen. They lined the awning of the cinema. Gathered in the eaves of the dole office. Congregated near the flower shop. Perched on goalposts in the football field. They even sat around the rims of beer kegs at the back of pubs. For the whole of that night and the following day, until Rhianon was buried, the town was stunned into silence, watching kingfishers as they burst their colours through the air. Her funeral was carried out, but talk of Rhianon was overshadowed – even at her wake the missing gaps in her life were not filled with the chatter of the locals, but with talk of how the strangest winter aurora had visited the dull grey town.

Rhianon left Ireland on a mailboat bound for New York in the spring of 1950. It was her nineteenth birthday, and by the time she wrote her first letter, three months later, there were so many rumours about her that the townspeople were a little disappointed, at first, to find out the truth.

She was, she wrote, on her way to Korea with American soldiers to help nurse democracy into the world. Rhianon had always cared for the sick and the dying. At the age of eight she had climbed the wall of the local lunatic asylum with a pair of scissors in her hand. The following morning the employees were amazed as old women with no teeth suddenly rose from their beds with beehives and bouffants. Bachelor farmers slicked back pomade at breakfast time. Young lunatics were proud of their short-back-and-sides, carrying tiny mirrors around in their overalls. Every Saturday after that Rhianon was seen in the asylum garden giving free hairdos, carefully applying lipstick, clipping nose-hairs, twirling cotton sticks in ears to take out wax. Some of the local people came to get their hair done, although they were always relegated to the end of the queue. During the week she bicycled to the houses of the sick and listened to their life stories as she gave them makeovers, rinsing their hair, chopping stray ends, taking away straggly fringes. She even took a short apprenticeship with the undertaker, dressing the dead, but the dead didn't tell interesting stories, so she soon gave up on that.

Everyone hailed her as she cycled along the curvy grey streets, with her pellucid blue eyes under a giant umbrella of electric red hair.

A party was held for her outside the local cinema on the day she left, and people came from miles around to wish her farewell, a line of them gathered under a red-and-white canvas tent to get tips on the latest make-up. Young men scribbled their addresses on the inside flap of cigarette packages. Old women listened carefully to hints about how to stave off wrinkles. Rhianon chatted with everyone, but was too shy to make a speech – she simply stood at the cinema door and hung her head as the townspeople clapped. A car beeped impatiently to bring her to the mailboat.

When she left, all colour seemed to drain itself out of the town, down through the rain gutters, along into ditches, and out to the lowlands, leaving the streets pale and monochromatic.

When the first letter arrived, the people imagined Rhianon in nurse-whites, landing in Korea in a plane with a giant red cross on the side. World atlases were hunted out of libraries and youngsters located the port of Pusan where she said she was going. Great consternation rose up when the butcher claimed that Koreans were apt to eat dogs. A whiparound was made to send food to Rhianon, fruitcakes and long-lasting soda bread, with a stern warning: *Stay away from meat, girl!* Pictures of General Douglas MacArthur were clipped from papers and the talk was of whether the North Koreans would sweep further south or not. Her mother hung an American flag outside Rhianon's cottage, and it flapped through rainstorms.

Rhianon, for her part, began to send letters as long as skirts.

Helicopters flew in low, she said, carrying the injured.

Korean women in the rice fields were shaped like sickles, backs bent into their work, stopping only to stare upwards at the flying machines. The canvas flaps of tents flapped in the wind. The hospital was a symphony of moans. Soldiers screamed about the loss of their legs or arms. Bags of plasma were scarce. She had no time for hairdos and not an ounce of make-up was to be found anywhere. At night the scratchy voice of Nat King Cole came over radios. American soldiers sat around and smacked chewing gum in their jaws. The Yanks called her 'Popsicle' because they said she looked like a long white stick under an icicle of red hair. When evenings fell, mosquitoes raved delightedly around her and she had taken to drinking spoonfuls of vinegar to keep them at bay. Another Irish nurse had come down with malaria. Rhianon was nursing her. *Don't worry about the meat*, she wrote, there wasn't a dog in sight. The most abundant wildlife was kingfishers, tons of them, radiant and mysterious – they were often seen to dart around the camp, dropping the seeds of plants, then flying off again. At night bats flitted above the rice fields and somehow made her think of home, the movement of shadows on the land. She always signed off by saying that she would write again soon, and drew a love heart underneath her name, with a squiggle coming out at the end of the heart, like a tail of a tadpole.

The letters were carted by the postman around the town, and people gathered in the tiny cinema, before Cagney appeared in a rerun of *Yankee Doodle Dandy*. Rhianon was discussed before the stream of light hit the screen. Women wearing headscarfs and brooches leaned into one another earnestly. Boys refused to believe that Rhianon didn't eat dogs. Men talked about the latest reports from the newspapers. And then one afternoon her letters burst into tropical bloom when Rhianon wrote that she was almost in love with a dying man, and people whispered of her affair even through the appearance of Hollywood stars in khaki uniforms re-enacting World War Two.

The soldier, Rhianon said, had so much shrapnel in his body that he could have been a fallen meteorite, heavenly in the way he shoved his stubby arms to the sky as if he wanted to return to the patient black Korean night and utter a final rage of light. At night the man gave off a glow in his army bed, the magnetism of the metal in his body attracting every packet of light in the tent around him. In the beginning the soldier had smelled of DDT – so much lice on his body that the tiny parasites had blocked out the light, but when a doctor doused him in insecticide he began to give off faint glimmers. Even the surgeons noticed the aura of light hovering around him, some of it coming from a sucking chest wound, more of it seeming to emanate from his eyes. They put it down to hallucination or perhaps chemicals – but Rhianon put it down to sainthood. He was the only one of her patients who didn't mind dying. He told her that there was a dignity to a good death, that to die well was the only thing that a man could do honestly in life. Having almost fallen in love the soldier was happy to die. The *almost* was important to both him and Rhianon – to them love was like innocence; once you became aware of it, it was gone forever. Rhianon wrote, under a bare bulb where moths careened, that she sat by the soldier's bed – a metal frame with green canvas – and held his hand, feeling the light flow into her. The soldier smiled back under the cloth, a slow and spectral smile. In the distance firefights cleaved the oriental sky. Days piled themselves into weeks. Rhianon sometimes wasn't sure if he was already a ghost or not, so she broke the rules and kissed him gently on the lips to make sure he was still alive.

Underneath the soldier's bed, in a bucket filled with ice, lay three of his mangled fingers.

He had lost the fingers in a firefight near Inchon, when a grenade landed in the branches of a tree. Two hours later an army unit found him lying on the ground, full of shrapnel, staring at his fingers spread out on his emergency blanket. He had been holding the detached fingers to his mouth every hour, trying unsuccessfully to spit the drying blood back into them. He was lifted from the ground and placed on a stretcher. The fingers were brought into camp with him, in the pocket of his fatigues, a trinity of remembrance. The doctors cast them into a bin, but Rhianon rescued them and tucked them into her nurse-whites. She placed blocks of ice in a bucket every evening, carefully packing it around the dismembered flesh. Each morning the vicious heat of that Korean summer turned the ice to water and the fingers lay there, floating, speaking to them of love and collapse, turning blue and black, the demise of another summer's day.

The fingers didn't give off any light but Rhianon was afraid to let them disintegrate. She picked them up one by one and fastidiously placed ice around them.

'I have only one wish,' the soldier told Rhianon one morning during the rainy season. 'Bury my fingers in a place where I was young, and someday you must return to see what grows there. Promise me that. You can do whatever you like with the rest of my body, but my fingers must be buried and you must return to see what grows.' Rhianon wiped the soldier's brow, from which light continued to fulminate.

When the letters arrived there were long novenas hailed to the heavens of Roscommon; rosaries were incanted at fieldside grottos; yellow votive candles were lit at the back of the church; the cinema was packed as Rhianon's mother read aloud the letters; some of the townspeople stared at their own fingers in a sad empathy for the unknown soldier. The complexion of gossip was changed. Talk of Rhianon was a grand diversion from idle chat about the weather, baking formulas and the disastrous milk yields. The postman swished on his bicycle through puddles, from house to house, carrying news. Some of the villagers even felt their own hearts creaking as they heard about the bold and inky handwriting: *My soldier will die soon, I am sure of it. The tent is full of light. I'm not sure what I will do without him. With all my love, Rhianon.*

It was soon decided that the soldier was an American corporal, tall, beautiful, with hair so slick and blond you could skate on it. The hillside he spoke of was probably somewhere in Nebraska or Dakota. He was a rancher's son, people imagined, hence the request for the finger burial – to see what would grow in the soil of his youth. His eyes undoubtedly held the chimera of blueness. He had probably been a hero in battle, maybe raging through the firefight with another soldier carried on his back, or pitching a grenade at an advancing line of Chinese communists, or gallantly planting a flag on a hill. He would have a quintessential American name – Chad or Buster or Wayne – names that invoked movie stars who were capable of rising from the ashes of their celluloid dying. And he too would rise phoenix-like from his hospital bed, recover fully, return one day to the country town with Rhianon on his arm, down main street, past the butcher's shop without a second glance, waving his fingerless hand at passers-by, using the good hand to fling his hat to boys on the bridge.

Mrs Burke, the dressmaker, made a white taffeta gown for Rhianon's return. Hurley, the publican, promised a free keg for the celebration. The funeral director said that he might even jazz up his hearse with white ribbons for the imminent wedding. Rhianon's mother rehearsed recipes in her mind – potatoes roasted in a bed of rosemary, flanked by a slicing of fresh carrots. And when Rhianon scribbled a single-line note that she was coming home, the excitement in the town was paralysing.

When Rhianon returned in the spring of 1953 – a warm day when yellow bunting was hung from townhouse windows – there was no blue-eyed soldier at her side.

She walked down main street, her hair unwashed and strung like strawberry jam on the top of her head, a hand over her belly where a child had begun to show. People came out to greet her, uncoiled from their houses like a giant rope, but they were shocked at the sight of the bulge in the smock. They shook her hand and welcomed her, told her how beautiful she looked, but soon drifted off, disappointed. Shouts from the doorway of the pub melted down into whispers. A gramophone in the window of a house was turned off and a needle slowly scraped across a record. The yellow ribbons were slack in the breeze. 'There's no soldier with her,' the butcher incanted from his shop counter, 'there's no soldier with her at all.' Somebody mentioned the word 'whore'. At a curve in the road near the river, Rhianon's mother slapped her daughter's face and that night the dress-maker sent a small plume of smoke above the town, burning the taffeta dress in an old oil barrel.

Rhianon wandered around town in a daze, telling the story to anybody who would listen, gently whispering that instead of the blue-eyed baby boy of an American corporal, she was carrying the bastard child of a black-haired Korean soldier who, when he died, had set off a backwards meteor shower over the landscape of his country, huge streams of light rivering upwards to the sky from some hillside where digit-shaped flowers burst out every spring in his memory. Nobody asked about the fingers and Rhianon didn't say a word, although a van arrived from Dublin to her cottage, carrying a giant fridge that nobody had seen the likes of before, with a freezer section on top, to which Rhianon attached a strong lock.

Her son, Jae Chil, was stillborn. Rhianon bought a twenty-acre farm, dug him a plot in the easternmost field, arranged him for burial, said a few Confucian prayers over the mound, dressed herself in mourning black from that day on. Two deep furrows inveigled themselves into the corners of her mouth, where she deceived her sadness by forever smiling.

She tended to a herd of twenty cows with a dog she called Syngman, and was often seen herding cattle down a laneway, a stick raised high in the air, her wellington boots covered in dung. She came to town carting pails of milk in a baby pram. She was still beautiful, walked tall and unburdened, offered her cosmetic services to the undertaker, who tentatively avoided her, hid himself in a back office when she came calling. She could be sometimes seen in the grounds of the asylum arranging the hair of patients as they sat in white garden chairs by flowerbeds, but for the most part she lived out the tedium of her days without bothering anybody, just working away silently in her fields. She didn't talk about Korea, although there were times when she was heard gibbering in a strange language to herself. Sometimes children sneaked up to her house and tried to peer in the windows. When she came out, in black apron with baking flour on the front, they ran away. Rhianon would stand at the door and stretch her arms wide, questioning them, almost imploring. From a safe distance the children would point at her and make a slant of their eyes, but she simply shrugged and waited until they left, the children bored by her seeming indifference.

On a few occasions, when travellers came through, she'd invite them to stay. They said that Rhianon seemed to always have words dangling on the very edge of her lips, but they couldn't figure out if the words were to be swallowed or shared. In the end the old woman said nothing, just sat with her guests and watched the sunsets slide by.

Rhianon stopped selling milk, only came into town from her farm when there were electrical blackouts and she would run frantically through the streets seeking anyone who had blocks of ice they could give her. She tore at the roots of her hair – corrugated now into rows of grey – and ran back with plastic bags of the ice to her cottage, a quirk soon forgotten when new, more reliable pylons were erected all around the county, leapfrogging through the lowlands. There were rumours, of course. She was hiding the soldier in a back bedroom. She was saving to make another trip to Pusan. She was going to get married to one of the lunatic farmers. But the rumours were tame and, like the ice, Rhianon herself might well have been forgotten but for her final trip to the undertaker, on a freezing Monday morning when, at first, nothing stirred in the deep cyanic vault of the sky.

She arrived in a floral dress, the black of mourning jettisoned for some reason. She stood at the undertaker's desk, twisting a curl around her finger, and said she would arrange herself for her own death, thank you very much, which would be on the following Wednesday.

'Absolutely no frills,' she said.

'None?'

'Not a sausage.'

'Pardon me?'

'None at all.'

She handed him a bundle of money in old currency and said that none of her clothes were to be touched, nor her pockets rifled, nor her fingers uncurled, nor her eyelids closed, nor her face made up in any manner or means, and definitely nothing should be done with her hair. Word of the gesture slipped around town and dozens of locals followed the undertaker on his trip to check out Rhianon.

It was the coldest day of the year. Berries had shrivelled on hedges. Puddles had been seduced by ice. The people came on foot and, as they negotiated the long laneway to the cottage, the distant flocks of birds appeared to the south. Men and women stopped in their tracks, lifted their anorak hoods and removed headscarves for a better view. Children whistled through their teeth. The skein of kingfishers seemed endless and the people were mesmerized by the sight, frozen to the spot.

Only the undertaker, rubbing his fingers like money, went into the cottage. Rhianon was found in bed, propped up by four pillows, a natural death, her feet frozen to the bedstead, her eyes open, her face painted, a curious look of contentment on her. A cup of green tea lay on her bedside table. There were no notes. She was lifted into a coffin hurriedly and arrangements were made, while outside the townsfolk still stared upwards.

The kingfishers continued their onslaught, a salvo of them through the Roscommon sky, with a liquid movement of their wings. A silence descended, like that of a half-forgotten prayer. Instead of going to the wake – Rhianon had prepared whiskey and sandwiches and left them on the kitchen table – the group of people stood outside and saluted the wash of colour. Even the gravedigger looked up as he slammed his boot on the blade of the shovel to lift the first clod of soil for the coffin. He kept straining upwards to see as the hole got deeper and deeper.

The birds left when Rhianon was laid down into the ground, in a plot she had arranged beside her son.

The locals walked home, chattering amongst themselves about the fabulous sight. They weren't even angry that two whole days had to be spent cleaning the birdshit from all the windows of the town, and sweeping feathers from the ground. A smell of ammonia hung for weeks. Everyone waited for another visit of the birds, but it never came.

They all stayed stupidly unaware of the three shrivelled fingers that lay dormant in the hip pocket of Rhianon's burial dress when they dropped her down into the ground. It never even crossed their minds that the Korean soldier had found the place of his youth, and it was only the following spring, when exotic oriental azaleas burst up wildly around the old woman's grave, that the townspeople pondered the idea that the kingfishers hadn't arrived for them at all.

LEO CULLEN

Tierra del Fuego

We were in the car another day. On the way home from a dark and lake-potted part of the country, very far away. We had been returning a dog. 'An unfortunate creature,' Daddy said he was. Two weeks ago Daddy had bought him. A sheepdog called Juice. We had collected him off the train. We had carried him home in the car boot, and the moment he was released he had slunk into the coalhouse to lie on a jute bag, shivering.

That day Daddy dragged him out to round up the sheep he was terrified. He drove the sheep across fields, through ditches, into the neighbours', so that I couldn't tell which, dog or sheep, ended up the craziest. I don't think Juice knew what ditches were, coming from a place where only ribbons of stone and sod divided the fields. Then Daddy gave him a cuff of his stick in the head and he somersaulted on the grass a few times and headed for the hills. It was that day that started the sad howling. He never let up the howling, never again touched his food. And never let up his shivering, so that here we were, having to return him. 'No good throwing good money after bad on that mutt,' Daddy said. 'We'll take him back in the car; it'll cost less.' I could see he was thinking of retrieving his money.

The journey seemed farther than any I had ever been on. The road was so dark and damp it made the car leather go clammy. The place we returned poor Juice to was up a mountain, and most forlorn. The children of the house stood in wide wellingtons and stared at my brother Richie and me as though they had thought themselves the only children in existence. We stood above a lake, black figures, looking at one another, and when one of them spoke I was so taken by surprise I jumped.

'Get into the house, get in be damned,' the boy said, and it was skulking Juice he was speaking to, not us. Then he looked at his brothers as though he had done an important deed. And his brothers looked back at him, on the alert for any other deed which required doing. Alert, yet still.

'Do I need that useless creature dangling around my neck?' Daddy said when the farmer told him to take him home because he wasn't going to give him his money back.

'Have you ruined him?' the farmer said, and began straightening a paling post by his gate. Vigorously he pulled it out of the ground, waved it in our direction, and stuck it back in again. His children watched, as if keen to help him.

'Get that dog back out here and put him in that car,' he said to them.

'Leave him where he is,' Daddy said. The farmer's sons fidgeted; balls of thread danced in agitation from their torn cardigans but none of them moved. Richie and I stood behind Daddy. I wondered how long we were all going to have to stand there. I looked away from the children with their squelchy wellingtons and flapping clothes. I began to count all the little lakes below us that glinted up at the sky, and the rain cloud that hung there as if about to come spiralling down and send us all toppling. Then there was a sudden commotion. A hen flew, squawking from a door, a dog after her. A mostly white dog, but with brown patches over its eyes which made it look mad.

'Get down, get down,' the man roared.

His children roared too. 'Get down, Sam, get down be Jeez,

and quick.' Sam did get down quick, his eardrums paralysed probably.

'A gun dog,' Daddy said. The dog had dropped to a crouch position. 'Trained, is he?'

And that was how, on the home journey, instead of a sheepdog called Juice, we had in the car boot a gundog called Sam. Just to show there was no hard feelings, said Daddy, just to show he was a reasonable man. And just to show he too was a reasonable man, said the farmer, for this dog, that could set a snipe in a storm, he would swap the sheepdog.

We were by now somewhere in the middle of Ireland, I decided. I said it to Daddy. I could see he was in a good mood, having recovered his dignity. We were well away from the hills and lakes now, big fields all around us, big and black in the dusk. And suddenly we stopped. 'See that tree.' Daddy pointed. 'What tree, what tree, Daddy?' An enormous shadow mushroomed out of the centre of the field. 'That tree,' he said. 'I've been looking out for that tree for the past few miles. That tree marks the dead centre of Ireland.'

'The dead centre of Ireland, Daddy?' Sometimes, if he was in good form, Daddy said great things like that. I looked again at this most important landmark. 'History,' I was saying to myself, 'geography,' thinking of far seacoasts all around me. What could I see? A few shadowy cattle. Already we were whizzing away. Daddy never delayed anywhere. And what I saw was what I always saw when Daddy showed me things: something lasting long and lingering, a mystery, in my mind.

Then Daddy stretched himself out a bit because of the wider road we had got on to. And I knew what was about to happen next. He stuck his hand in his pocket, dug out the rosary pouch. That time of night had arrived: 'Richie, like a good lad, get out my beads. With the help of God we'll say the Rosary. In the name of the Father and of the Son and of the Holy Ghost.'

The Holy Ghost, where was he? Beneath the tree in the middle of Ireland? Here was shadowland indeed.

Then a real ghost loomed up before us, hand outstretched. We were speeding. But Daddy put on the brakes, and after about a hundred yards the car stopped.

'Damp night. Are you going far, boss?'

'A bit. Down the country.'

'I'll get in with you so.'

Daddy always picked up hitch-hikers. He liked the company. Kept him awake, he said. So did I, usually, but a hitch-hiker in the car during rosary time, I didn't like that.

He climbed in the back alongside me, wheezing because of having to run to catch up with the car. I smelled his coat, oily, a smell like sheep's wool. He wore a cap. In the dim light of the dashboard I made out a long nose and big eyebrows. His arrival delayed the Rosary because Daddy had to talk to him a few minutes.

'Are you from these parts?'

'Indeed I'm not, these parts are the middle of nowhere.'

Daddy could not think up anything that would make the man more cheerful about the parts we were travelling through. I said to him, 'We're near the dead centre of Ireland, you know. We saw the tree.'

A minute passed. I thought he had nothing more to say, like some of the hitch-hikers we picked up, either too timid or too hostile to say a word. The sort who caused a strain in the car. I was relieved when he spoke. 'You're right, young fella, dead centre.' He spat, making up for his minute's silence. It landed in the dark at his feet with a thud soft enough to give me hope that Daddy mightn't have heard. Was he a spitter? I wondered. If he was, the back of Richie's seat was going to be in a bad state.

'You're not from these parts, young fella?' He seemed pleased when I told him where I came from.

'I've been there,' he said. 'Worked a circus there once. Considering places I've been, not a bad spot.' For one moment I lived in the hope that Daddy would not begin the rosary. Not even Daddy, surely, expected a circus-man to know the rosary. I dreaded a hitch-hiker in the car during it. Why? Because sometimes he didn't know a word of it. Then Daddy had to recite both his own and the hitch-hiker's parts, his voice slowed down with disappointment. Daddy expected people to know their rosaries.

Sometimes we passed a light on the road and as it flashed through the car I got a look at him. He wore a scarf. A car came against us. Its headlights filled our car for quite a while. The shadow of Daddy's head swam around the back of the car. Richie's low shadow barely jumped beyond his seat. The shadows beneath the hitch-hiker's eyebrows flew sideways. And I saw staring watery eyes.

I suppose Richie had been holding Daddy's beads all the time. As the headlights swooned away out of our car Daddy took them from him.

'The first sorrowful mystery of the Rosary, the agony in the garden.'

The rosary, unbearably slow and sleepy rosary. For once I found myself wide awake for it. I think the man knew when it came to his turn. But he said nothing. Daddy started it for him: 'The fourth sorrowful mystery, the carrying of the cross'. As Richie and I began to mumble the response he called out, 'Wait a minute.' He told us he couldn't believe in rosaries any more. And we shouldn't either. Daddy said we did.

If we could only hear ourselves, the hitch-hiker said. We sounded like the savages.

'Like who?' Daddy said.

'Like the savages, like backward people I've seen. Casting spells on themselves, codding themselves.'

'Well, I'm not codding myself,' Daddy said. He continued then with the rosary. He finished off with the litany, slowing down only at the very last word and then he turned around to the hitch-hiker.

'So you've travelled,' he said, with not the slightest annoyance but with real interest showing in his voice. Peaceful after the recitation, even without the hitch-hiker, of the rosary.

The hitch-hiker told us of his travels. He was a sailor. I wondered was he still one, why was he so far from the sea if he was. But I was impressed with all the places he had been. I could see Daddy too was impressed. 'Amazing world,' he kept saying as he asked the hitch-hiker for more details of his travels.

'Tierra del Fuego,' the hitch-hiker said. 'The Land of Fire.'

Daddy asked him why it was so called.

'Ice on fire,' he said. 'Frozen solid wall of fog and ocean on the edge of the world. Lit by the sun's flames. Only if a fellow was driven by something did he go through it.'

'What drove yourself?' Daddy asked. There was a laugh in his voice, he was enjoying the story.

'Oh, a woman,' he said. 'What else, only a woman could drive a fellow around Cape Horn.'

That seemed to stop Daddy. I wanted to hear more about Tierra del Fuego. After a long time he asked: 'Are you married now?'

'No, sir, no thank you,' the hitch-hiker said, so definitely that I thought the conversation was over for good. But he himself started it up again, asking Daddy where he was coming from.

When Daddy told him the story of the sheepdog and the gun dog he laughed. 'So now you're without a sheepdog,' he said. 'Are you looking for a sheepdog?'

And that was how, when Daddy heard about the time the hitch-hiker had settled among the Indians of Tierra del Fuego – the people whose incantations had sounded like our Rosary – and heard he had kept sheep there, had managed them without any sheepdog other than himself, that was how Daddy hired him.

'Take me out of this godforsaken hole of the country,' the hitch-hiker said. 'I worked a circus once in Tipperary, take me back.'

That was how our journey to that faraway place found us a gun dog and a sheepdog.

And how along the way home an image arranged and rearranged itself in my mind: A place of ice and fire. The hitch-hiker's Tierra del Fuego. But fading, no longer the streaks of sea and sky as when he had described it. Shadows getting in the way: a lone tree, ragged children. Then the hitch-hiker began to snore, his head lolling and banging into mine, and Daddy asked Richie to get out his beads for him like a good lad so that we could start on the Glorious Mysteries because they would lighten the journey home.

MIKE McCORMACK

The Angel of Ruin

From the beginning they called him the kid, sometimes the Irish kid but mainly just the kid even though he was eighteen and taller already than any of the men in the crew. But he was thin, desperately thin and pale, and he looked like a stricken tree standing in the gravel yard fronting the warehouse. He was wearing black jeans and a T-shirt and his hair hung lank in his sunken face. He was a detail in misery, looking as if at any moment he was going to burst into tears.

His new boss, now striding from the warehouse towards him, was John Cigali, an Italian American in his mid-thirties, a self-made man with a broken coke habit and four years' military service abandoned after amnesty was handed out to Vietnam draft-dodgers. He now eyed the kid with unhidden scepticism.

'Have you worked with fibreglass before?'

The kid shook his head wanly.

'Never mind, you'll learn. From now till the end of summer you'll be eating and sleeping fibreglass.' He peered more closely at the kid. 'Is there no sun at all in Ireland? You look as pale as shit.' He then turned on his heel and returned to the office.

Mike, the kid's cousin, emerged from the office clutching a sheaf of pink forms. He was in his mid-twenties, over six foot tall and with his head cropped to the bone. He thrust the pink forms at the kid.

'Signatures,' he said. 'State and federal tax, insurance, that kind of shit.' He took a pen from his shirt pocket. 'Welcome to America, sign up and piss away your soul.'

The kid signed the forms on the hood of the Oldsmobile nearby while Mike fiddled with the locks of the loading bay doors. When they were opened the kid saw tools and buckets stacked neatly on the metal apron.

'All this shit has to go in the truck,' Mike said. 'Start loading while I finish writing up these documents.'

The kid began loading up. There were several rolls of fibreglass matting, buckets of chemicals, paintbrushes and rollers, a giant vacuum cleaner that looked like a huge reptile, several hand tools for the tool rack and, lastly, two massive jack hammers weighing nearly a hundred and twenty pounds each. The kid could barely lift them; he staggered rigid-legged to the truck and dropped the first heavily among the other tools. His face was flushed and a pulse throbbed frantically on his jawbone.

'Out of the way, kid.'

Mike had come quietly up behind him. He was carrying the second jack hammer, handling it easily before lowering it lightly into the truck. He grinned at the kid.

'This is as good as it gets,' he said, making no concession towards the kid's embarrassment. 'From here on out it's all downhill. We're ready now so let's go. We have to be there by midday. The others are there already and John's going to follow us in the car.'

The kid took his seat in the front of the truck and they moved off, driving for two hours through the claustrophobic New England landscape where beech forest grew right to the margins of the road, through the small cities of Holyoke and Springfield and on into Connecticut where the terrain rose steeply and his ears popped, past intersections in the middle of nowhere where no traffic flowed but where traffic lights still swung from overhead cables, and finally on to the interstate hewn from raw rock. While they drove, the radio blasted out retro rock, Lynyrd Skynyrd, Led Zeppelin, all classic seventies music. When the kid asked him did he listen to any post-punk music, the Smiths for instance, Mike told him bluntly that he didn't listen to faggot music.

Beyond the suburbs of New Haven, where the country opened up into a grey wasteland that spread as far as the sea, they pulled in at the entrance to an immense wired-off compound. Over the entrance hung the logo of the CHEMCON company. After Mike signed in the truck and two men at the security booth, the red barrier lifted and they drove up the pitted road to the plant. To their left, in front of a warehouse complex, a small, vile lake spread itself out over two acres, bordered on one shore by a multicoloured refuse tip. All about its edge yellow drainage pipes had their ends uncovered, all carrying spill-off and waste from the plant beyond; on the lake's surface floated languid clouds of grey scum.

Mike motioned to the lake. 'Nothing in that sewer but two-headed fish and unspeakable things. It's a real cesspool.'

They rounded the farthest shore of the lake and pulled in between a decrepit warehouse and a series of brickwork laboratories. Up ahead a battery of chemical tanks blocked off the end of the alleyway. The kid got out of the car and stood in the silence: silence like a coma.

'How come it's so quiet?'

'The whole plant is on shutdown, three weeks of it. Bar a skeleton crew to keep it ticking over there are no other workers here but maintenance and repair crews. That's why we're here, we have a heavy schedule of work to complete before they get back from their holidays.' Mike's voice trailed off in fatigue. 'It's a waste of time if you ask me, this place is only a shithole.'

The kid looked about him. Corrosion and decay seemed to

work in the air like a virus. The metal storage tanks raised on concrete platforms stood like shabby monoliths, their seams and rivets weeping with rust. Pipes dripped from cracks that needed sealing and some of the entrances to the laboratories gaped blankly without doors. All around, the brickwork added a terracotta tone to the corroding metal, and some of the brickwork itself had been graffitied over with obscene hiero-glyphs, a lurid psychedelic detail.

Mike was handing him a yellow hard hat and safety glasses.

'See those pipes? Last year we lagged every one of them, tried to dry them off and coat them with fibreglass. We said at the time it was useless, told them that the resin would never take to the corrosion and that the whole thing needed replacing. But it was no good, that was what we were contracted to do. Look at the mess now.'

Around the storage tanks the lattice of supply pipes was hung with a filthy bunting. The fibreglass matting had come away from the corroded metal and hung in strips, flapping lazily in the warm breeze and streaked through with a green hue from the acid; it was an unspeakably doleful sight.

A car approached behind them and slouched to a halt beside the truck. The boss got out. He was already wearing a hard hat and glasses and he spoke directly to the kid.

'Go nowhere without that hat and those glasses. We don't want you going back to Ireland with a patch over one eye or daylight showing through your head. No smoking either,' he said. His voice then lowered to a note of fatigue. 'This whole place might go up in a bang any second.'

He was holding a massive torch, inserting batteries and flicking it on and off.

'OK, if we're ready I'll show you the work.' He paused for a last moment in the sunlight to look around him. The ruin and decay of the plant seemed to find a raw spot in him. He spoke softly to himself. 'I hate this fucking place, it burns a hole in me every minute I'm here.' Then he was making strides towards a darkened doorway in the warehouse, calling in his wake for them to follow him.

Inside, out of the sun, the kid couldn't see a thing: he just followed in the wake of the boss's torch. Underfoot he could feel the concrete crumbling wetly, slewing sideways into treacherous pools. All about was a kind of serpent hissing and a heavy dripping of liquid. In front, high up beyond the torchlight a red neon sign pulsed, DANGER TOXIC. The kid slowed and clamped the hat down further on his ears. He had a feeling that terrible shapes and creatures were straining out towards him in the darkness, trying to lay mangled claws upon him. But worse still was the total presence of decay which seemed to agitate the darkness, working in it as it worked in every pore of the concrete and metal.

'This is it then,' John declaimed, swooping the torch in a low arc. 'One thousand square yards of corroded concrete, eaten away by acid and God-knows-what shit. It has all to be lifted down to the subfloor and replaced. That's all there is to it.'

The kid's eyes were now attuned to the murk and he had a dim view of the shambles all round. On all sides the floor was breaking down into pools of sludge, the acid raining down from the web of overhead piping feeding the phalanx of holding tanks ranked against the opposite walls. A flooded conduit ran the length of the floor and against the farthest wall a massive fan chopped the air lazily.

'This is hell,' the kid breathed.

'Not at all,' the boss retorted, his voice ringing off the metal. 'This is smoke-stack America, a piece of living history.' He turned to the floor. 'I have to go and get those pipes emptied. We need those lights fixed as well and I want to get that fan moving properly, we need some air in here or we're going to suffocate. Mike, take the kid to the canteen and show him the rest of the crew. I'll get you when everything's set up.'

Mike led the way from the warehouse, out past the brickwork labs where no one worked and past the silent workshops littered with discarded tools towards a raised timber shack that may at one time have been painted. Inside, seated in a booth, he was introduced to the rest of the crew. There were three in all. Jeff, the boss's younger brother, a heavy slob in his early thirties with none of his brother's military bearing. He was sprawled out blowing smoke rings at the ceiling, his Adam's apple exposed. Kevin and Leo were in their early twenties, friends of Mike and both bearing the grey hue of a binge that had not entirely been purged from their systems; both were drinking black, unsugared coffee. In true American fashion he shook hands with them all and they made room for him in the booth. Jeff was curious.

'So what brings you to America, the land of the fee and the home of the bribe?'

'A student visa.' The kid tried to smile but gave up when the corners of his mouth wouldn't work. He lowered his eyes. 'For three months.' It sounded like an apology.

'No need to be ashamed, boy, we're all doing life here. What are you studying?'

'English and philosophy. I hope to graduate next year.'

'We're all graduates here too,' Leo said. 'Honours students from the University of Budweiser, doing postgrad in booze and beaver.'

'You know Jack shit about beaver,' Kevin said. 'Pam and her five sisters is your limit. Leo is all talk, kid, all talk and no tackle.'

The kid finally managed a smile, a thin, composite expression, more pain than mirth.

'One thing's for sure, you'll find no women or booze in this fuck of a place. You're not likely to learn much either.'

'Is it as bad as it looks?'

'No, it's a lot worse. This place is the devil's asshole, kid, once you're here there's no getting away from it.'

'Do you not go out after work, for a beer or something? It's real hot in that warehouse.'

Jeff shook his head. 'There's no time, we work nearly eighty hours a week on this contract, anything to get it finished. Take it from me, you're not fit for much when you've done a day's work in this place, you just crash into bed. Pussy will be the last thing on your mind.'

They talked and smoked a while longer, downing more coffee to kill off the deep-rooted hangovers. The kid learned quickly that there were only two topics of conversation in blue-collar America – sex and money – and it wasn't always obvious which of the two was at issue. Presently the boss arrived, carrying a clipboard, all business.

'Are we ready?' he asked. 'Have we scratched and smoked enough? If we have then it's time to rock. I've got lights set up and the fan working, so let's go.' He swung his arm in a beckoning arc and the crew got up and followed him.

In the warehouse two carbon arc lamps had been mounted on stands and were casting a lunar glow over the floor. Against the farthest wall the fan now moved at full speed, tumbling heavy wads of warm air through the length of the room. The pools glistened blackly all around, heavily cast over with fleeting rainbows. John was handing out rubber moccasins and heavy gloves.

'Pull these on, those boots will fall off your feet in two days if you don't. Keep these gloves on too.' He turned to the floor. 'First thing we do is unblock that conduit, see if we can get as much of this fluid as possible to run out into the manholes. Mike, you and Kevin get shovels and work through its length. The rest of you, get squeegees and start moving that slop towards the door.' As the rest of the crew moved off he turned to the kid and gave him one last appraisal.

'OK, kid, this is your chance. Now we get to see what you're made of.'

Working under the carbon lights, in the sharp reek of the acid, they spent the rest of the day drying out the floor, slopping the heavy sludge with the rubber squeegees and then using the vacuums to suck up the residue from the pools. By the end of the day the floor glistened like a sand flat and they brought in a series of blowers to continue the drying overnight. As they were leaving the kid was standing by the truck, inspecting his blistered hands.

'Piss on them,' the boss said, coming up behind him.

'What?'

'Piss on them,' he repeated. 'It will wash them out and the salt will harden them. You'll get no infection either.'

'Yah, sure,' the kid replied.

'Have it your way then.'

But as they drove to the motel they made a stop at a drugstore and the boss presented him with a small package – a bottle of meths, some cotton wool and a roll of lint.

'Thanks.'

'Don't thank me, it's an investment, not a present. I'm not losing any time with those hands.'

'You won't.'

'Damn right I won't.'

*

The real work began the next day, breaking up the floor with the massive jack hammers and barrowing out the rubble to the refuse tip near the lake. The kid vied gamely for his turn on the jack hammer and then caused much guffawing among the rest of the crew when he was thrown off balance in a heap by its first surge of power. But he got up and tried again, gritted his teeth and hung on for twenty minutes before handing it over to Mike. He stood clenching and unclenching his numbed hands, shaking from the vibrations. In the canteen his hands still shook and he slopped his coffee at the first gulp. So, for a time he drank from a straw, and for long after it was necessary, just for the clown value of it.

But very quickly, after a few days, he found nascent muscle in his arms and back and he was able to take his full turn. He stood with his legs braced apart and his arms stiffened, the massive vibrations shaking every bone in his torso, his head pounding with rhythm and his whole being running with adrenalin. A definite change had come over the kid: he was happy and he had begun to smile and his hands were healing fast. Best of all he knew that he had hacked it, knew it in his heart and knew it from Mike that the boss was well pleased with him. He had no worries about holding down the job for the rest of the summer.

By the end of the first week the kid was having a feeling of almost total rejuvenation. The chemical plant became his element and he thrived in it like a hothouse orchid. He began to flex the new-born muscles in his arms and back and they were wondrous as wings, and he took to walking around at every opportunity with his shirt off, singing crazy fragments of songs, his white torso glowing in the pale light. The boss was unimpressed.

'Put it back on,' he told him curtly. 'You are not Charles Atlas yet.'

*

Beneath the arc lights, with the compressors and blowers working, the warehouse grew baking hot. After the first hour's work their bodies ran with sweat and their shirts clung like second skins. They took it in turns to foray into the daylight for fresh air. The kid preferred to walk to the refuse tip on the waste ground behind the warehouses and stand on its low peak where he caught the thin breeze that blew in over the lake. He would stand there on the summit for the duration of a cigarette, slick and steaming like a new-born thing.

He was finding himself enchanted by the place. Like a child his mind took in the palette of decay spread all around him, the green murk of the lake, the copper tones of the rusted metal and faded paintwork, the blackened chimney of the incinerators; all these colours fixed his imagination into a coherent spectrum of ruin. The kid now knew that there was no other fact in creation, no other dynamic in the world except this corrosion and wearing away, this attrition which seemed to level everything down to a uniform plane of ruin and which had this chemical plant as its centre and origin. And he stood there in the middle of this desolation, a newborn god, lithe and keen-eyed, ready to spread his wings.

He never stayed long in the open sunlight any more, he would stub his cigarette and return quickly to the sanctum of the warehouse. Sunshine no longer had anything to offer him.

While he worked the kid developed a theory about the plant, it became a pet project. One evening at the motel, sprawling among the empty pizza boxes and beer tins, he spoke about it, it was his longest soliloquy so far.

'The way I see it, the whole plant is a kind of monument, a cautionary symbol of waste and deterioration, emblematic of all the piss-poor aspirations and materialist dreams of the century. The whole place is a work of art, a piece of kinetic sculpture.'

'Is that so?' said Mike, his voice thick with doubt and hash. He was lying on the bed blowing heavy smoke rings. 'Then what am I doing here? I'm not an artist, all I do is work with fibreglass. I'm a repair man.'

'That's just it, you're not a repair man.' The kid was real excited now, his eyes like two pitch bores in the middle of his skull. 'This place is not broken, it does not need repair and no matter how it looks it's not falling apart either. All it's doing, day after day, is refining itself, coming more clearly into its own identity. And its identity is one of rot and decay and corrosion. That is why we lay down a new floor or lag a few pipes every year. It gives it something new to feed off.'

The kid was aware that the rest of the crew was looking at him in slack-jawed amazement; the boss seemed to be staring at him with special intensity. He could feel the flush on his cheeks from the fervour of his words and he had the horrible feeling that he had made some sort of fool of himself. Then he saw Mike grinning at him, shaking his head as if he had caught him doing something obscene.

'I think you're full of shit,' he said, without losing his grin. 'Full of shit like a whore's outhouse.'

The kid sighed with relief.

'Fuck you too,' he said, well glad of his escape.

They now had the entire floor lifted down to the foundation and they spent most of their time vacuuming the uneven surfaces, preparing it for the readymix. They spent three days shovelling the concrete, three days of backbreaking labour bent close to the ground with short shovels carrying massive blades. Then they got down on their knees and moved over the floor, section by section, with a four by two on its edge, screeding it to a smooth finish. When they had finished the last section more time was needed for it to dry out completely.

'We'll give it two days,' the boss said. 'Two days and no more. Till then I've got work set up in a few places. Mike, take the kid to the opposite warehouse. Inside you'll find a series of flues. Their inner surfaces need relining. Show the kid how to work with fibreglass, give him his first taste of it.'

In the warehouse they found the flues, four of them dismantled and mounted on trestles, their inner surfaces black and pitted. There was an assortment of paintbrushes and fibreglass matting among the other tools on the ground.

'There's only a good day's work here,' Mike concluded.

'Well, maybe at last I will get to work with some fibreglass. I haven't seen one bit since I started this job.'

'We'd better make a start then,' Mike said. Reaching for one of the grinders he handed it to the kid. 'OK,' he said. 'Grab a hold of this.'

The kid was shown how to clean out the inner surface of the flues and how to use the grinder smoothly and lightly in long, curving strokes and how to sweep out the dust and apply styrene. He was shown also how to cut the fibreglass mat with a minimum of overlap and how to lay it seamlessly within the curved surface before coating it with chemical resin, and finally how to get a smooth finish by carefully laying down the thin veil of gossamer fibre on the glistening surface. The kid relished this change from the brute labour of the floor. He had proven himself in that sweat-and-muscle arena, now was the time to pick up a skill. The kid learned fast and the work went well; by mid-afternoon they had nearly half the flues completed.

'Let's take a break,' Mike said. He was wiping his hands on a rag steeped in acetone. 'We're well ahead, there's no hurry. Let's get some coffee and a cigarette.'

The kid shook his head. 'I'm going to take a walk around the plant, have a last look at it before I go. We've only got a few days left.' He jammed the hat on his head and walked from the warehouse. Mike watched his stark form disappear through the brightened entrance of the loading bay, and for one instant he could have sworn the kid exuded all the light about him.

The kid walked beyond the tool crib and canteen, past the lab complex which sidearmed round one shore of the lake and on to the waste ground that ran as far as the perimeter fence. It lay strewn with fragments of brick and timber: saw-grass grew heavy over treacherous lengths of abandoned piping. From the perimeter fence he had a full view of the plant. It was laid out like some childish construct of cubes and cylinders. From its centre the blackened chimney sent up a plume of heavy smoke that curved out over the far perimeter, a beacon to the wider world. At the base of the plant the lake reflected the sky like a tarnished mirror.

The kid felt a sudden pain in his chest. To his amazement he found himself on the verge of tears. He began to talk to himself.

'I love this place,' he said. 'This is my home and I belong here. I know everything it says about decay and ruin and corrosion and they are all truths to me. And now look at me: have I not grown strong by them?'

At the far end of the waste ground he saw the boss walking towards him, picking his way cautiously as if he was walking on marsh land.

'Having a last look?' he asked when he finally drew up.

'Something like that,' the kid said. 'A kind of overview before I leave. I'll miss this place when I leave. I've learned things here.'

The boss nodded. 'When I saw you first at the tool yard I didn't think you could hack it in this job. But I was wrong. You've thrived in this place, you've got stronger and you even talk more. In all my years of working with different men I have never known anyone to be so affected by such a place.'

'It's this place all right,' the kid replied. 'I think it's beautiful. This place is a work of art and I've reacted to it as I would to a work of art. I've been transformed by it, I've been inspired by it.' The kid seemed to glow in the sunlight, his face and arms luminescing against the scorched colour of the grass – for a moment the boss had a vision of insect larvae. The kid was staring vacantly at the plant, lost in some idyll of ruin and decay, totally unprepared for the vehemence of the boss's attack.

'I've heard enough of that shit,' he said suddenly. 'Enough of that crap. This whole place is a death trap, nothing more and nothing less.' He swung the kid round by the arm, facing him into the perimeter fence. 'Two miles down the road from here there is a small village called Wickhurst, no more than a hundred people. Three years ago it buried four infants, all of them with skin blued over from arsenic poisoning. Ground water contamination was traced to this plant. On the far side of this plant a dairy farmer opened a pit on the margins of his land and buried a third of his herd in it, all of them asphyxiated by windborne emissions. Their carcasses couldn't be used for dog food. So no more shit about this place being some sort of monument: it's a death trap and that's all there is to it. No more theorizing or philosophizing. You work for me now, so just make sure that you do good work and check once in a while to see that your head has not run away with your ass.'

He threw his cigarette to the ground in a lavish gesture of disgust and strode away heavily through the grass.

The kid needed the isolation of the perimeter fence to get over his shock. The boss's words and violence seemed to have sprung from some personal wound. The kid could not believe that he harboured any resentment towards him. He found himself trembling, unable to account for the vicious turn of mood. He stayed a long time at the perimeter, leaning against the wire, feeling the lattice pattern imprint itself in his skin. Presently, he pushed himself away and returned to where his work was among the cylinder and cube abstract.

As he worked the rest of that evening he thought over what the boss had said about the deaths and contaminations. He was not surprised to find no revulsion or horror within himself, just a clear forensic curiosity prompting him to seek more information.

'Do you know about the deaths and contaminations that this plant is supposed to be responsible for?'

Mike nodded. 'Sure, we all know. This plant has paid out over five million dollars in environmental lawsuits during the last decade, spillages, ground water contamination, emissions, the works. Even now it's tied up in more court cases than you can count. Why do you ask?'

'Just now I met John and he gave me a fucking about my attitude towards this place. He thinks that I'm besotted with it and he told me to get a grip on myself. Then he told me about the dead babies and the dead cattle. He wasn't pleased. How do you feel about working here?'

'I hate this place, I begrudge every moment that I have to spend here, I wonder what it does to my soul. I imagine it corroding away every minute I spend here like one of those pipes or tanks.' There was no trace of irony in his voice, just a dark knife-edge of bitterness. 'But it's work,' he continued, 'and that's why I do it. I've worked for John for six years since the mid-eighties, the boom years when we could pick and choose work. But it's not like that now. Work is real tight and we need this contract. It can get us over three slack months and all the winter months are slack ones. Besides, if we didn't do it, someone else would.'

'And John doesn't like it either?'

'Not a bit. He took over this contract from another company who abandoned it after those kids were killed. This contract saved his company from going under. John used to employ ten men back in those peak times. Now his crew is down to us.'

'Have you ever thought of doing other work?'

Mike shrugged. 'I like this work. Besides, I owe John, he took me on first and I became his foreman. Now he's over a barrel. He hates this contract but he needs it to keep his company. He's got kids and alimony as well, so he can't afford to let it go. But I think he worries about his soul also. And he's worried about you too. What he does not like is your enthusiasm for the place. You've been working and singing and talking your head off since you've come here, like a man possessed. I think it scares him. I think he believes you might have caught some sort of bug here.'

'Maybe he's right,' the kid said. 'Look what's happened to me since I've started working in this place. I've never felt happier or stronger. I'm sure if I checked I'd find that I've put on weight. Now I'm told about all these deaths and pollutions but it doesn't change a thing for me. I don't feel any different towards the place. I'd be telling a lie if I said I did.'

'You can't deny what you feel,' Mike said dryly. He had just tidied away the last of the tools and the flues now glistened like split fruit. 'Just remember that you are the only one who feels that way. Unlike you, most of us would give a lot to have this contract somewhere else. Remember that when you start eulogizing next time.'

During the final days, as they laid the fibreglass covering, the kid seemed to reach a new peak of well-being. His body now soared with such energy he seemed to have difficulty just standing still, and despite Mike's cautions he could not stop himself singing as he worked, bawling out isolated phrases and choruses over the clamour of the fan, making the others grimace, not entirely in mock pain either.

> *Pour shame all over us*
> *Harden it into a crust-cement*

The boss did not hide his annoyance. 'Shut the fuck up,' he yelled. 'Thank Christ we're moving out of here in a few days. Maybe then you'll calm down and quit acting like you've got a belly fully of amphetamines.'

'I can't help it,' the kid said. 'I've never felt better in my life. Look at this.' He held out his arms from his body and bunched up his biceps and pectorals like a body-builder posing in a competition. 'Charles Atlas or what?'

'Only a sick fuck could thrive in a place like this,' the boss retorted.

'Then I must be a sick fuck,' the kid said. 'Where do we go after this?'

'Maine, one week at an Ocean Spray plant. Good clean outdoor work relining concrete containers. You might get some sun on that white ass of yours.'

'Or I might fry. I'll be sad to leave here. Home is where the heart is.'

'It's news to me that you have one.'

The kid just shrugged.

The fibreglass was laid quickly, the glistening strips advancing over the floor, slick and heavy like an oil spillage, drying finally into a dull sheen. On the third day they laid down the final veil covering, bonding it down with a last coat of resin. Then they stood back at the doorway, taking a last moment to appraise their work. The floor shone with nocturnal radiance, like a pool seen in a dream. From above, the metal containers were reflected in its illusory depths.

'How long will it last?' the kid wanted to know.

'It should last forever,' the boss said. 'But nothing lasts forever in this place. Too much heavy chemical will be spilled on it and too many heavy weights will crash down and crack it. Probably next year whole sections of it will have lifted up and ruined, like every other piece of work we've done here.' He turned quickly in disgust. 'Come on,' he yelled. 'Get these tools rounded up and let's get the hell out of here. I'm sick to death of this place.'

It was only thirty minutes' work to gather up the tools and place them in the back of the truck. They worked quickly, rejuvenated at the prospect of leaving. As he came out of the warehouse the boss squinted in disbelief when he saw the kid walking to the truck carrying the last pieces, the two jack hammers dangling at the ends of his arms, his whole torso a knotted cartography of muscle. He lowered them gently into the back of the truck and then turned with a wide grin on his face.

'When I started this job I couldn't lift one of those hammers. Now I can measure my well-being in pounds and ounces.'

'So now you're twice the man.'

'Not twice the man. Just different, different altogether. Listen,

I've even developed a singing voice.' For the last time the kid broke into song.

> *Forget the glamour*
> *And mumble a jack hammer*
> *Under your breath.*

The kid was dancing now too, prancing by the side of the truck in some improvised step, swinging his arms in the failing light to hold his balance. The boss watched him carefully, and for a fleeting moment he had a vision of the kid taking flight, his fingertips finding some impossible grip on the air and hoisting him higher into the gloom, up by the warehouse wall and out over the lake like some cancerous angel. It was an epiphany of beauty and ruin and the boss was lost in it for a few moments until Mike rounded the side of the truck, an unlit cigarette jammed in his mouth. He gazed for a long moment at the dancing kid.

'That kid needs his head seen to,' he said solemnly.

The boss nodded, moving his head slowly, as if supporting a great weight.

'His head among other things.'

They stood looking a while longer, and all the time the kid continued dancing, his broken image soaring in the curved surfaces of the holding tanks. And he continued dancing, dancing, dancing even after he had stopped singing.

UNA WOODS

The Letter

There was no one in the parlour. The light fluttered like a heart. Then it whimpered like a sound. Shudder-lit, the wallpaper peeled in places. The church bell rang.

Mr McKeown grabbed his hat from the hall-stand. Mercy be to God, he said. Mrs McKeown moved about in the kitchen. Out through the window the yard fell instant. Like an atomic silence. Inside Mrs McKeown moved an ornament slightly into place. The front door closed. At the centre of the bang Mrs McKeown paused. Then she looked around the walls.

Mr McKeown peered into the monastery glow. His hands behind his back. Stooped forward. Celebration stopped short as incense. There were no seats. Standing at the back Mr McKeown joined in with the prayers. Rolled his eyes to the high ceiling, supplicating.

Outside in the street the deadened drone could be heard. A bicycle rang but it made no difference. Slates were more like it, weakened as they were by evening light. There were no birds. So much was happening the evening shortened, drained through stained-glass. Light on its last legs.

Mrs McKeown moved her parlour curtain. In the flattening gap children glided. Mrs McKeown fixed her eyes on the hidden scene. From where she was the shimmer-stopped evening played like awakening. Stone-frail voices sudden as brick. Then ripples.

*

Mr McKeown got up after the blessing and brushed the knees of his trousers. The organist launched into music that caused chaos on the altar. As people made their way out into the straight light their clothes were already drab. Mr McKeown amongst them stopped and looked around as if at an alien race. Merciful Jesus, he said rocking on his heels. Ha-ha.

Then he vanished out through the gates into the dim-sparked evening streets. All the rest went their separate ways.

The door closed. Merciful heavens, Mr McKeown said, placing his hat on the hook. They were the only two sounds in the house. When he broke into the kitchen like a man home, his wife slipped out of the shadows. Then when he went to open a cupboard door she whispered, Don't touch that. He looked up at her, still crouched.

Till you've washed your hands, she whispered.

Jesus, Mary and Joseph, Mr McKeown said, wringing his hands.

Later he sat in his chair counting coins. Children could be heard faint in the street. Mrs McKeown came from the scullery. Give me a penny, she whispered to her husband.

I'm not sure I can afford it now, Mr McKeown said, looking down at the coins. I was going to give it to the monastery.

Mrs McKeown whispered nothing. Then she went over to the sideboard and lifted a tin. She took the lid off and poked in it. She replaced the tin and hurried out to the door. She barely opened it but drew the attention of a child by wagging one finger.

I'll give you a penny if you go away, she whispered.

The child took the penny and went back to her friends. They moved a few doors down the street. Lamplight flickered just on where the street hung before darkness. As endless as that.

*

The next day pale quiet opened on houses like an empty book. Bleary unwritten pages basked on slate. Weak-lit clouds hovered thin as another day. Mrs McKeown walked into the parlour. Light tinkled on the net curtain, where her fearful eyes fixed. No one sees me from here, she thought. Then things happened together as if they were life. Mrs McKeown began to move like a participant. First I must go out to the shop, she thought, and get Mr McKeown some eggs for his breakfast. It's a lovely morning. Clouds make possible the sun.

Immaculate Mother of God, Mr McKeown ejaculated, coming down the stairs. Saint Anthony and all the saints.

Mrs McKeown waited till he had gone into the kitchen. Then she slipped out into the hall, took her coat from the hall-stand, tiptoed down the hall and out through the front door. When she looked down the street she saw futures flickering in wait. She chose the one that lay ahead, still hopeful. I must walk here, she thought. Ahead the corner stopped like a light off, but only out of sight. Mrs McKeown took each step against the air that lightened her passage. Dizzy bits of dust glistened along the road's dull edge. Half a dozen eggs, she whispered over to herself, and a couple of soda farls. She reached the corner and continued on.

Where's that blessed woman? Mr McKeown said out loud. He walked in his stooped way into the scullery, leaning forward as if in the dim glimmer he might see her. Then he rocked on his heels, hands behind his back. He shook his head. Lord the night, he murmured, give me patience.

He turned back into the kitchen and went over to a picture of the Sacred Heart hanging on the wall. He lit a small red lamp underneath it and, kneeling down before it, began to pray fervently.

Mrs McKeown stopped in the doorway. Preserve us, she whispered, and went into the scullery with the groceries. Mr McKeown finished his prayers, then got up and brushed the knees of his trousers. He went into the scullery and opened the door out to the yard. What's it like out, eh, woman? he asked his wife. Grand, Mrs McKeown whispered, putting an egg into a small saucepan of cold water.

Later that morning Mr McKeown was out doing his laundry round.

Mrs McKeown took a chair out into the yard and sat in the early sun. I'm safe here, she thought, so long as nobody comes to the back door. She took a letter from her apron pocket and opening it out began to read it. Her most pressing thoughts, when she came to the end of the page, were, How did she know I was still somewhere? How did she get my address? And then, How can I reply? Like the silent aftermath, the lone survivor of an explosion, she read again the words of warmth from an old friend. She felt herself beginning to shake. Then she shuffled herself up in her chair until her body was erect. She stared at the back door a minute, then quickly folded the letter back into the envelope and stuffed it into her pocket. It's too late, she thought defiantly, I'm almost pleased to show her.

Mrs McKeown got up from her chair, lifted it and carried it back into the kitchen. Then, like resentment, she plotted to clean the house from top to bottom. I'll show her, she thought, on her hands and knees, scrubbing the scullery tiles, I'll show her what's become of me. Who does she think she is anyway? Outside, the dull air flickered then dissolved. All that could be heard in the distance were the numb sounds of every day. Inside, the soapy scrub angered hope. It was all she could do to continue, against knowledge, moving the bucket on like a pained clang across the floor. Now and again the letter made little crumpled noises in her pocket. Yet its meaning opened a world away.

Unless I could go, Mrs McKeown thought suddenly. She knelt upright on the dry tiles. Unless I could go and see her, I've lived like a fool.

Mrs McKeown's throat fluttered like the last piece of snow on a sunny yard wall. Or the first primrose in a lonely country lane. In other words, like possibility against all odds.

Mr McKeown said goodbye to the nuns at the nursing-home door. Then he drove his van down the long driveway, through trees with shades of brown and yellow like nothing on earth. Nothing on the treeless street where he lived, the lamps ordinary, lit or unlit. He drove through the strange golden glimmer and out on to the stuttering road. When able he turned left. Of all that's good and wonderful, he muttered to himself. Saint Brigid and Saint Patrick. People walked in both directions, no further away, and the light spread and flattened on the pavements.

Ha-ha, Mr McKeown laughed and shook his head. Who would have believed it? Who in their right minds, that I would be with the laundry all this time.

Then he saw the spire of the church ahead, he saw it narrow up to a weak sky. Like liquid identity. His eyes stared at the road beyond, height swam in their reflection of light. When he turned into the streets Mr McKeown felt eternity as solid as the houses on either side. His life vindicated, his years in the laundry. Mercy be to the heavens, he said. Praise be to God.

Children played at doorways, their voices sudden as beaten tin.

*

Mrs McKeown felt a different person. It was easy. Silence was enough, and walls as thin as years. When she walked on the floor the ice of imagination smoothed her way. She touched things as if she controlled them. The suddenness of freedom came back to her. It's the same place, she thought, after all this time. She took the letter from her pocket and out of its envelope. She smoothed the paper on her knee, then read the words like magic. The address at the top of the page was shocking and exciting. Saudi Arabia. I could get the plane, she thought. I could fly out, these streets are dead.

She slipped into the parlour and looked through the net curtains at the soundless grey. No hope of reawakening, why did she stay? Then a reminder as dull as prevention, the drone of the laundry van. It pulled up outside the door. In the stone-smooth grey of afternoon Mr McKeown jumped down on to the pavement. The sound of his feet closed the scene, the future here impossible. Mrs McKeown heard the thud like confirmation. Then she fixed the corner of the curtain slightly into place. Brick flickered on the far side of the street.

Divine light, Mr McKeown said as he came to the door. When he was in the hall and had closed the door behind him he said, Merciful Jesus and his Holy Mother. Then his feet walked sure as yesterday on oilcloth. Mrs McKeown stood still by the window, rigid with detachment, the house balanced around her like imminent collapse.

Then from the scullery came the sound of water bouncing on stone.

Good, Mrs McKeown sighed, he's washing his hands.

When she appeared in the kitchen door he said without looking up, Ah, now, sure the nuns were in good form today, what? He wrung his hands under the gushing water.

Use the kitchen paper, Mrs Keown said, I've washed the

towel. The words fell like boredom on the clean floor where she looked down out of habit. Then as if nothing had changed Mr McKeown crumpled up the wet kitchen paper and threw it into the bin.

They passed each other on the scullery step almost touching.

Saudi Arabia, Mrs McKeown thought.

Lord the night, Mr McKeown said.

Days merged into winter. Cold air gripped the fading light like a brick wall. Mrs McKeown got no further. Day after day secret thoughts swam in circles until they met the dusk and disappeared. She could not make plans.

One day she put pen to paper. Seated at the kitchen table, a fiasco of feeble light on roofs beyond. Almost still and clear like a flimsy gold-thin glow. She stared ahead at the back wall, something further, further than wall. What she had to say hung like memory. It took up the whole evening. When she looked down at the paper she couldn't think what to write. Then words came stilted as daily chores. As the odd light in a window coming on, the blind abruptly closed. What could she reveal? 'I' seemed too much after all the years of hiding from its statement. 'I' closed before her on the page. It could not live up to the expectation of the new writing-paper and envelopes. And Mr McKeown due home from the laundry in no time. Like a rabbit darting its head out of a burrow only to hear the sound that threatened its whole life, Mrs McKeown snapped the writing- pad closed, and scuttled over to put it at the back of the drawer.

The house stunned into evening. Mrs McKeown's eyes stared out the kitchen window at nothing moving. But the moment moved imperceptibly so that the faint fidget of dusk seemed everywhere. In comparison to the evening light wasted on slate. In comparison to the high yard wall like glass. When she touched the letter through the wool of her cardigan pocket, the crumpled petals opened in the sun. The house sank slowly in the growing glimmer but when she tried to put it into action she couldn't move. Then from a street behind a voice deadly as unbroken days hit the grey. Mrs McKeown hurried to put on the kitchen light.

Tomorrow, she thought, I'll go to the Travel Agents.

Sweet Virgin Mary, Mr McKeown said as he hung his brown laundry coat on the back of the kitchen door. He took some coins out of one of the pockets and counted them. The infant Jesus, he said, shaking his head.

Mrs McKeown set a heavy pan down on the stove like the end of marriage. Then she came as far as the scullery doorway.

Is there an atlas in the house? she said more inaudibly than she meant.

Mr McKeown was banging coins in his trouser pocket. He swung round.

Speak up, woman, he said, speak up! Then he looked at his watch. He flung his arms in the air. Jesus, Mary and Joseph, he exclaimed, I'm doing the collection.

I said, Mrs McKeown raised her voice just above the sound of bacon frying, is there an atlas in the house?

Mr McKeown rocked on his heels. Ha-ha, an atlas, he laughed. When did I last see an atlas? Then he frowned across at her. Why, are you thinking of sending some money off to the missions? Do you want to know where Africa is?

Then he rushed out of the room and up the stairs. Christ on the cross, he could be heard saying, Mary Magdalen at his feet. Soon he moved about in the room above as if the heavens rumbled, the house below waited in anticipation. Mrs

McKeown turned the bacon with the small knife. Bits of fat spat like secrets exploding where she stood on the spot.

The front door banged. Mr McKeown looked up and down the dark street, lamplit with reverberation. A still yellow glow. Lord have mercy, he said, beating his chest. Then he lurched across the road and into the entry opposite by way of a short-cut. Christ have mercy, he said in the entry like an echo landed on walls. There was no light save where the street dimmed ahead. Mr McKeown hurried out into the dim opening. Opposite two young girls were tying a thick rope on to a lamp-post. Stark as amazement, their voices hushed in the drained air, their faces raised in the ghost-glow. Suffer the little children, Mr McKeown said as he passed by.

Hallo, Mr McKeown, they answered in unison. They sang.

Houses all around joined in silence. In solid dark. In the scale of things they stood on either side. Shadows made no difference. Then out on to the main road suddenly where Mr McKeown glanced up and down as if mankind could be lying in wait. Its intention withheld door to door. Tall lights were more like it, leaving dark as it was. Pray for us sinners, Mr McKeown said as he turned abruptly left. A few people walked ahead. Now and at the hour of our death, Mr McKeown said in a low voice. He blessed himself.

Mrs McKeown walked past the Travel Agents for the second time. Through the large window genuine travellers were chatting to clerks. Coloured posters showed the blues and yellows of sea and sand and cloudless skies. People on the pavement ignored Mrs McKeown, or looked at her with hardened faces. I'm out of place here, she thought, where people don't know me. They pass like strangers, far from where

I live. She stopped and looked into a shoe-shop, then moved slightly to right and left pretending to examine different pairs of shoes. But how can I get to Saudi Arabia without going into the Travel Agents? she thought. Without asking questions that will give me away? Without hearing answers that make everything impossible?

Mrs McKeown hurried past the Travel Agents without as much as glancing in. She reached the corner where opposite the City Hall stood bare in the bright morning sun. It rose like a closed door against the sky, even to pass it seemed impossible. I'm so small in the city, Mrs McKeown thought, and the bus for home is almost out of reach. There it is at the side of the City Hall. When able she crossed the wide road diagonally like one beaten under a desert sun. Her feet sank one after the other in the hard cement which made her progress all the more difficult . Once on the bus light flooded the sky just where buildings parted. I'm on my way, Mrs McKeown sighed. She poked in her purse for the fare.

CLAIRE KEEGAN

The Ginger Rogers Sermon

Don't ask me why we called him Slapper Jim. My mother stamped his image in my head, and I was at an age when pictures of a man precede the man himself. The posters verify: Thin Lizzy with a V of chest exposed, Pat Spillane's legs racing across my bedroom wall, his hurley poised. I was the girl with the sweet tooth and a taste for men. And pictures.

I have a photographic memory. I can see every tacky page of my cousin's wedding album, the horseshoe on the cake with the man slightly taller than the woman and their feet sunk in the frosting. I parcel out my life in images the way other people let the calendar draw a line around them every month. That time of Slapper Jim was the time of the strangest pictures.

We killed pigs then, ate pork cracked in its own fat with a pulpy sauce. Plasticine grey and apple green, those were the colours of my home. Ma held my dinner plate with the tail of her skirt and talked through her day while I tucked in.

'You should see the new lumberjack your da hired. Slapper Jim, they call him. A great big fella he is! Walked in here and I'll tell ya nothing but the truth, he leaned up against the partition there and I thought the whole yoke was going to cave in.'

My brother, Eugene, quacks his hand behind her back. I spear a slice of pork and in my mind I see a giant, the earth tremoring where he walks. A man who doesn't know his own strength. That can be dangerous. I've seen my father crack a cow's ribs with his fist, just trying to slide her over in the stall.

'I gave him his bit of dinner and he reached over for the

handle on the saucepan without getting up. Ate eleven spuds. Eleven spuds if ya don't mind! Yer lucky there's aer a one left.' Ma rummages in the cutlery drawer for a spoon.

Tapioca and stewed apples, I suppose. I hope for sherry trifle, gooey caramel, dollops of ice-cream.

'What's for afters?'

They leave me here alone on Saturday nights. Eugene goes too, even though he doesn't dance. Him staying home with me is a sissy thing to do because he's so much older. Seven years older. I was made out of the last of my father's sperm. I found that out just recently. My mother says I am The Accident in the family. My father tells people I am The Shakings of the Bag, which I suppose is much the same thing.

Dance mad, my parents. Ma says a man who can't dance is half a man. She's taught me the harvest jig and the waltz, the quickstep and the Siege of Venice in the parlour. She says dancing is good therapy, makes her feel like she's in time with the world. Mostly we move where we're put, stooping under the rain and such, but dancing frees her up, oils her joints, she says. Everyone should know how to move in their own time. She puts the record on, I shake Lux across the lino, and we whirl around the parlour floor like two loonies. I am the man loony. I pretend I don't see her watching her reflection in the mirror of the sideboard as we pass. The Walls of Limerick requires two-facing-two, so we hold our hands out to imaginary partners and move them into their places. I like this knowing what Ma will do, where she'll go before she does, not having to think about it.

Saturdays smell of girls: wet wool, nail polish and camomile shampoo. In the kitchen, Ma sets her hair. We call it The Salon. I hold the pins between my lips and roll her hair around the spiky curlers, stiffen them with setting lotion. Her head goes into the net and she sits in under the hood of the dryer we bought down at the auction. I hand her an old *Woman's Weekly* and imagine it's *Vogue*. The last page is ripped out so Da can't read about women's problems.

'Do you want a coffee!' I shout above the noise.

There was never any coffee in that house. She stays under there, deaf and talking loud like an old person and I hand her a cup of frothy Ovaltine and an hour later she's out, relieved and pink.

Then the daubs of shoe cream, the shush of the steam iron smoothing out the creases. The shuffle of the entertainment pages and Da working a lather for his face and sticking the headlines on his chin to stop the blood. Ma wriggling into her flesh-coloured roll-on, a big elastic knickers to keep her belly in. Pot Belly, I call her.

'Are ya going dancing now, Pot Belly?'

'Where's the beauty contest, Pot Belly?'

'Where did yer pot belly go, Pot Belly?'

She calls me The Terror. 'Shut up, ya terror.' She dots Lily of the Valley behind her ears with the glass stopper and slides her tapping feet into her dancing shoes, ready to take off.

'You won't fall into the fire now will ya?' Da always having the last word, jingling his keys like they belong to the only car in the parish.

'No, Da.'

Eugene pulling on his corduroy jacket, giving me a look like I shouldn't be alive.

The film comes on after the nine o'clock news. I change into my pyjamas and find the biscuit tin. She hides it in the washing machine or the accordion case or the churn. Once Eugene left a note that said,' Find a better hiding place next time,' but Pot

Belly went mad, so now we leave nothing and she says nothing.
That's the way it is in our house, everybody knowing things but
pretending they don't know.

I turn off all the lights and sit with my feet up and play with
myself in the dark and hope the actors take off every stitch and
go skinny-dipping in close-up. *The Birds* is the name of tonight's
film. Crows line up on the wires, watching the children with
their black eyes. Ready to swoop. Even the teachers can't offer
them protection. I think of the grey crows picking out our ewe's
eyes. I hear a noise but it's only the milk strainer hammering
the glass in the wind. Looked like a metal claw, a wiry hand. I
slide the bolt across the door and let the setter up on the couch. I
squeeze my eyes when the birds dive on the town.

It's after midnight when the headlights cross the room. Ma
wobbles in, opens the fridge, its light shines pink on her cheeks.

Da slides the kettle over on the hot-plate and warms his
hands, ready for a feed. 'Saw the Slapper down in Shillelagh. He
was out on the floor with a one.'

'And the size of her,' Ma chips in. 'No bigger than a bantam
hen she is, sitting up beside him. And neather one of 'em has a
step in their foot. Fecking useless.' She bites into a tomato with a
vengeance and Eugene heads for the stairs before she starts her
Ginger Rogers sermon.

'How's the bantam?' is the first thing I say when I meet Slapper
Jim. He laughs a big red laugh that sounds like the beginning of
something. He has plump lips and blond hair and standing
beside him is like standing in the shade. He's as big as a
wardrobe. I feel like opening all his shirt buttons and looking
inside. 'Haw' is the word he uses all the time.

'Who's this bantam now, haw?' Sounds like he's talking
down a well.

My father sits at the head of the table and rubs a wedge of tobacco between his palms and packs his pipe. He has no teeth to distract the smile away from his eyes.

'Ma says your one is like a bantam,' I say.

'Haw?'

'Do ya leave her sitting on the nest all week?'

'Maybe she's not nesting at all.'

'Pluck her.'

The bantam jokes went on until the end. The hatching, plucking, sideways-looking, gawky jokes carried us through summer and beyond.

Slapper doesn't wear a belt. If he pulls his trousers up on his hips, the hems almost reach his ankles. On real wet days, the men stay home and do odd jobs around the yard. They fence, pare the sheep's feet, weld bits and pieces. On Saturdays Eugene watches *Sports Stadium* and bites his nails. I help Slapper split the sticks. I am a girl who knows one end of a block from the other, know to place it on the chopping block the way it grows, make it easier for Slapper. But I don't suppose it would make any difference. That axe comes down and splits that wood open every time, knots or no knots. Even the holly, which my father calls 'a bitch of a stick to split', breaks open under his easy strike. We have a rhythm going: I put them up, he splits them open. With other people, I take my hand away fast, but not with Slapper Jim. He and I are like two parts of the same machine, fast and smooth. We trust each other. And always he gives his waistband a little tug when I'm putting them up, and that waistband slides down with the swing of the axe and the crack of his arse shows every time.

I too am a lumberjack in summer. Pot Belly says it is no job for a girl. Girls should flute the pastry edge or wash the car at best is what she thinks. I should wallpaper my room, practise

walking around the rooms with a book flat on my head to help
my posture.

'Keep her away from the saws. If that girl comes home from
that wood with no feet, don't come home here.'

We've all seen such things. Toes sawed off, an arm mangled
in a winch, and once, a mare gone mad with the sting of a
gadfly, pulling the slig out on to the road and scrapping the car.
But when morning comes I'm up and ready, watching for
Slapper's Escort on the lane.

Following the mare is the job for me. A grey Clydesdale with a
white face, she's seventeen hands if she's an inch. And the smell
of her, the warm earth smell like the inside of a damp flowerpot.
I put my nose on her neck and breathe in. And she's smart too,
knows to stop when she snags and bikes up without putting out
your shoulder. No dirt in her, but still she'll give you a lash with
that tail if you're not quick. We're clear-falling every second
line on the slopes. Slapper and Da fall and trim, sitka spruce
mostly, and larch, the trimmer's dream. I hook the chain
around the slig and follow the mare down the lines on to the
car-road, drawing the timber as close together as I can, keeping
the butts even. I unhook the slig and lift the swing back up on
the hames and then my favourite part – holding on to the
mare's tail and letting her pull me back up the line after her.
Slapper says I have brains to burn, thinking of that. Da says I
should give some to Eugene because he does nothing, only sit
around on his arse with his nose in a book all day.

We drink mugs of tea from a flask at nosh-up, and milk from
an old Corcoran's lemonade bottle. Soda-bread soggy with
tomatoes and sardines in red sauce. The tea tastes bitter
towards the end of the day. Slapper dents the bumper where he
sits, talks with his mouth full.

'Uckin' lies,' he says when he swats the flies. They light on the horse-dung and the bread. They chase me up and down the lines and drive the mare cuckoo. I sit on the mare backwards with my feet up on her flanks while she grazes the bank and wait for somebody to open the biscuits. Jim lifts me up there. Peaches, he calls me but I am nothing like a peach. My father says I'm more like a stalk of rhubarb, long and sour.

'Ya have a way with that baste, Peaches. She bites the arse off me.'

'It's always hanging out anyway, Slapper. Here,' Da says, handing over a wad of baling twine, 'until ya can buy yerself a real belt.'

'Haw?' Slapper smiles but he doesn't tie his trousers up. He just looks at the twine in a way that makes Da put it back into his pocket, and gives his waistband a tug the way another man might push his glasses up on his nose.

Slapper teaches me the tricks of the trade. He holds his big finger up but doesn't stoop when he says these things. 'Don't open the slig until you've unhooked her; if she takes off, yer fingers will be dogmate. Don't stand in front of the saw; if there's a loose link and the chain breaks, you're fucked.' He opens up that forbidden world of adult language and invites me in. Then he leaves me alone to be capable.

We stay at it until dusk. The foresters come around with their kettles in the evenings and paint the stumps with the pink poison. We hide the saws and the oil and petrol cans under the tops up the line and let the mare loose in the field down the road. The lorries drive up with their robot claws and load up the lengths. Twenty-five tons is a load for them, a cheque for us, and a pound of wine gums and a *Bunty* and *Judy* after Mass and two choc-ices and gobstoppers for me.

'What do they learn ya in school?' Slapper asks as we're driving the mare down to the field.

I know trigonometry. 'I know that the square of the hypotenuse is equal to the sum of the squares on the other two sides.'

'What's a highpotinuze?' Jim pushes back the passenger seat to make room for his legs, but his knees are snug against the dashboard. He holds the mare's reins out through the open window as she trots next to the car.

'Go on, ya lazy cunt ya! Whup! Whup! Ya hairy farting fucker ya. Go on!' He claps the outside of the door with his hand.

'The child, Slapper. The child!' Da admonishes.

Slapper looks back at me. My father's eyes watch me in the rear-view mirror. I pretend I haven't heard a bad word.

'What's a highpotinuze?'

Those are the pictures of that time. Three dirty lumberjacks sligging out timber, the wood slick and white beneath the bark. Eating packets of coconut creams, spitting, listening to Radio 1 in the car when it rained, sharpening chain, files grinding on the rakers, the cutters shining all round like some deadly necklace. Slapper asking what they learned me in school, his file sharpening smack-on with the slant of the cutters every time. Da says Slapper's a great man with a saw. The last fella Da had working with him slid a matchstick in between the spark plug and the petrol tank so she wouldn't start, but Da found out and gave him his walking papers. I tell Slapper Jim the things I learn in school. I know that Oliver Cromwell told the poor people 'To hell or to Connaught' (I can see him on his black horse, pointing west), that Jesus lost his temper. I can recite William Blake: 'Tiger! tiger! burning bright / In the forests of the night, What immortal hand or eye / Could frame thy fearful symmetry?' I can see it on the page, the curve of the question mark at the end. Slapper holds my hand and stands me up on the bonnet of the car in the rain, telling me to say the poems. I read them off my memory. He asks me what 'immortal' means but I don't know. He says I am the morbidest child in Ireland.

'Get that child in out of the rain!' Da putting a damper on it from the driver's seat. 'Do ya hear me, Slapper? She'll catch her end and you can be the one to bring her home!'

But Slapper just smiles. 'Say the poems, Peaches.'

I shoot up like the rhubarb stalk Da says I am, and the transformation begins. I take an interest in my cousin's old dresses. Flowery things with thin patent belts and matching pointy shoes that pinch my toes. I limp home from school and make the announcement. Ma says Shusssssh! and gives me the elastic belt and towels. I think it's the equivalent of Da's newspaper for his chin.

'Don't let yer father see them,' she says. Her always hiding women away, like we're forbidden.

Now that I am thirteen, I am sectioned off from the men. It happens in school too, in gym class. I play basketball and jump over hurdles and come back all red-faced and sweaty and talk non-stop in class. Nobody sits beside me because I smell like an afterbirth. I wear the pads and the Lily of the Valley and go dancing down the pub. Slapper Jim is always there with the Bantam. I waltz around in the cigarette smoke with old men my father knows. Watch Sam Collier prancing across the floor in his patent shoes, swinging Pot Belly around, and him with his left hand up so high, she can barely reach it. Foxy, we call him, with his head of slicked-back silver hair, his horse's eye. The men's hands grip me by the waist and swing me around, same as I'm a bucket of water. They hold me close as an excuse not to let me go. The backs of their shirts are wet. I drink Babychams out of long-stemmed glasses. They taste like warm honey and soften the pictures. Eugene sits with his elbows on the bar, watching the dancers, his shoe tapping in perfect time on the rung of his stool.

Slapper cannot dance. If his feet move on the beat, it's an accident. He doesn't catch the rhythm. He takes me out on to the floor and puts his arms around me and shifts his weight from one leg to the other, taking huge strides for the waltz. My head comes up to the fourth button on his shirt. I could almost see past him if I stood on my toes. I can smell him, get the whiff of the sticks on his chest as if he sweats out resin. Reminds me of the mare, the hair and the warmth under his shirt, the big feet moving over the floor. I try to lead him into the rhythm, exaggerating my sways, but he does not feel the music, and I wind up stepping on his toes.

'Should have worn me steel toecaps,' he says.

His Bantam isn't even as tall as me, a dark, plump woman with a mouth like his. She wears a royal blue blouse with gold sequins blown across the bust. He could scrape her sequins with the buckle on his trousers, if he had a buckle. That's how funny-looking they are.

At closing time, the couples stand against the gable wall: women with their backs against the wall, the men leaning against them, both hands against the bricks, kissing. Snogging, we call it at school. I want to see Slapper snogging the Bantam, I don't know why but I want to see what that looks like. I think he'd have to put her standing on a beer barrel. I look for them, but they're never there at the gable wall. I wonder what it would be like to kiss Slapper, to have the tough, hard hands inside my dress and his mouth on my mouth. Ma puts her arm around my shoulders and leads me to the car, shielding out that world of romance and men and women touching.

The winters are dark here. I shiver from the chill behind the curtains, piss without touching the toilet seat. Downstairs, the paraffin oil heater throws shapes like tears on to the kitchen ceiling. Ma turns up the wick, making the shapes dance when Slapper comes in. I think of the way she turns up the oven when she puts the second loaf in. She braids my hair in two long plaits while I eat spaghetti hoops and a fried sausage. She wets her thumbs on her tongue, catching up the stray hairs. I listen to the suck of Slapper's pink mouth slurping tea, the cast-iron pot swinging on its hinge outside the window. I don't want to go to school.

I crack wafer ice on the puddles in the lane and smoke twigs until the bus comes, blow my breath out white. I bring home nits from school. Da holds me down with his farmer's grip while Ma douses my head with turpentine-smelling lotion. She pulls the comb along my scalp and catches the nits between the teeth and crushes them with a crunch beneath her thumbnail, saying, 'There, we've got him.'

The snow has come this Saturday. I have taken everything but the blinkers off the mare, left the men to pack the gear. I am riding her the whole way home to keep her in the stable until the weather improves. When the car passes me on the road, the mare whinnies and trots on after them, but soon we are left behind. Slapper's hand waves from the passenger window. Sometimes you'd think he was the Pope or somebody. The road is quiet, but the mare's ears are up. Then further on, I see three yearling colts leaning up against a field gate, waiting. I try to pull the mare to the far side of the road, but there's no bit in her mouth, and it's impossible. She puts her nose to theirs, and squeals. I dismount. The colts have their willies out, the pink and black hoses almost reaching their girth lines. They snort and push the gate until I think it will fall over on to me. The

mare kicks out with her hind leg and squats to piss on the road. I
pull the reins down hard but she is oblivious of me now. Her
snorts deepen and the colts bite each other, their mouths fast
and open. They scrape the bars with their hooves. I throw
stones at them and they eventually launch into a farting gallop
down the field and back again, trotting inside the ditch beside
the mare as I pull her home. I am afraid to mount her until I get
well away from the colts, knowing she will canter back given
the slightest chance.

When I reach home, Slapper's grey Escort is still parked in the
yard. He comes out of the barn and reaches up and pulls me
down into his arms.

'Are ya frozen, Peaches?' he says.

'She's horsing, Slapper!' My teeth chatter. My hands are stiff.

'Haw?'

'I'm not joking ya. Them colts nearly climbed over the gate to
get at her.'

Slapper says nothing but smiles as he rubs her down.

We walk across the frozen mud towards the house. Pot Belly
has made beef stew with the bone from the round steak sitting
in the soup. Dumplings bobbing on the surface. Eugene's
reading a book called *Seven Deadly Nights at the Edge of the
Universe*. His eyebrows have grown together since the last time I
looked at him. Pot Belly gives out and tells Slapper he's not to be
going home in this weather. He's staying the night.

We make up the extra bed.

'I hope the shagger doesn't snore and keep me and Eugene up
all night.' I try to put her off the track.

'Your mouth's getting worse, young lady. I'll have to have a
word with Slapper about that.'

But she never would. She, like the rest of us, thought the sun
shone out of Slapper's arse.

*

He doesn't know I'm watching. He stands where the slant of blue light partitions the room. I am glad of the snow. Slapper closes the door behind him and doesn't bother to open the buttons on his shirt. Instead, he holds the back of his collar and pulls it over his head. He doesn't wear a vest like Eugene. There's hair all over his chest and more on his back. His stomach is a plank of muscle. He slides the zip down, exposes his legs, sits down, pulls the waistband down over his feet. I imitate Eugene's breathing in the far bed. Slapper comes over to my bed in his navy-blue underwear. He bends down and I close my eye. His breath fans my face. I am just about to let him kiss me when I hear the creak of the other bed.

His feet hang over the mattress. I know by the quiet that the snow is still coming down outside. The light gets whiter. We are safe inside the drifts. Snowed in. Tucked up. Perhaps the drifts will come and he will have to stay another night.

'Are ya asleep, Slapper?'

'Haw?' For a long time he says nothing and then says, 'It's a cold fucking house.'

I go over to him, wrapped in my blankets. I pull his bedclothes down and get in, compounding our warmth. I lie up against his back and breathe on his neck. My hand slides around his waist, wanders shyly down through the curls of his pubic hair. I feel him stiffen. I think of the colts. He moves to the edge of the mattress but I follow him. When he turns over, his hands are cold. Big and gentle and precise. 'Jesus, Peaches,' I hear him whisper before his will subsides. Eugene's breathing is steady in the far bed and I am thankful that the bed does not creak.

Three feet of snow has fallen over Ireland, the wireless says. I find a bonnet from an old Volkswagen and Slapper and I spend the afternoon sliding down the top field, right over the ditch, across the lane and into a nice curve in the field below. The track gets a little longer every time, but when we get off at the bottom and look back up, I cannot resist doing it again. He pulls the bonnet in one hand and mine in the other and hardly says a word. Suddenly, I am somebody no one is supposed to know about. At last I know the reasoning behind my mother's secrets. Men are weak and women must hide themselves to keep them strong, must rip out problem pages of the women's magazine, must hide the flow of blood, be sexless.

I saddle the mare and take her the full circuit through the snow, down the lane and up past the bog-field. The moon brightens the dark sky like a fake sun, but the land is white. The world's turned upside-down. The evening is edged in blue like TV light. All the chainsaws have stopped. I listen to the puff of the mare's breath and her hooves compressing horseshoe tracks through the snow. The smell of the pines is everywhere for the snow has bedded down all else. We have just eased into a canter along the car-road when she shies. A pheasant flutters out over the trees. Horses frighten easily at night. Especially when there's wind. I pull her up and listen. It may be deer. I dismount and lead the mare down between the trees. The ground is dry, the moss smooth underfoot, and the mare stumbles. It's black beneath the branches. And then I get the smell. The mare pulls on the reins. I stop and listen. The wind pheews through the treetops, like somebody learning to whistle. We walk towards the smell and then I see the source. Slapper's boots are at eye-level. They are resting on nothing. As I draw closer, I see his face, darker than bark. Christ, the smell. The wind spins him gently on the rope. I can't even cut him down. I leave him there, hanging in his own dung, and gallop home.

That was the hardest part, taking the others up there, letting them see him like that. The way they stood and looked and cursed and said Jaysus and Holy Mother of Divine Jaysus and Why in the name of Jaysus? and took their caps off and carried him down the hill on the bonnet of the Volkswagen we had used as a sled, my father's coat draped over his body. I was sorry I hadn't stayed longer with him among the trees.

Eugene stood there looking at me like I did it.

We come home from the wake and sit in the parlour. The room is like a second-hand furniture shop, the walls painted lime green, a border of faded roses creeping below the ceiling. Pot Belly produces a bottle of Bristol Cream from the sideboard and fills four glasses to the brim. The padlock on the yard gate beats its clasp, hammering down the silence of the room. My father watches the sparks lifting into the soot. Eugene has no nails to bite; they are bloody at the quick. When his eyes meet mine, they are full of accusation and blame. I am aware of my own breathing.

Pot Belly brings candles down out of the kitchen, white blessed candles she got at Easter, and lights them from my father's match. She stands them upright in their own grease and places them about the room. She takes a record from its sleeve and turns the light off. The room is lit by flame. On the mantelpiece stand trophies, silver-plated couples frozen in mid-swirl. They quiver in the firelight. Pot Belly catches Eugene's hand and pulls him upright. He does not want to dance, but her pull is steady. I know what she is doing, and from my father's evasive eyes, that look he has when Ma is changing her dress, I know that something's going on, know my parents have spoken of this. They have it planned. Ma has always thought a man should know how to dance. The only flaw she could see in Slapper Jim was his leggy, graceless motion on the floor. She is teaching Eugene, as a precaution, as if him knowing these steps will carry him through, prevent him from tying a noose around his neck later on.

She begins the slow waltz and he follows her reluctantly, shifting his weight, his body stiff, his feet imitating hers. My father keeps his eyes on the fire. Pot Belly takes Eugene around the furniture whispering one-two-three, one-two-three until the music stops. The stylus crackles in the groove and the rhythm changs to a quickstep. Da stands up and pulls off his overcoat and takes my hand. The steel of his suspender digs into my side. The voice of a travelling woman, clear and stern, pushes us together. Pot Belly counts the beats into Eugene's ear. One, one-two, one. We dance around each other, cautious of the space we're taking up. And then the song changes to a reel and there is nothing but the primitive da-rum of the bodhrán, the sound of wood pounding skin. Da-rum. Da-rum. The near screech of a fiddle, the pull of hair on string, the melodeon, the wheeze of bellows catching up, and the slight imprecision of the live instruments playing. We lift the furniture to the edge of the room, and I shake the Lux across the floor. We swig our drinks and exchange our partners. Eugene starts moving with the beat, throwing himself in time. Ma removes her shoes. A V of sweat darkens the back of my father's shirt. The music is raucous, ornamented. Our shadows are larger than we are, doubling our statures, bending us up on to the ceiling. It is two-facing-two. We face each other. Eugene jumps up and down like a highland dancer and although he does not know the moves, he has found the rhythm. We move him into the places he should go. First the ladies exchange places, then the men. We take the man facing us and go right for seven and back again. We swing our partners and begin over. The fire heats the room and I peel off my cardigan when the tune ends. We gulp the sherry. Ma gets the stand from the hair-drier and sings into it like it's a microphone. Eugene puts his hand up very high, imitating Foxy, sticks his belly out and we move around in circles.

'Do ya come here often?' he says.

'I do when the ewes aren't lambing.'

'Do ya live in a disadvantaged area?' He belches.

'Yeah, I get the subsidy.'

'God, you're lovely. There's nothing like the smell of a hogget ewe.'

He breathes me in with his sherry breath. We move with the squeal and squeeze of the uileann pipes, we are pulled in with the bellows. The quavering lilt and sway of a tin whistle curls through the dark room. The long swathe of hair that covers Da's bald patch falls down and almost touches his shoulder. Ma pulls off her roll-on and swings it like a hula hoop on her index finger, keeping her left hand at her waist. The last picture I remember is the roll-on flying across the room with the snap of elastic and Eugene asking, 'Can I interest you in a snog at the gable wall?' as he swings me in a perfect twist.

MAXIM CROWLEY

Writing Cookbooks

John Ambrose was a writer of cookbooks. Nothing in his earlier life had seemed to predestine him for this profession – born when his mother was thirty-four, his father forty-one, he had grown up siblingless in a quiet family, in a quiet area of Athlone, the centre of Ireland, midway between Gael and Gall, the centre of his universe. Sometimes he visualized, in greyish images, the flow of the Shannon and the small boats, colourless, moored near the nineteenth-century bridge linking Athlone east and Athlone west, Ireland anglicized and Ireland anglicized less.

Looking out over Dublin Bay from his three-storey house – his study on the top floor, where he sat at his desk positioned in front of a large bay-window with exactly forty-two small panes set in wooden frames, reducing his potential view by roughly one third – he saw a murder of crows picking at some substance, food presumably, on the beach. He wondered what crows ate – not fish, surely? He had noticed that more crows now swarmed on the beaches, starkly and darkly contrasting with their environment, flapping helplessly in the strong winds and often hopping, blackbird-like, rather than flying, low over or on the ground. Gulls, on the other hand, moved further inland every year, perching motionless in fields and meadows, as hopelessly out of place there as the crows were on the seacoast, no longer floating effortlessly in the strong breezes that hampered the flight of the crows so much.

What did the crows eat? They fed on carrion, of course, but

not on live fish. How did the gulls provide for themselves? Had they become vegetarians, stuffing themselves with seeds, varying their diet with the odd worm and insect?

Perhaps, Ambrose thought, he should include a recipe for worms – fried – in his new cookbook. This had been commissioned by his regular publisher, who, driven by a desire for originality and a need of substantial profits, had suggested that Ambrose should produce a smallish book – 'a hundred pages, say, no more' – with exotic recipes, the exoticism remaining unspecified, for Ambrose to specify. Ambrose had once, years ago, eaten ants, from a tin, when these were on offer during an African festival – some Third World do, yet another attempt to interest non-Africans in African culture – and he remembered that they tasted of tar. Or at least what he thought that tar would taste like. Macadam. A Scotsman producing road surfaces that smelled and tasted like what Africans ate. A sort of bitterness, a texture of coarseness.

He remembered that shrimp in their diverse varieties – scampi, prawns, crayfish, langoustes – were as disgusting to Africans as locusts, say, were to Europeans.

An exotic cookbook. This would have to include recipes for various living organisms available in Europe but not ordinarily eaten there. Worms, of course, were a good beginning. Australians ate them, and they were Europeans, surely? Pickled ants – another possibility. Lots of ants in Europe. He would have to check which species were edible. The bark of trees. Some kinds could be consumed, apparently, though he had never bothered to try. A simple cookbook, set out along conventional lines – first courses, entrées, desserts. Some soups as well. Elephant meat, whale meat, bear and monkey, lizard soup, snake meat – there was no end to the filth people would eat. Brains, sheep's stomach, seagulls – somewhere, somehow, someone would cook it, eat it, proclaim: 'An acquired taste.'

There was a child moving about in the house somewhere. Stanley, aged four, brought up by his wife rather than by him. There was a wife about in the house as well, part of the day. In the afternoon she went out to work, a part-time secretary with a firm of chartered accountants. He didn't see his family often, being locked up in his study, third floor, most of the day. Writing cookbooks.

A pinch of salt. Some nutmeg. Cook well. Pepper from the mill. Catch a rabbit.

Whenever he went to Athlone, twice a year, he had dinner at The Prince of Wales. Irish cuisine strictly. Irish cooking, he had come to realize, was unique. It wasn't French, much simpler than that, but it wasn't English either. He had often wondered why the English were perhaps the only nation in the world unable to prepare food. They cooked it, for hours. They had no sense of taste, nor of combinations of taste. Nothing to do with sophistication. He realized that Irish cooking was similar to Japanese cooking – not as far as ingredients were concerned, not in *fanciness*, but in simplicity. The Japanese took fresh ingredients and prepared them carefully, but simply – the Irish did the same. It was all based, not on sauces or spices, but on a harmony of tastes, of flavours. Chicken and ham – the bland taste of the one supplemented by the equally bland taste of the other. Different blandnesses combining to create a superior dish. A superior bland wine to go with it – a Montrose for example.

He stood up from his desk to go to the toilet. Slight stomach pain again, bearable but bothersome. The sort of nagging ache that doesn't incapacitate one, but does spoil, destroy, one's temper and peace of mind. A water torture, lethal.

He was forty-seven years old, so that when walking down the

two sets of stairs to the first floor where the toilet was his legs creaked – or at least he *felt* them creak, inaudibly. The continuous process of eating, elimination, decay. Death and being decrepit. His desire for heaven had been weakened, when young, by the realization that food was a superfluity there. He enjoyed food. He wasn't sure if sitting peacefully on a cloud, without any need to partake of fleshly meats, would be satisfactory. Eating was what he liked most in life.

It showed. His was a portly figure, a strongly fleshed belly, a round, filled face. Once, in a bar, he had been with some friends, a young girl, twentyish, among them. She had asked everyone, rhetorically, what they enjoyed most. 'Nothing compares to a good fuck,' this girl had argued, describing in some detail what she meant by it. When it was his turn to answer, Ambrose had disagreed. 'Good food,' he had said. What use is sex if you can completely absorb organic material and truly become one with it?

He opened the bathroom door. Where was the child? No sound filtered through to him, no noise echoed from the recesses of the old, cavernous and uncared-for house where he lived and spent his days. The boy would manage, he decided. He sat down on the toilet, his pants pulled down, and pushed, hoping that the ache in his stomach would go when he emptied and cleared his guts. It did, for a moment, which made him feel joyful – twenty years old again. A young man, who loved eating. Not yet physically corrupted. Layers of fat only developing. Brains not quite arteriosed. Lean meat.

When he stood up, the pain already coming back, his trousers still down to his ankles, he noticed, looking, some red in the toilet bowl. Not as bad as it had been a couple of weeks earlier, when everything had been a clear red, gallons of it, seemingly. Just a strong reddish tincture, mixed with the asphalt black. Dark as a tin of ants. Smelly, too, like a newly tarred road.

It would have to be his masterpiece, this new cookbook with the exotic recipes. It would have to change the world. No more chops, steak, pies, stews – no more beef, veal, lamb. No more shrimps. Worms, ants, tree bark, locusts, shark and crow, gulls and spiders – these would constitute the delicious new basic diet in Ireland and the rest of the Western world.

Thank God, he thought, that I won't have to eat the stuff. He was no lover of exotic things. A reasonable existence, lived out in comfort, no financial worries and three square meals a day. A snack at night-time. A bottle of good wine, and a fine malt to finish the day – Lagavulin preferably. His life had centred around food. As has anyone's, but Ambrose was conscious of it.

He walked up the stairs, slowly. The necessity of sleep, he thought, was one thing. The necessity of food quite another. He wondered about people who thought of food all the time – his natural peers, as it were. Who were they? Cooks, of course, and chefs, and other cookbook writers. Professionally interested, all of them. Housewives, having to prepare another meal day in day out for the rest of their natural lives. Ambrose shuddered. He *hated* cooking. Eating he loved, feeding even, and writing about food was all right. Preparing it was not.

Hunger-strikers, African villagers, concentration camp inmates – these were another category of his peers, of people whose every thought centred on food. The operative word, of course, was food, not partaking of it but thinking of it.

Going up the stairs, Ambrose tried to categorize the food freaks he had just listed. Chefs, housewives and the general public were not eaters – they prepared. Chefs and housewives were preparers, using recipes, inventing them, cooking them. They differed fundamentally from him. Hunger-strikers,

Africans were no eaters either – lacking food, they abstained from it, voluntarily or otherwise. They were not like him either. But they also differed from ascetics, who used food sparingly. Ascetics were users of food, much like himself, but in smaller quantities.

Chefs on the one hand, hunger-strikers on the other, ascetics in the middle – it was an orderly, pleasant world view, provided – or so Ambrose thought – that one was outside it, looking at it, and not involved. Eat or be eaten. A divine position. But heaven, with its lack of interest in food, was not for him.

He opened the door of his study, sat down at his desk and felt the pain increasing. A blasphemy escaped him. The only way he knew how to get rid of the pain now, after defecating, was to put a finger down his throat and throw up. He had tried this several times before and it had helped, but lately it had helped less. The pain had become sharper, the ache more lingering – and it was the ache, permanent, never-ending, that he wanted to be rid of. A bit of pain he could bear, a permanent ache would eventually destroy him. Intestine torture, continuing for years.

Sitting at his desk, his first notes for his exotic cookbook in front of him, he disgustedly put his finger down his throat. He gargled and gagged, his stomach heaving. Cramps and pulsations passed through his body. Nothing came up, except a tiny bit of internal fluid, a mere half-drop, virtually tasteless. He swallowed and wiped off the sweat. The ache continued unabated.

God damn it, he thought. I cannot finish my cookbook in this condition. Hack work it may be, routine it may be based on, but the pain is simply too severe. There must be some intervals at least, some moment of calm, of – what, relaxation? – when I can sit down at my desk and put some uninspired words to paper.

He looked out through his window with the forty-two panes. Motionless, several gulls wafted on the wind, some crows continued their flapping. The tide was changing.

He heard the sound of his young son downstairs. What the hell was the child up to now? He could hardly walk. He shouted at him, 'Stanley, is there anything you want?' Silence ensued. He shouted again, 'Are you all right?' The child remained silent. He stared out of his window. Stillness outside as well. It was ten past five. 'Stanley,' he shouted.

Athlone consisted of one long street, a bridge, and a river touching the town. And shaping it. His next trip was six weeks away. He would take a taxi to Heuston Station, get on the Galway train, have a few drinks in the buffet, ogle the girls sitting near him. More of them every year, he thought, getting younger every year, less interesting. He would live in suspension on the train, live in anticipation as well, arriving in Athlone in the early evening, walking to The Prince of Wales, having his usual dinner. Good soda bread.

Where was his wife? She should take care of the child, he must not be bothered, certainly not now, when he was writing, or rather reflecting on his cookbook. A dull ache. His notes in front of him. The child downstairs was silent.

He looked at his computer screen. It was empty. He touched the keyboard. This will serve four, he wrote. Next line. Ingredients. Two pounds of tree bark, to be collected on a moonlit night. He erased the last part of the sentence. Two pounds of tree bark remained. Spices and herbs. Marinate the bark for twenty-four hours in a mixture of olive oil, with some lemon juice and a pinch of kerry. Pinch of salt. Fools would eat this, he thought, the *Irish Times* would run it as a special recipe. The Dublin 4 crowd would love it, if they thought it was fashionable.

Follow this unusual but hearty hors-d'oeuvre by an equally unusual but tasty entrée, he wrote. Worms, ants, horsemeat, the most disgusting organic matter you can think of. Spiders. Crabs and lobsters were spiders, weren't they? Another cramp, and the feeling that his intestines were going to empty into his trousers. Ah well, anything was better than this persistent ache.

He should see a doctor, but he knew that he suffered from intestinal cancer, so what was the point? He could let them cut him up, through yellowish fat getting at the red meat, fry for five minutes according to taste, but what use would it be? Having considerable lengths of his intestine removed, to be cleaned thoroughly and fried in butter, *tripe à la irlandaise*, it would be thrown away, put out with the rubbish, at the back of the hospital, together with the other bits and pieces, the discarded parts of God's creation. And God's children. Bits of foetuses.

Could one eat foetuses? One could eat afterbirths – some feminists apparently did. Could he think of a good recipe for fried afterbirth? Yes, he could. But it wouldn't go down well in Ireland. Eating oneself. The opposite of self-maiming. Or merely the same thing in reverse. The human condition.

He heard the front door open. His wife, presumably, returning from her daily toil. What can a man eat? he thought. Praying mantises ate their mates. Swallowed them. Gone and done with them. He felt like vomiting. The thought of food disgusted him.

Again he felt a cramp in his stomach. Sit down, he thought, sit tight, and write. He had to write his exotic cookbook, his masterpiece. Shit, blood and women, what did he care? His *magnum opus* would be written.

What will they eat? he thought. Anything, of course,

provided the recipe was right. One hundred pages. Thirty menus. Thirty main courses, thirty entrées.

Think. Whale, snake, monkey, worms, ostrich, crocodile, horse, dog, rat, ants, tripe, brains, gull, swan, bear, locusts, shrimp, spiders, wood lice, crab, cat, pig's feet, crow, goose, duck, gnat, chicken, the occasional mouse, hare, the glands of animals, any.

Basically, he thought in desperation, this wasn't all that exotic. He remembered having seen on television an Eskimo tearing apart the body of a sea lion and gobbling it up, blood, lard, everything, the cold, snow and ice contrasting seriously with the gore.

Athlone was such a grey city. But then, most of Ireland was. He wasn't sure who had thought up the fiction of a green island. Lush green. A thousand shades of green. Bord Fáilte, no doubt. But there were several colleagues of his – well, literati, no cookbook writers, but writers still, pensmiths, no swordsmen – who had referred to Erin's greenness. He knew only Ireland's greyness, interspersed with garishly painted front doors in yellow, purple and pink, and with the thousand shades of brown of Connemara. One shade of grey, he thought, and a thousand varieties of brown. No greens, except the greenery on one's plate.

The child was silent now, taken care of by his mother, presumably. He was not to be disturbed – strict orders and strict discipline prevailed in the house.

Would he be there in six weeks? he wondered. Would he live that long? He could do the book, if he focused on his task and concentrated in spite of the distraction of the pain, in two weeks. Usually he tasted his own recipes first. He would not this time.

The food he described would be inedible, and besides, he

could no longer eat. Sometimes it wasn't all that bad, but mostly even a single bite of anything substantial produced such gruesome stomach cramps that he desisted almost at once. Fat and rotund, he could live on his lard for a while.

His body wasting, all the consumable bits being consumed, until only the hard matter remained, ribs, skull, teeth. No edible or consumable bits left. A skeleton even before the worms got him. Those worms could be fried.

His cookbook was a parody, he decided, but it must not be regarded as such. The introduction would be crucial. If he wrote the introduction with the right amount of seriousness, mixed with some humour, but *earnestly*, people would eat the abominations he would think up for them. You can fool all of the people all of the time, he thought, they'd go to any lengths to get ahead of others provided they remained with the pack. Stand out, but belong. It was the great motto of all mankind.

'This is an unusual cookbook,' he wrote, 'containing recipes of unusual foods.' That much was true. 'Unlike your run-of-the-mill, common-or-garden variety of cookbook it does not offer the trite dishes that your guests have been served so often. Every dish is original, nourishing and dramatically different.' Silly drivel, he thought, as Joyce had done before.

God, if only he could eat! Nothing, absolutely nothing on earth matched the glory of good food well cooked. How he had eaten in his prime! Large plates of every delicacy, small bits of tasty morsels, and the best of it the combinations of a hundred different tastes, harmoniously coming together, never blending, but always combining.

Cramps of unusual intensity racked him. He went downstairs again, to empty his empty bowels somehow.

There was no blood, or not so he noticed, and the pain settled again to an ache. He went to the kitchen, took four aspirins, swallowing them whole – he had always been a man of large appetites – and knew they wouldn't help. He should see a doctor, if only to get some painkillers, but they would want to operate, cut out his intestines, his stomach, his eating apparatus. It would finish him, and he wanted to finish whole.

His wife came into the kitchen, to prepare the meal. Her name was Carmel. They had been married twelve years. She did not share his interest in food. Food, to her, was simply something to stay alive, a necessity. It had no place in her life and he had resented her for it for a long time.

'Had a good day?' he asked.

'The usual,' she said. 'Except there was a report on Dixon's firm. The bank has foreclosed and I think they'll go bust.'

'Dixon's?' he said. 'Are you sure?' His father had been a friend of the firm's founder, and even though he was no longer in touch with the family, and even though the family didn't in fact own the company any more, he was unexpectedly touched by this bit of news.

'What's for dinner tonight?' he asked, knowing full well he couldn't eat it anyway.

'Smoked halibut,' she said, 'for starters. It was on offer at Macy's. Amazing, isn't it? Then lamb chops, garlicky. French beans to go with them. Is that all right?'

'Yes,' he said, though the halibut was prepackaged, dead in taste, deep frozen, and the smokiness probably came out of a chemical factory.

'I'll leave you to your labours then,' he said. 'I'll be down in thirty minutes.'

He went back to his study. The ache persisted, the aspirins had not, or not yet, had an effect. He could not eat. He hated it.

Thirty minutes. He wondered if he would even live that long. Probably. Athlone in six weeks was doubtful, but thirty minutes before the lamb chops arrived was manageable. The pain increased. He would not be able to eat them. Work his mouth around them, yes, work his teeth on them, yes, swallow them, yes – and then, four or five minutes later, the pain would be unbearable. He would be dead in thirty-five minutes. He was dead now.

He would not eat in heaven, but he might be eaten in hell, be gnawed at. He preferred that. Worms or vultures eating him, lost souls gnawing at him. It gave him a sense of satisfaction. Eat or be eaten. If he could not eat, he wanted to be eaten. Give pleasure.

He started to write. Never mind the introduction, that would come later. 'This nutritious and unexpectedly tasty menu,' he wrote, 'starts with a cocktail of peppered mouse in a mint sauce. It is amazing how succulent mice meat is, tangy and yet sweet.'

Pain tore through his guts and he began to sweat. He looked out of the window. Crows and gulls whirled and balanced and ate. Edible, inedible. He felt the sourness of his insides rising in his throat.

The Walking Saint

Once a year, Mr John McManus made obligatory contact with his past. Choosing the most dismal of Sundays in late winter, when there were no sports to settle him in for an afternoon of hooting and cheering, he announced the trip to see his great-aunt, a nun, commonly referred to as 'the walking saint' by McManus. He began in earnest meditation at the table. 'I've an idea now for what we could do with ourselves for the afternoon.' The *we* gave it away. 'We're dressed to the hilt, and there's no better time than the present,' McManus said.

'You mean there's no football matches on the telly,' his son Johnny groaned.

'That's enough of your lip'. McManus listened to no protests, nodding with practicality as he gnawed on a piece of fat. 'How many people can say they're related to a walking saint, tell me that?' He pointed menacingly with his fork. 'You'll need the saint's prayers when the Leaving Cert comes around, and if you want a good job. Do you know that when I came up here to Dublin I had to sit an exam against over a thousand others for my job? And do you know what?'

'They chose only twelve men,' Johnny said with a mocking guttural country accent. 'And you were one of those twelve apostles of the Gas Board. Hallelujah.'

'We'll have enough of that, walking atheist.' McManus rolled his eyes at the brazenness of his son but did nothing. He knew his son would get into the university by himself.

His son didn't need the intercession of faith or walking saints.

While the girl cleared off the table, McManus went upstairs and parted his hair with oil and a comb. Dabbing on aftershave, he whistled away to himself, participating in a long-standing ritual that went back to his boyhood: the yearly visits to the walking saint. There was always a reverential tip of the head when the words 'walking saint' were pronounced. Not that much had come of her, really. When he'd first come up from the country to Dublin for the job interview with the Gas Board, the walking saint had arranged for him to stay at a priest's residence so he wouldn't have to waste money on lodgings. But of course, you couldn't get out of a priest's clutches without dropping a fair few bob for Mass offerings, which added up to what a boarding house would have cost and more. That was usually the way of it. The walking saint cost you more than she gave you. Her mission was not of an earthly nature. She had the commission of eternity. Still, she'd blessed his pencil box on the morning of his exam.

'Right, have we got everything – the communion and confirmation medals and the wedding ring?'

Mr McManus's eldest girl of seventeen, Martina, with long stringy black hair and a rat's twitch of anxiety for a face, held a pen in her hand. 'Do you think she could bless the pen I'm going to use on the Leaving Cert?'

A pen! It was a shock to McManus that such stupidity had been inherited so completely. But thank God it had afflicted the girl and not his son. 'Jesus, I don't know about that, Martina. It's . . .'

'It's vulgar,' Mrs McManus said from the kitchen.

'Yes, that's right. It would be vulgar all right. Do you have your confirmation medal? She'll bless that for you.'

Martina made the horrible reflexive twitch, the eyes watering. 'I don't have to tell her what the pen is for. I'll just tell her to bless it for . . . for a special intention.'

'I wouldn't have her bless a sneeze,' Johnny laughed behind her back.

'I'll make sure she gives you a good blessing, walking atheist,' McManus said severely, but there was no conviction in what he said. The walking atheist was a bad bastard, no doubt, but McManus took an edifying pride that he was rearing the sort of creature who would grow up to badger other men the way *he'd* been badgered and looked down upon in his years of service at the Gas Board. McManus couldn't figure how he had managed such a son with the likes of himself and his wife, but accounted for it simply: 'The whole is greater than the sum of its parts.'

The Sunday afternoon rain had the roads desolate, how the earth would be if everyone died. McManus was in good form since there was the odds-on prospect of getting a good afternoon tea up at the convent. His rheumatism acted up though, and he managed to keep the leg warm by depressing the clutch erratically, changing gears more than was necessary, which kept everyone's head rocking forward slightly as the car moved along. His wife eyed him cautiously. McManus raised his index finger off the steering wheel to indicate silence. He would endure his suffering alone. His solace was simply that, without speaking of it, his family was aware of it. They knew this was the hazard of walking the streets, rain or shine, to read gas meters.

The teeming humidity of the rain made McManus sweat

profusely, and the damp turned the windows misty. McManus had to keep wiping the window with a handkerchief. He finally stopped off at a small sweet shop. 'Martina, go on in and buy a few lottery tickets, a bottle of Lucozade and a box of Rose's chocolates, and a pack of Sweet Afton.'

'And a bottle of holy water,' Mrs McManus insisted.

'Jesus, wait a second. Didn't we buy holy water at this very shop last year, and it's up in the bathroom untouched? We should have brought that. Does holy water have an expiry date?'

'It does, Dad. Celestial disclaimer. Miracles are not guaranteed after date of expiry.'

'Listen here, walking atheist. I don't give a shite if you damn yourself to eternal oblivion, but have the common decency not to do it in a moving car with your family in it.' With a flourish of his handkerchief, McManus cleared the window, waited for his daughter, then bucked away from the small sweet shop as a spasm of pain ran the course of his right leg.

The car proceeded through the old part of the city, along a great wall behind which lay a succession of great old structures, a maternity hospital, a jail, a convent for the aged and deranged and a graveyard. It had a strange effect on McManus, for wasn't it the sum of human existence set in brick? There must have been a great municipal and philosophical presence of mind in days gone by, a fixity to the simple things, before it all got complicated. McManus wanted to give the walking atheist a good puck for himself.

Dwarfed by the wall, the black car crawled slowly along, with McManus looking for the small entrance to the convent cut out of the brick. The convent had the look of an eighteenth-century prison, but had actually been erected by the Sisters of Charity for the care of the infirm, the deranged and the plain old.

McManus checked his face in the mirror, mechanically licking the tips of his fingers and patting down the parting along the exposed thin line of his pink scalp. In a way he felt slightly ashamed of what had become of himself. To present his own mediocrity once a year had a humiliating effect now in his later years. His own job at the Gas Board approximated to what one could expect of a competent nine-year-old, since all he had to do was go around to the sides of houses and read the gas meters, jotting down the numbers and submitting them to the accounts department. There was an unspoken accountability in his visit to the walking saint, the small-talk and chat. It was as much as to say, 'Is this what's become of you, my favourite nephew?' For all of her spirituality, that was the way the walking saint must have felt. There was a knowing practicality behind the walking saint. She had a way of quizzing the children when they came to see her. Questions in their sums and trick questions about percentages. 'If there was a cake there on the table, and someone said to you, "Would you like one sixth of the cake or one third of the cake", which would you take?' And she had a certain smiling sympathy for the one-sixth takers, and a wink for the one-third takers who might then get a question from their catechism on the Trinity: 'How many persons in the one God?' A certain logic with numbers seemed to be her way of judging character and future prospects. McManus's grandfather said that when the walking saint was a girl she only talked about land and money. She'd a great head for figures.

McManus brought the car to a stop. The great outer walls had long since turned a grimy black from the soot of coal fires and car exhausts, adding a gloom of overbearing antiquity. 'I'll ask you now to be on your best behaviour.'

Johnny shrugged his shoulders.

'Everyone agreed, then.' The flood of years, of his own dead parents and the times they came up on the train for this pilgrimage, filled McManus's head. He had to catch his breath.

Mrs McManus, wearing a bit of crocheted white knitting on her head, bowed her red face. 'We should say an act of contrition,' which they did in sorrow for their sins.

Mr McManus knocked on a heavy iron-studded wooden door.

A small man opened the door and stepped back. McManus entered the small enclosure, followed by his family. They entered into an ill-contrived purgatory, a sort of dark stable crowded with old men in ill-fitted herringbone tweed suits. These were the sane (or at least non-violent) residents who had the privilege of going to this makeshift room to talk among themselves. Most of them sat quietly with half-open mouths, gawking into space. McManus looked at a small group seated at a table. 'Good day,' he said congenially, assaulted by a smell of distilled whiskey. He could see there were piles of matchsticks for betting and steel tumblers for whiskey before each of the men at the table. The cards had disappeared, though.

McManus announced that he'd come to see his aunt. The men began murmuring, civil war medals on their suits jiggling.

The attendant on duty, with his big belly bursting through a buttoned cardigan, wavered in obvious intoxication on his stumpy bow-legs. He had been sleeping on the job. Only a ridiculous black cap he wore, with a silver badge saying porter, distinguished him from the patients. In McManus's estimation, the attendant looked like an overgrown school bully.

Clearing his throat before speaking, the attendant balanced himself by holding the back of a chair. 'Were you called for, sir?'

'We never needed an appointment before.' McManus leaned forward. The attendant smelt of whiskey. 'Is there something wrong?'

The attendant jerked his head back. 'Ah no, sir. I was just wondering, that's all.' The chair scraped against the cold floor. He showed a set of cracked teeth that looked like they'd been glued back together. 'If you'll have a seat now, sir, please.'

McManus rolled his eyes and shuffled his family on to a church bench pushed up against the wall. He was used to this sort of bravado down through the years. The attendants were of the lowest order, fiddlers who were always 'on the make' as they said, bringing in whiskey and taking bets for the men. Sin, it seemed, had been recognized and allotted its own room out by the walls of the convent. This was what McManus loved about the old days, the unspoken pragmatism. Evil was a living creature which had to be cordoned off and contained.

The attendant picked up a black phone receiver, cupped his hand over his mouth and waited anxiously. He motioned to one of the old men to open the front door to clear the air in the room. McManus watched as the attendant inserted a Silvermint sweet into his mouth.

Martina and Mrs McManus had the same perplexed look. The smell of the men scared them. The girl was the slim image of her mother. Mrs McManus seemed on the verge of saying something, but Mr McManus gave her a severe look.

A mildewed dirty skylight had turned everything a ghoulish green in the small waiting room, and the men looked like etiolated stalks with heads craned towards the failing light. This was the first defence of a cloistered medieval insularity, the small, darkly lit rooms preparing the penitent for entrance into another realm. Everything about it said that sanctity could only be ensured by a removal from vice, a retreat from the vicissitudes of earthly existence. Beyond lay the domain of a walking saint.

McManus touched the oily sleekness of his hair. He caught Johnny's eye and saw the sombre mood the place had brought on to the walking atheist. The boy had his head partially down-turned, the eyes averted from the old men. McManus wanted to say, 'You see now, walking atheist, we weren't such eejits as you thought.' Faith propagated itself like moss in the small enclosure of dank walls.

The attendant crunched away on the mint. He took his cap off, exposing a shining egg head which he wiped before setting the cap down again.

'We need some air in here,' he said gruffly to one of the men. 'Fan the door, will you?' His eyes looked uneasily at McManus. 'Mother Superior will be along presently, sir.'

A man looking over rounded spectacles smiled at the family.

McManus gave a knowing nod in the men's direction. He was always struck by the strange affability of old men who wanted to tell you something, men who had been abandoned within the walls of a convent to die. As a boy it had terrified him that old age could bring this on. His mother, and even the walking saint, had made mention of what happens when men have neither family to care for them nor money to keep themselves. It had provided the unconscious push in his youth, the phantom room of dying men reminding him of what can and does happen to those who go astray. Most of the men had been manual labourers all their lives, earning little and now abandoned by their children, who had fared just as badly. The demon of ignorance and, no doubt, drink had done its damage, but the sorry end of it was simply that without money you could depend on nothing and nobody. This was what these men, in their inept gesturing and agitated winking, were left to contemplate, until death, which awaited them just one hundred yards away in the cemetery.

An old fellow breathing quickly through his lips as though blowing on a spoon of hot soup rocked back and forth as he sat. 'Could you spare a cigarette, sir?' he shouted, making everyone jump. Obviously he was partially deaf. The words had a nasal slur. He pulled at McManus's arm. 'Just one cigarette, sir. Just one.'

McManus reached into his pocket for the extra package of Sweet Afton, knowing from experience that you couldn't give just one man a cigarette. The men became agitated, coming out of the gloom like curious cats. McManus distributed the cigarettes. In a minute the room was choked with smoke and coughs. It hid the smell of whiskey.

'I'll tell you something for nothing there, sonny.' A man winked at the walking atheist. 'I know your sort through and through. You'd do well to follow this advice to last as long as us here.' He pointed at the other men, who took a particular pride in their age, straightening up and looking at the walking atheist. 'If you don't have to run, walk; if you don't have to walk, stand; if you don't have to stand, sit; if you don't have to sit, lie down. And remember this: always eat whenever you can.' He punctuated everything with a blink of his moist eyes. 'That should see you through life, sonny.'

'I'll remember that, sir. To paraphrase: sit around on my arse and do shag-all.'

At that the old fellow faced McManus and grinned. 'You've a job with him, I'd say.'

'Don't be talking,' McManus concurred.

*

The crunch of gravel and the jingle of keys announced the approach across the no man's land between the convent and the guard house. The heavy attendant put on a black coat with a theatrical flourish, raised his cap, wiped his forehead and munched down on another mint. As he pulled back a heavy bar on the door he was already shouting, 'And aren't you looking great, Mother Superior.' His silhouette merged with the Mother Superior and they exchanged some words. A wave of cold grey light poured into the small room.

The men instinctively rose, and a low, reverent hiss of 'Ssssister' filled the room as the Mother Superior came in.

She acknowledged them with frank condescension, a dismissive movement of her sleeve. She saw the men at the table and the matches. 'There wasn't anybody playing cards out here, was there?'

'Not at all, Mother,' the attendant answered, waving his hand over the men.

The Mother Superior had a huge jailer's ring of keys tethered to a string that disappeared into her pocket. 'Well, there better be nothing going on out here.'

The men stayed silent. They waited, the cigarettes pinched between the thumb and index finger, glowing in the cup of their hands.

The family sat lined up like dismal convicts before a firing squad.

Mother Superior moved towards McManus, who winced as he stood up. He touched the fastidious knot of his thick navy-blue work tie like some earnest schoolboy.

The Mother Superior came within a foot of McManus's face without saying anything. She had a terse leanness about her, a gaunt, mannish face with eyes set unnaturally far apart. 'The once a year McManuses,' she said.

'The very people.' McManus smiled for lack of anything else to say, trying to take a step back, but found himself wedged against the church bench.

'The McManuses from down the country always write us a fortnight in advance to let us know they are coming.'

'We'll do that in future, Sister,' McManus managed, retaining a level of decorum and subservience, enduring the galling spectacle of having himself shown up in front of the walking atheist. This was all the walking atheist needed to make a show of things, which he did, emerging from the smokiness in the room to brazen the Mother Superior with a strange defiant stare, saying out of the blue, 'Father, Son, Holy Ghost, boiled some ham and burnt some toast.'

'Johnny, please,' Mrs McManus beseeched.

The attendant pulled on his cigarette, glad to have attention drawn away from him and the men.

The Mother Superior took account of the walking atheist's words and gave a nodding gesture of silent scorn, but meditating all the same on what she'd have done to him if she'd half the chance. With her usual frankness she stared at McManus and said, 'Your aunt is very sick.'

McManus hesitated. 'Sick . . .'

'Sick, Mr McManus. Yes, very sick.'

The smoke curled, drifting towards the open door. The old men strained to catch what was being said. McManus felt the stifling quiet of the small room as the Mother Superior hesitated.

In the end she took a step forward and wheeled McManus away by his elbow. Her face was inches from his. Her breath was horrible. McManus stiffened in a way that made his joints crackle. 'It's a situation of a delicate sort.' She was trying to manhandle him into a mutual complicity. 'You understand of course, Mr McManus,' she persisted. She showed the inflexible resolve of a creature who got her way.

McManus didn't, but he felt the pressure of her fingers on his arm. 'The children would be better served if they stayed here.' Her thick caterpillar eyebrows moved on her forehead.

McManus nodded obligingly with a simpering religiosity.

'I'm taking your husband up to the house to talk,' she said, turning to Mrs McManus. 'I'll have tea and sandwiches sent out to you.'

McManus added, 'It'll only be a short while.'

'The pen,' Mrs McManus said hesitantly, egged on by Martina, who held the pen out.

McManus averted his eyes to the Mother Superior's face, and she dismissed the gesture of the pen, leaving the girl holding it sheepishly.

The walking atheist spoke loud enough to be heard by the men: 'They've probably buried her already,' which made the men issue a hiss of consternation and cross themselves with their cigarettes.

Again, Mrs McManus pleaded, 'Johnny,' while Mr McManus rounded out the pantomime of dissatisfaction by compressing his lips, making the clicking sound of an agitated insect.

The Mother Superior vented her frustration by leaning down and brushing the small piles of matches on to the floor. 'I'm not a fool, Mr Bennet.' She glared at the attendant. 'Shame on men who can't even keep the Sabbath.'

McManus caught the grinning face of the walking atheist and the bewildered men scrambling for their winnings as the bar slid across the door once more.

In the cold, narrow corridor McManus sullenly followed, in tow, with a perceptible halting gait, his right leg scraping the cold tiled floor in which he could see his reflection. Everything was meticulously polished and smelt of carbolic acid.

McManus drew the stares of old men and women gone in the head who were held in chairs by leather straps. He smiled at them. There were others who stood looking bewildered at the walls or the ceiling.

The fervour of the visit was long since lost. McManus's odds on the afternoon tea had drastically diminished, and there was nothing ready back at the house. Still, McManus instinctively picked out the clank of pots from some distant kitchen on the lower floors. A strong smell of meat permeated the cold air as they moved into the desolate recesses of an old passageway with little rooms off to either side.

'If you will, Mr McManus?' The Mother Superior led McManus into a small windowless room with an empty fire grate, a plastic bowl of fruit on a round table, a single chair and a lone light hanging from a high ceiling. He had just been directed to sit down when the Mother Superior began in a dramatic, yet sombre manner. 'Your aunt's condition, Mr McManus, concerns the very foundation of this order.'

McManus tensed his face in a manner which he thought was necessary under the circumstances. 'What's wrong with her?' he offered.

'She suffered a stroke that has left her partially paralysed.'

McManus leaned forward in his seat, sensing something more.

The Mother Superior took her cue and proceeded. 'With the shock of something of this nature, there is a, how shall I say it, a fear of death that sets in. Mortality has a way of . . . of fixating itself in the brain . . . ' She touched her head, intimating the brain.

'I see,' McManus said when he didn't see at all, pressing his knees with his hands. The bulb cast a clinical starkness, making him uncomfortable.

The Mother Superior pushed on. 'You see, Mr McManus, your aunt's faith was tested in . . . the ordeal . . . ' That is what it had come to be called, as McManus was to learn, 'The Ordeal'.

'But she's the very rock of faith itself.' McManus puffed up his cheeks in a show of exasperation. 'She's . . . She's a walking saint.'

The Mother Superior's eyes looked heavenward, her hands following in the way the religious do, invoking space, shaping the unseen into something real. 'That is the mystery of His ways, Mr McManus.'

McManus extended his right leg as a twinge of pain ran to his big toe, making him bang the floor with his boot. His face reddened. 'How has her faith been tested?'

The Mother Superior seemed to hesitate, as though she'd gone too far, but then saw the copper bracelet on McManus's wrist that he used to stave off the rheumatism. The tight cowl around her face pinched a taciturn expression. 'She wouldn't sleep without the light on,' she finally said, with a level of self-consciousness that made her cough slightly and blink anxiously.

McManus looked up and wanted to have a good laugh. What the hell did wanting a light on have to do with anything? He showed his teeth to register a moment of contemplation and hide the laughing inside his head.

'It's not a laughing matter, Mr McManus,' she said severely, with prescience. 'I'll have you know she screams if the light is turned off. Everybody knows about it . . . the other sisters and the residents and . . . ' She straightened herself. 'And the Cardinal has been informed, I may tell you now.'

McManus had the sudden foreboding notion that the Mother

Superior had done something to his aunt. She was after all the keeper of women and men out in the hallway who were restrained with leather straps on their arms and wrists. She had a capacity to immobilize and detain, a staunch defender of the faith with the resolve of the inquisition. 'This is not the Dark Ages, for God's sake,' McManus burst out. 'Maybe she's deranged from the stroke. That can happen when someone gets sick . . . ' McManus found he was half-shouting. 'Yes . . . You . . . you can't test the faith of someone who doesn't have their senses about them.'

The Mother Superior raised her hand in protest, the loose arm of her dress flapping like the wing of some restless bird. 'Mr McManus, this convent will not veer from its duty no matter what the circumstances or the consequences. In her final hour your aunt has abandoned the Almighty. A life of charity and poverty has been undone in her last hour. God came and tested her faith and she was found lacking.' She pointed heavenward with her long finger. 'Lacking!' She broke off for a moment and then began, 'I am talking of her salvation, about her soul and where it will spend eternity.' She trailed off into a whisper.

McManus looked distraught, making a clumsy gesture with his own raised arm. Trying to point to where his aunt was, but of course he didn't know. His extended hand took refuge on his brow and then slipped quietly into his right trouser pocket where it found his leg trembling. He felt the jingle of change in his pocket. It suddenly struck him: maybe it was money they were after him for?

The only reason the walking saint got out of the convent once a year was to participate in a national collection campaign, to extort money out of decent people who couldn't refuse. Well, if that was the way, he'd set them straight there and then. He persisted, though less resolutely, feeling it was really the money she was after, but disinclined to broach the subject. 'But there are insane people who can speak all sorts of gibberish and they're not accountable for what they say. She's had a stroke, and that mde her lose her senses. Any doctor would say that she is suffering from the effects of the stroke.'

'We do not hide behind doctors, Mr McManus. The word of a doctor is nothing to the word of God. We will not lie on her behalf, we will not let her die without begging God's forgiveness . . . '

'But wanting a light on . . . Surely to God . . . ' McManus shook his head in a venerable posturing, feeling the burden, that he was fighting an abstract philosophical battle. After all, he hadn't seen his aunt in a year. There was no point of reference, no sense of what she'd become. He drew himself out of his chair.

'Surely you understand, Mr McManus?' The Mother Superior seemed to stalk him, her head thrust out of the habit, the eyes following him. 'What is the greatest fear children have?' she whispered.

'Wetting the bed,' McManus said, as a point of goading.

'Fear of the dark, Mr McManus, that's what. And why? Because children have no faith in God, in the Almighty's ability to vanquish darkness with the light of faith.'

McManus could see there was nobody who believed in the Devil like the religious. It was as though the Devil slept in their very beds, whispering into their ears. As McManus sat there he began to see through the fixed look in the Mother Superior's face. It was more than likely that it was her faith that had been tested by the walking saint's ordeal. How could she reconcile it with her faith when the walking saint was off in some room screaming if the light was turned out?

The Mother Superior was saying something . . . McManus looked up.

'Make no doubt about it, your aunt's faith has been tested by the ordeal.' There was a moment of apprehensive quiet. A trolley rolled somewhere out in the hallway. McManus pricked up his ears like an alert dog.

It was in this moment that the Mother Superior slipped in slyly, as though in mid-thought: 'Why indeed was she picked out for the ordeal by the Almighty?'

McManus drew himself back to the issue at hand.

'That boy of yours perhaps . . . ' Her thick eyebrows came together in a desperate, pensive way.

'What?' McManus saw the way it was now, the insufferable indignity of it that she should even dare to think she could get away with the likes of that. His face became imbued with blood. The leg twitched violently. To think that she had casually offered up the possibility that his son was in some way to blame for what had happened to the walking saint . . . And yet McManus hadn't the outright conviction to speak his mind. He had been sized up well, trapped in the religious fear of his upbringing. Hadn't he set up his son as an evil solace against the world? Indeed, there was the dark notion that what she was saying made some sense to McManus. After all, this religion was one of retribution. That was how it had been handed down to him and his kind, and from the stories in the Bible, the blood of lambs splattered on doors, plagues delivered unto the oppressors . . .

The Mother Superior whispered softly, 'God works in mysterious ways, Mr McManus.'

A knock at the door interrupted further discussion. A plump nun in white brought in a tray with tea and sandwiches along with slices of brandy cake and a bowl of whipped cream. With silent discretion, the Mother Superior directed the nun, putting her body in front of Mr McManus to obscure his view.

They thought he could be bribed by food. He was being made the right eejit and yet he remained steadfast. The tray emerged again on the table, and McManus was left staring down at the usual delicate triangular sandwiches of cold meats, ham and roast beef with the peculiar extravagance of salad dressing, a layer of taste unto itself. His eye finally fixed on the depression of the nun's thumbprint on the soft white bread.

The Mother Superior stood back as the nun leaned over the table, arranging the solitary meal for McManus. Of course, he obliged, but not before he said in his stern voice, 'I should like to see my aunt,' as a sort of vague but commanding protest.

The door closed behind, and McManus was left like an ignominious Hansel stuffing his face at the witch's gingerbread house.

Twenty minutes passed before the Mother Superior appeared again.

McManus, satiated by the brandy pudding, looked up from his seat, holding the ear of a cup of tea. He'd licked the bowl of cream clean in a moment of bravado to offset the tension, even though he had a condition when he ate dairy products.

The Mother Superior eyed the bowl, understanding his intentions. What was not said was important. The clairvoyance of the subjugated had occupied the time of the walking saint when the country was under foreign control and everything was said in silent subterfuge. As his father used to say disparagingly about talk, 'When all is said and done, there'll be more said than done.'

'In circumstances of this nature years ago you would have been sent away, Mr McManus.' She hesitated. 'But this is the time of the doubting Thomas.' She was a creature who had not reasoned with anybody in years, ill-equipped for inconsequential gentleness or diplomacy, as was McManus himself. But in that moment of expectation, McManus felt a bout of indigestion rumbling inside himself, and finding the need for the relief of open space, forced the point curtly, 'If I could see my aunt?'

Silently, McManus followed the Mother Superior at an appropriate distance. They went down a staircase, along a windowless passage that held the coldness of interment. The quarters had the stark lunacy of a saint's mortification, a place of pure cold, everything conceived to make the body useless and infirm, to rob it of heat, to let cold enter the marrow of bone. A diffused reddish glow emanating from beneath the bleak representation of the twelve stations of the cross provided the only light. McManus passed the eighth station, and shuddered, seeing the wounds on Jesus's feet had been worn away by the silent adoration of lips.

A smell of fresh-cut roses drifted out of the small cell which contained the walking saint. The walking saint was on her back. McManus had to assume a reverent stoop to keep his head from touching the low ceiling. He crossed himself, his eyes filling with tears for a moment. McManus hesitated to move, afraid to cast a shadow.

The left side of the walking saint's body had died in paralysis, the flesh the colour of aged, jaundiced leather. Her tiny hands had been joined together. The left eye, half-closed, floated aimlessly in its socket. A perpetual tear flowed down the withered cheek and into the ear. The other eye, transfixed, stared at the light. This eye was the only source of life on the face. Existence had come down to this one solitary sense, to this solitary image of light.

McManus collected himself soon enough. He could see the walking saint understood nothing.

The Mother Superior instructed McManus to a chair. It was warm. Obviously, someone had been keeping vigil. McManus's big rump spread out on the chair as he looked at the walking saint, too afraid to touch her. A collection of rosary beads, a bottle of holy water and a prayer book were set on a small side table. They'd been at her to repent and offer up a good confession.

To McManus, the walking saint looked like one of those disinterred doll-faced mummies that are stuffed away in the recesses of side altars in cathedrals.

'Can you hear me?' McManus whispered, inhibited and self-conscious of the Mother Superior behind him.

The walking saint had passed beyond pain and recognition. It was as though God had forgotten about her, as though she was so far removed from the real world, down in this crypt, that she was hidden from God's eyes. Or at least, that was the impression that came over McManus at that moment. He even found himself wondering why the dignity of death had passed over her . . . The walking saint had spent her life in the service of the aged and infirm, given up a life in the outside world. She had endured the decrepitude of others' old age and dementia, subjected herself to the grotesqueness of what human flesh can emit from its orifices.

The Mother Superior turned off the light.

McManus had to catch his breath as a sudden strange crying filled the pure silence of the cell. 'Turn it on,' McManus shouted. Sweat turned cold on his flesh.

The light filled the room again.

'Jesus, what are you trying to do to her?' McManus managed, getting his breath again.

'There is no light in eternal darkness,' the Mother Superior answered stiffly.

The small lips of the walking saint had parted slightly from the screaming. McManus took a glass of water and a cloth from the table. He gently poured a trickle of water into the small hole of the mouth and waited. The walking saint's body jerked, but the water disappeared. McManus dabbed the lips. His face was over the eye, which seemed to see him for a moment. Then silence returned to the walking saint, the right eye again fixed on the light.

The Mother Superior had not calculated the effect of the screaming on McManus, who had become afflicted with shivering. He got up but there was nowhere to go. He had to almost back up to move away from the bed, turning slowly to face the Mother Superior, who had a horrible look in her eyes of disquieting despair. McManus could see the look of madness. The Mother Superior had become unnerved and resentful of what the walking saint was doing to everyone. McManus could imagine her coming down at all hours of the night and turning out the light only to hear the sudden screaming. The walking saint had become incidental in a way. Really, all the Mother Superior was concerned about was herself. She wanted her personal faith restored.

'She should be under the care of a doctor,' McManus said softly.

The Mother Superior shook her head. 'A doctor comes and sees her . . . '

McManus was aware of his own limitations. He hadn't the power to have her removed and there was no point causing a scene and disgracing both the Church and his own family's name. Maybe it was better to leave things as they were? What would have happened if he hadn't come today? But of course he had, by the grace of God or coincidence, who knows?

'You will have to leave her now,' the Mother Superior said.

'One more minute, please . . . ' McManus turned again and sat down. He touched the walking saint's icy fingers, feeling the small wedding ring of her vocation: a bride of Christ for over half a century. Everything that was said and done amounted to nothing in the end, only death . . . And hadn't that been why the care of the old, the infirm, the mad had been committed to the care of Christian charity through the years, to nuns who gave up their lives in this world for the glory of some other world?

McManus could see his own father in her face, the same McManus face that the walking atheist had inherited. He put his lips to her wet ear, tasting the salt of the perpetual tear.

'Mr McManus . . . ' The Mother Superior's voice rang anxious, afraid that McManus was whispering something into the walking saint's ear. 'Your family is waiting for you, Mr McManus . . . '

McManus hesitated, and then, in his most pure moment of atheism, committed his most religious act. He raised his hand to the light and whispered. 'Don't you see . . . Mother?' The shadow of his extended arm ran the length of the walking saint, bisecting her. He was working with very little, light and dark, yet wasn't it after all the essence of religion? 'She is staring at God,' McManus whispered. 'Staring at God . . . '

The Mother Superior stepped back, afraid that McManus had gone mad as he began to shout: 'Don't you see it?' Tears streamed down his face. He was taking no chances.

The Mother Superior stepped back to the door and then her hands came together in a shock of revelation or a moment of uncanny pragmatism. It didn't matter, what mattered was that McManus saw the effect and kept up the waterworks of tears and the shouting. 'The light of God,' McManus shouted. He knocked the jug of water off the table, stumbling forward.

'The light of God,' she whispered, nodding her head as recognition broke on her face. She stared at the light, McManus at the dark of the shadow.

'She is staring at God,' the Mother Superior cried, and went out into the passageway weeping. They had not understood, that was all. 'She is staring at God.'

That was how McManus the gas meter reader, father of the walking atheist, saved the walking saint from a sorry funeral on a rainy Sunday afternoon in early December.

The walking saint died a fortnight later in the contemplation of the light. The Cardinal offered up prayers in the graveyard next door on a glorious winter day with a pale yellow sun and the wintry stars up in the clear blue sky. The herringbone-tweed men acted as pallbearers, decked out in their war medals. Their breath showed in the cool light.

McManus, as surviving relative, read from the gospel up at the church and was fed the usual compliment of sandwiches and brandy pudding afterwards. And there was a barrel of stout on hand. McManus indulged himself, dressed up in his Sunday best and his hair parted with oil.

There was great talk of the walking saint's faith, of her devotion. The word saint, or more exactly 'saintly', was used by the Cardinal. Of course, pronouncements were premature at this stage. As it says in the good book, 'lots had already been drawn' for her clothes, which had been torn to shreds for the usual relics – the first order of business when you went about getting someone into the running for sainthood. It seems the diocese had the little glass casing with the bit of blood-red backing in stock.

The Cardinal was pressed on the matter by a few newspaper

reporters. The aura of saintliness was fostered by the honey light of the mid-winter day when you couldn't help but contemplate the glory of God's creation. The reception was held out back of the home in the great expanse of gardens. Off in the distance other men in the same herringbone-tweed suits tilled the land, growing greens and spuds and raising livestock. The bleat of sheep travelled on the stilled air. In an old city tram that had been converted into a sun room sat the industrious women, like fat cats sunning themselves, smiling, glad of the weather, their hands mechanically working away to the click of knitting needles, making socks and jumpers for the residents. Everything had a self-contained efficiency to McManus's mind as he supped at the warm stout and circulated among the throng, receiving the words of those in attendance. Yes, it was a great day all round.

The Mother Superior made herself scarce when McManus roamed the garden. He saw her avoiding him, and sure it was best for things to be left unsaid. They were in agreement on that point. It would only be awkward . . . You answer your own conscience in your own way. That's how McManus thought of it, and anyway the drink had made him mellow and satisfied.

The Cardinal was holding court near a fountain of St Francis feeding birds. The reporters were scribbling away on pads of paper. The Cardinal was explaining the process of beatification, canonization and finally sainthood as best he could. He said the way it worked was that a committee would be set up in the diocese and strange occurrences, cures or outright miracles due to prayers offered up to the walking saint, or by the placement of her relics on different parts of the body, would be documented and duly forwarded to Rome, where a commission would convene to see if the reports deemed the testimonies true and worthy of further investigation. Of course, the Cardinal intimated that the process could take centuries, and there were no guarantees. 'You could be an early runner, but what matters is staying power over the centuries. Name recognition is everything in a run at sainthood,' the Cardinal said decidedly.

'As it is with dishwashing liquid,' the walking atheist laughed at McManus. He had really let the walking atheist go to hell of recent times.

The Cardinal paid no heed to the walking atheist and continued with his blabbering.

The walking atheist had said to McManus the week before, 'Do you know that human intelligence is limited to the size of what can fit through a woman's pelvis?' It was due to the size of the brain or something, and what could McManus do except wink and say, 'Well, don't tell your mother. She'll be very upset, son.'

Out in the garden a glass of sherry had gone to Mrs McManus's head and was making her cry. Martina was all concerned, leaning into her mother, earnestly shepherding her over to the sun room. McManus watched the two of them. God, his daughter was the spitting image of how his wife had been. Yes, the faces don't change down through history, the death mask is inherited from generation to generation . . .

'There now.' McManus smiled at his wife, intercepting her and leading her into the tram. He took his handkerchief to her stained lips.

'Isn't it beautiful weather for it?' she whispered.

McManus was off again, continuing his rounds, slurping away at the old drink. Port was produced for a final comment from the Cardinal. Only time would tell, keep your fingers crossed and all that, and who knows, but the prayers might be answered.

McManus remembered reading stories of the Church remorselessly pursuing prospective saints from the Middle Ages into their graves, prying open coffins only to find scratches on the insides and pronouncing the sin of despair on the corpses. Some plague or other had rendered the victims in a 'suspended animation' of sorts, and they had been buried alive.

Sin, it seemed in McManus's religion, could follow you beyond the grave. But the main thing now for McManus was that the day had been a great success, and he had got the walking saint into consecrated ground.

PETER McNIFF

Peddling Air

The subbies' trucks sail by and back again, the drivers eyeing old familiars. There are fifty of us strung out along the pavement, cold and hungry from sleeping rough; strung out from drink, and more drink, stamping our feet, flapping our flippers, steaming on the frosty air. We've been here an hour watching the city rouse itself, hearing its dull roar grow louder as the streetlights pop out.

The sun cranks up, low and yellow. Tanner, beside me, blows into his hands. He stinks like death. When the tar-truck pulls in with a kid leaning out of the passenger side wagging three fingers at anybody, Tanner hobbles into the mêlée.

'Three skins – we want three skins,' the kid calls. He's ten going on twelve years old. His red hair is cut to the bone, his freckled face ingrained by outdoor life and shaped by generations of breeding from the same old crop of potatoes.

Mixer buffets a bunch of hands away, blocks with his bulk, drawls, 'You got 'em, sonny.'

Mixer cannot read or write though he carries sums easily in his head and collects ten per cent of everything. He is deep-voiced, has all the deep, quiet moods of a slow and strong river working its way through chaos. People mistake the pain in his eyes for anger.

'What's in it?' Mixer says to the kid.

'Two hunnert'n'fifty,' the child says. 'To finish.'

Hard labour, sixteen, seventeen hours maybe, then cash for some B&Bs with bathtubs instead of freezing under cardboard in the park. We are going down. Peddling air. None of us has worked in weeks. We need money or treatment. Valium to steady our hands. We don't eat much any more because nothing stays down. Mixer looks at me, then Tanner, still pumped up by the quart we slugged for breakfast. Our last quart.

'Ye're on,' says Mixer, spits on his palm and shakes on the deal with kid.

'Gerrup,' the kid says.

Barrelling along on the back of the wagon the cold sucks the heat from our bones. We arrive numb as dumbstruck sheep. A button pushed somewhere adds mystery to the silent opening of the black iron gates. The drive is half a mile long, a curve through leaning, leafless trees. A fortress-like house appears, high and mighty and carved from cheese.

'We'll never get this done in a bloody day,' Tanner says, panicking.

'You want the job or dontcha?' the old man growls, climbing from the cab. He might be eighty years old. The thumb and finger of his left hand are missing.

'There's no better men,' Mixer says, dropping over the side and tossing a tough glance at Tanner.

Mixer helps the old man unhook the tar boiler from the truck's tow-bar. Blue smoke curls tarry, warm and sweet. Lungs haul it down. Tanner reconnects the gas bottle, tosses a match at the burner. We lob tar bars to each other and stack them. Tanner breaks them to brittle, plops the pieces into the bubble of black soup. The kid snaps orders – wheelbarrows to Mixer and Tanner, shovel and rake to me.

'Come on, move it!' the kid yaps.

'Young fellers n'more knows what work is,' the old man mumbles, unbolting the tailgate. He spits a grey gob into a bush, climbs back into the cab and then tips the fill in ten different spots along the drive.

'Don't take no shit,' he tells the child as he passes. 'You kick ass. Hear me?'

The kid nods, wearing the face of an old man like a mask. We could squash him flat. He leads us up the avenue, tells us the driver of the truck is an uncle; that the job is to fill a few potholes and pour tar over the crumbly bits. There are sixty-three chalk marks, some up to three feet wide.

'Yaw,' the kid yelps at me. 'Clear the potholes.'

'You and yaw's on gravel and tar,' to Mixer and Tanner.

The kid lays to for a while, sweeping gravel, grows bored, pisses on the lawn, walks around the house, returns with water for the kettle. We sweat unabated into the afternoon. The kid fries up beef sausages, doles them out wrapped in bread. Pours pint mugs of sweet tea.

His name is Sean. After the meal Sean fires up a cigar, the real thing from Cuba. He calls up his uncle on the mobile. Swears vile stuff down the 'phone. Walks about while he talks, pisses like an untrained pup all over a shrub. The owner flings open the front door of the cheese castle and charges out – a woman of fifty in a fluffed-up pink pullover and tweed skirt.

'Will you for God's sake tie that child down,' she rages. Her eyes bulge at me. 'I have guests and they've been watching you. You're nothing but animals.'

'Nought to do with me, missus,' I tell her. 'He's the boss. I'm just doing my job.'

'He's the boss?' she says. 'Do you think I look like a fool? He's a child.'

'He tells us,' I say, 'and we do it.'

The kid zips up as she whirls on him, looks back at us, betrayed. Slaps down the aerial on his mobile.

She says: 'Where's the old man I paid the deposit to?'

'Boss is at another job, missus,' he says, turning his tough freckled face towards her, arms akimbo. 'We do be busy betimes.'

'Well!' she says, bunches her fists, goes off into the house ranting.

In the afternoon my nightmare explodes. I am on my back watching this Rottweiler's jaws juicing. He will eat my face off and I can't move. My voice vanishes. I know that if, somehow, I can manage to wriggle my toes I can escape. The dog's fangs snap at my cheeks.

Mixer is pinning me down, slapping my face.

'Come on, boy,' he soothes. 'Easy does it.'

'What's happening to me?'

'Just one of your fits.'

'Yeah?' My body shakes violently.

The child noses the air above me. 'What's the fightin'?'

'He's just overheated,' Mixer says. 'Needs water.'

The child brings water in a mug, holds it to my sore lips and I gulp it down.

The tedious day moves on in digging, hammering, raking, picking, pouring, wheeling, flattening. Hours with sores, scalds, blisters, aches and pains. Pints of tea and sausages again. At ten, the owner inspects by torchlight, begrudges the quality of work but yields all the same to the time and effort taken. The child summons the uncle for the pay-out.

So we hit the all-night store for provisions, then retire to the park to celebrate at an open fire. We will take a bath tomorrow. Shadows wander in from the bushes. A dozen pairs of eyes surround us. Friends and enemies. Bottles get sucked all round. Laughter. A couple of fights break out. A woman's legs are exposed in the firelight, her coat flung back reveals wrinkled skin on bones, scant grey pubic hair. More laughter. A shadow drops upon her warped frame. Her face rears up under Tanner. It is Martha, slender Martha once exquisite. I take a walk with a bottle and somewhere along the way wake up aching, fog in my eyes. I'm lying on a canvas bunk surrounded by cream-painted walls, an electric light caged in the ceiling, a metal-plated door with a peephole. Beyond sound muffled voices, footsteps, Eventually the door bangs open. A shirt-sleeved peeler steps in.

'Anything you say will be taken down, blah, bloody blah. Right?'

'What?'

'You should bloody see your bloody self,' he says. He has bright blue eyes and a blue moon-shaped scar on his cheek. 'You bloody stink.'

'Is this my nightmare?' I say.

'Into the bloody shower with you, me lad. Come on, quick about it.' Down a corridor of cells, out across a yard with a high brick wall crowned with barbed wire, cameras, into a prefab. 'Right, knickers off.'

The water hits like a fire hose.

Back in the cell, shivering again, the peeler returns with a tin tray, porridge on a buckled plate. Tea in a chipped mug.

'Get that down you, ugly,' he says.

'Come here. What did I do – tell me?'

'Scared people shitless. Smacked a bobby resisting arrest.'

'I did?' I says. 'I didn't.'

'Get that down you.'

'What'll happen?'

'Ho-ho-ho. It's the nick for you, my lad. For the rest of your natural.'

In the rats, my hands won't stop shaking. I can't lift the tin mug. My face twitches. On all fours I slobber over porridge. Nothing swallows. My stomach turns over and over.

'Mixer!' I shout. 'Mixer!'

Echoes.

'Shut yer bleedin' face or I'll shut it for yer.'

In the witness box I stare into a pit full of dickheads in dark suits, white collars. A pink-faced peeler tells them I was screaming Rottweilers. The curs in court raise their fierce eyes, lick their chops. Drunk and disorderly, the peeler says, very disorderly.

Among a choice pick of words the Beak says, 'I'm binding you over to keep the peace for twelve months. You realize I could send you down for six?' Six what? I wonder. Long pause. Smacks the gavel twice. 'Next case.'

Back at the station they empty a plastic bag with my bottle opener, lucky pebbles, St Christopher, copper clips to stop rats running up trousers, spoon, tobacco papers, matches, money, string. Fourteen pounds. No knife.

'Where's me cutter?'

'Offensive weapon. Confiscated.'

'It's an eating iron . . . for cutting things . . . '

A week passes but there are no sightings of Mixer or Tanner. Maybe they're dead. Making my rounds, hand out along the way, I collect enough for hostel nights and half a bottle of redeye. The place is full: ex-army types who still polish their boots. Accountants with quick mad eyes who scrawl and screw up scraps of paper.

There are others. A man with no memory wanders in with bank rolls for Sister Venezuela. The bald Nathaniel, who freaks if people touch him. Naomi, who saves photographs of sunny places from magazines – shafts to drop down when she's lonely, drunk, wet, robbed, raped or rented like the other child whores, child addicts, child thieves, child drunks who learn to suck off rich old men and smile as they kneel in back alleys or black cars that flash by crooked-boned women bending into windy corners, grim and grimy-faced, humpbacked and bow-legged, hauling rubbish in squeaking prams; women who have loved and lost companions to death, to drugs, to drink, to poverty, to a world that frankly, my dear, doesn't give a damn.

And there is Martha: *'She must have been a beautiful baby. She must have been a beautiful girl . . . '* My, how that song hurts, Martha my love.

She occupies the stairs of the hostel. Dressed like a man in grey grease-stained slacks. A man's tweed jacket and red knitted hat, shape of a woollen bowl, pulled hard over her ears. A refugee from flapper days. She chirps to herself, a parrot on a perch, preening; rubs her legs with slender, tapered fingers.

Her bones are fine bones, exquisite. Elegantly is the way she may have walked once. You think, she's from a good family, aristocratic, big house, wide lawns, deer under the oaks, hounds on the porch, daddy a duke. Nobody knows where she's from and she never says. It's when she raises her head, looks at you suddenly, locking you on to her eyes, that you see the wild and fierce and frightening aspects of her being sparking her lonely madness.

I go into the hostel and queue for the shower. Sister Venezuela hands me a clean shirt in exchange for the filth on my back.

'Promise me, no more drink,' she says.

'Sure, Sister. Bless you. I'm going into detox next week.'

'On your word of honour.'

'On my mother's grave.'

Being between drink and detox is like falling off a cliff. No parachute. No brakes. Alice in Wonderland. You plunge on down, down, down. In terror. You think there's no way up, no way back. No way out. No wings. No hope. You burn. Behind your eyeballs roars the hell scenario, devils, mad face-eating dogs. Detox my arse.

Soaping in the shower, Fizzer pops his head in.

'How're you doin', maan?' he drools. 'You lookin' good.'

'Been here, there, workin' my butt. Dropped in for the sunshine,' I say. 'Here, ye haven't seen Mixer and Tanner?'

'Mixer an' Tanner?' he says. 'Dey buy stuff offev me.'

'When?' I say. 'You're lying in your face, Fizzer. I know you.'

'Honest to God.' Fizzer is a jockey from the Grenadines. Once led the winner of the Derby into the paddock. 'Sold dem stuff coupla months back. Good stuff. You wanna buy some?'

'I don't have no money.'

'How about a new shiny pair ob boots,' he says. Stumpy white teeth in his big-lipped grin. 'Only four pounds.'

'New? Who're you kidding?' I am in a heavenly haze. Steaming. Glistening. No shakes. Benevolent with good liquor in me. 'So beat it.'

But I think 'twould be nice to have shiny new boots. There is a dent in the toecap of my own which annoys me.

'You can try dem for size,' Fizzer tempts with a gleam of leather under newspaper wrap. I am towelling. Eyes darting, he peers around the lockers. Goes to the door, opens it, closes it. Returns. Lets me peep again at that gleaming leather.

'They're not new,' I say and offer him a slug from my brown paper bag.

'Honest, I on de dry.' He pushes the bag away. 'What about dey boots, man?'

I love their shine.

'Nicely broken in. Soft as fleece. Smell dat shine – don't touch!'

'How much?' I say and gulp from the bag.

'Four poun',' Fizzer says. 'I givin' 'em away.'

'Two pounds.'

'Three seventy-five. Fit you like a glubb.'

'OK,' I say, firmly. 'Three pounds.'

'Three fifty. Listen, I only holler once and they'd be fists bangin' fivers on that door. Everybody want these boots for dey shine.'

'Three pounds.'

He looks at the door.

'OK,' I say and crack. 'Three twenty-five and not a penny more.'

Next day I go back to beating the pavements for Mixer and Tanner. Feeling lucky in my clean shirt. Striding out in snug, light-blinding boots. I walk six miles beside the river. Scour the arches, the gardens and parks. Pass the House of Parliament. Pass gougers and bums. Pass peelers who glare. Pass seagulls and boats, tugs and restaurants. Pass palaces and men's private clubs, pass tube stations and statues of horsemen. Pass Nelson and Japanese tourists, pigeons and lions in bronze. A long, thirsty plod across the city.

The sun dips. My bones ache. My feet burn. Mixer's gloomy baritone peals laughter out of the dusk, plucks chords on my brain. I find them pitching for the night in the Park of Rhododendrons.

'I thought you was both dead,' I tell them.

'Thought you was in stir,' Mixer says. 'Saw ye hauled off in the wagon.'

'Look at him. Clean as shit,' Tanner says. 'Must have regular work.'

'I grubbed hard to get here,' I say.

'He was round the hostel,' Tanner says, 'shagging Sister Venezuela.'

'Bought myself new boots.'

They look at me. They look at the boots.

'Dope,' Tanner says, bending closer.

'What's up?' I say.

'You was done. Right, Mixer?'

'Been cleaned out.'

'Stop winding me up,' I say.

'Where'd you get 'em?' Mixer says.

'Black feller, ex-jock.'

'Fizzer,' Tanner says. 'Bloody Fizzer!'

The two of them laugh. Mouths open wide. Mixer has no back teeth. He says, 'Where's yer old boots, ye great tick ye?'

My face twitches. I look down and that old dent cracks up through the bootshine.

'So what?' I shrug as if I could not care less, but the twitch gouges into my face.

SHEILA BARRETT

Fortune-Teller

The summer I didn't marry Maury, I went to the fortune-teller. There were two that year; the one in Fort Worth was a numerologist and the one closer to home an astrologer. The women in the office spoke well of both of them, but the astrologer won out for me because she had known that Jane Ann's child was an adopted boy. Also, she was accessible; she lived just north of downtown in an old part of Dallas that had once been wealthy and was still gracious, with brick and frame houses and dried-out front yards.

The astrologer's house had a porch all the way across the front. She herself was old and bustling. Someone was already there, she told me; would I wait on the porch? Would I like a glass of water? Yes to the first, no to the second. She went back inside, with a creak and a clatter of the screen door.

I didn't believe in fortune-tellers, of course. I felt a little ashamed, knowing this and waiting on the shady porch, looking at the old woman's pots of busy Lizzies. I had really come out of loneliness and curiosity; I want to be more like the other women at the office. The more they talked about their husbands, their children, their divorces, their boyfriends, the more mysterious they became. I had only Maury, and he wasn't the sort of person you talked about. For one thing, he was too kind; he would never make you pregnant out of wedlock, or marry you when you were seventeen and then leave you with three kids, or cut off your money. In fact all the excitement that summer came from my own family, and I wasn't about to tell anyone my mother had left home. Mothers did not come into these discussions unless they baby-sat or were senile.

I was wondering what I was doing there, without a life to be commented on, when an old man walked around the side of the house. There was a little dog with him. The man, who was talking to the dog, didn't notice me until it began to bark. He was already on the porch by then, and he blinked at me with blue, innocent eyes that reminded me a little of Maury's.

He hushed the dog and said, 'Are you waiting to speak to my wife?' with a flop of his hand towards the screen door.

'Yes,' I said, sheepish.

'To get your fortune told.'

'Yes.'

'She's good. She's very good.' He sat down on the broad rail of the porch. 'She'll tell your fortune, all right. You got to be careful, though,' he said, shaking his head. He looked perturbed.

'What about?'

He got up and peered over the railings of the porch until sure he wasn't overheard. 'The Masons.'

'The Masons?'

'They listen to what you say. You got to keep the radio on all the time.'

I thought the Masons must be the next-door neighbours. My eyes followed his to the side of the porch. He nodded, satisfied that I understood. Then his forehead creased. 'I can't even eat my dinner these nights!' He met my eyes with his candid blue ones. 'The lima beans,' he said. 'They poison them. Right in the store.'

'The Masons? I mean, wouldn't you notice if . . . ?'

He shook his head, tired. 'They do it under the label. With a hypodermic.'

When I think back on my innocence, I wonder how Maury, who was smart as a whip behind his lazy-looking façade, had any time for me whatsoever. Maybe I just entertained him.

The man and I could hear the old woman, though not what she was saying. She was somewhere in the back of the house, and she had a very loud voice.

The little dog, who had coarse fur interrupted by disease, scraped at the screen door with a stiff paw. The man gave him a moody look, but he did not get up. 'He's no good. He doesn't even bark any more when they come. They've got their microphones in the bathroom now. I can't even sit in the tub. Behind the tiles. Talking at me.' He jerked his head towards the screen door with a hurt look. 'She tells me it's just the radio.'

At that moment the astrologer opened the screen door, and a woman from the office walked out. It was strange seeing her on a Saturday. We exchanged embarrassed looks. She seemed confused and a little upset. All of a sudden I wanted to go home. The old woman, whose untidy grey hair and plain cotton dress were a little like my grandmother's, noticed this. 'Do you still want to come in?'

'Yes, thank you.'

The house smelled like all frame houses in summer, of dry wood and shadows. We walked past the front room, which had large pieces of furniture in it. They seemed to be carelessly arranged or half-forgotten. The back room of the house, where she invited me to sit down beside a heavy oval table, was the same but more so. Magazines and papers littered every surface. There was a screen door to the back yard at the far end of the room. It was almost noon, and the door was a rectangle of overgrown shrubs and blazing sunlight. Then the front door slammed, and in a moment the little dog thumped down beside my chair and began to scratch itself.

The astrologer pulled at something beside her ear. 'Hearing aid,' she explained crossly. 'Gives me trouble.' She pulled a clean sheet of paper closer to her and picked up a chewed pencil. 'Well – when were you born?'

'June third,' I said, my heart racing a little. 'Nineteen forty-three.'

'Time?'

'Time?'

'The time of day you were born.'

I stared at her. 'I was born on June third, but I don't know what time.'

She rubbed her cheek, pulling the fine wrinkles this way and that. 'I can't do a chart for you if I don't know the time you were born,' she said in a disappointed voice. 'Can you call up your mother and find out?'

I shook my head.

'Well. I can read your hand, then,' said the astrologer, her eyes flicking to my five-dollar bill, which I had put on the table between us.

'All right.' I held out my hand a bit sullenly and she took it in her plump, crumpled-papery one. She jabbed her forefinger in the air above my palm, pointing towards four dangerous frays in my life line. 'Now, that's coming up pretty soon. You better look after your health. See this? Now, that's in about ten years' time.'

Then she dropped my hand and went pale. Her face twisted; she leaped from her chair. Her hand flew to her cheek in the ancient sign of grief. In that moment, I believed. A dreadful revelation was on the way.

Instead of turning to me, however, she trotted towards the hall. 'George!' she shouted.

The old man said something in the front room. There was a sudden burst of sound. She came back.

'That radio!' she said. 'My husband turns it on when I'm having a consultation.' She sat down again, still rubbing her ear. 'Blasted thing comes through my hearing aid.'

She looked at my hand and talked some more, but I believe it was just as opaque to her as it was to me. 'Someone'll come back into your life,' she said, disconsolate.

That evening Maury brought me to a fancy restaurant not far from where the astrologer lived. Maury fed me all that summer. He'd watch quietly while I made my way through steak or lobster Newburg or baked Alaska or cherry pie. Maybe he looked like that when one of his patients was on a drip and he stood beside the bed, fingers on the improving pulse. Mother hadn't taken the cook with her, but there was still Thursday night and all of Sunday to deal with, and my father didn't like to be seen at the Club without her. He wanted to keep the lid on things in case Mother decided to come back. We weren't starving at home, but we were bewildered and empty, and that's what Maury picked up.

I told Maury about the fortune-teller while he ate and listened in the Southern way he had, that made everything seem effortless.

'And what brought you to an astrologer?' he asked, fine eyebrows raised.

'I just wanted to know what it was like. What was going on.'

'Was there?'

'What?'

'Anything going on?'

'Maury . . . who on earth are the Masons?'

'Do the Masons figure in your fortune?' Maury's blue eyes got a gleam in them.

'No,' I said, huffy. 'They seem to be figuring prominently in

somebody else's. This nice old man. Her husband. He thinks –
he believes they poison his food.'

'Senile dementia,' Maury said. 'Are you going to eat those
beets?'

I passed him my salad plate, and he speared the repulsive
slices on to his own. I said, 'I'm surprised you like beets.'

'It shouldn't be an obstacle.'

Perhaps my never knowing when Maury was joking and
when he was serious was the real obstacle in our relationship.
'Those beets don't remind you of work?' I asked, then waited
while Maury, swallowing sedately, rose to the occasion:

'Livers were last fall and placentas were over in May.' He took
another bite. 'Do you reckon beets have anything to do with
senile dementia or the Masonic Order?'

'It was lima beans.' I told him how George thought
hypodermics were being inserted under the labels.

'Now that's interesting. I wish I'd had him. Usually it's
communists, up and down the ward. Those communists come
all the way from Vietnam to climb under Mrs Barrington's bed
and interfere with her slippers. I tell her, why would somebody
who can travel in a light ray want to stay under your bed? All
those communists go to Paris, France.'

'That's mean, Maury.'

'Mean?'

'It isn't funny, Maury, they're scared.'

'Well, Mrs Barrington isn't scared; she is irritated. She wants
them out of her shoes. Oh, she wouldn't speak to me for two
days. She was incensed that I would imply that a communist
could prefer Paris to Dallas, Texas.'

I thought uneasily of my mother's and my trip to Dubrovnik
the summer before, and Mother's refusal to discuss our
reactions to the country while inside the hotel. Luckily this only

lasted for about an hour. After that the electricity failed, and she lost patience. I wondered if the utilities worked in the apartment she had gone to. I just saw it once. There was a lot more carpet than furniture.

Discussing the fortune-teller got tricky that night. For one thing, I hadn't told Maury about Mother. She and his mother had gone to high school together; that was how we knew each other. It didn't seem right to tell.

'I reckon some tall, dark stranger's on his way into your life, then?' Maury asked, with the scornful look of one who read fortunes through the lens of a microscope, in blood cells and tissue.

'Tall, dark stranger, yeah,' I told him. 'And I'm supposed to travel.'

'Any place in particular?'

'Oh, far. Maybe Paris, with all the communists.'

'Well, shut my mouth.'

Maury used that old Southern expression to be ironic, but it certainly described both of us that summer. I couldn't put my bewilderment into words, and Maury didn't give much away, either. That's why I can't remember many conversations we had. I remember the way he looked, with soft, fine dark hair that tended to drop a little over his forehead, and of course his eyes. His dress, too. That was always immaculate; he always wore a sports coat and a tie. No, I can't remember what we talked about, only things like his catching my elbow when I tripped.

The fortune-teller – she had been demoted from 'astrologer' by my not knowing my birth time – had indeed told me a tall man would come into my life. Maury was medium. Even when he was thirteen and I was eight, he was a comforting size. I remember him showing me where the Parcheesi game and the checkers were kept in his house with exactly the same quiet decorum that he had in the middle of downtown Dallas one day when we noticed, simultaneously, that I had gone to work in odd shoes. I laughed when I saw one was black, one navy, but there was a look in Maury's eyes that I couldn't read.

'Don't get married right away,' said the fortune-teller, with a sorrowful tightening of her mouth and a glance towards the hallway. She had seen me patting the little dog when she came back into the room after turning off George's radio. She concluded that I was prone to being kind to feeble things, and I had better watch out. It was when I stood up to go that she remembered to say I would travel.

My fortune sounded like the other women's; we just had different starting points. The women at the office, Jane Ann and Marilee and Polly, weren't any older than me, but life had not allowed them to daydream their way into college. Most of them had already been kind to feeble things. They married them. As for travel, the only tickets they would get were on Boomerang Airways – their children would always call them back.

It's strange about that visit to the fortune-teller. Of all the things that happened that summer, it's the clearest. In the end, it seemed like everything coalesced inside the fortune, like components in a land mine, hidden beneath the faint map of my palm. There was the fortune-teller's husband George and his madness, my mother's absence, the embattled domesticity of the women at the office. Then there was Maury.

The fortune exploded in slow motion, its ingredients floating out in strange directions. Mother 'came back into our lives' that August, and two years later I married a tall man from another country.

By then Maury was already on a hospital ship in the Tonkin Gulf. It was Maury, not I, who had the soft spot for feeble things.

Maury photographed the boys as they were brought in, their faces and torsos like Stone Age steaks. He wanted people to know.

You never really get rid of anyone. In the office, the women didn't talk about their husbands while they were still married to them, but they never stopped after they were gone. I travel Maury's broken life in my mind and wonder sometimes if my visit to the fortune-teller uncovered something that shouldn't have been disturbed. Yet what is there but separation, reconciliation, ageing, death, and if you're unlucky, a dollop of madness along the way? And of course there's the certainty that you can never know what will happen to you unless, like Maury, you diagnose it some day.

I never exactly told Maury I wouldn't marry him. Maury never exactly asked me to. He might have, actually, one time when we had already said goodbye and I was putting the phone down. I heard his voice, faint, like the voices poor George heard over the bathtub; but that summer, I couldn't stop my hand on its way to hang up.

EUGENE McCABE

Heaven Lies About Us

Half thinking, half dreaming, she could make out from the cold light of her bedroom window Jesus sitting in the sun at the root of a great tree outside Nazareth or Jerusalem, where her mother had gone on her wedding holiday. Marion knew she had to be careful not to say honeymoon. It wasn't a bad word like the ones she heard at school, but her mother didn't say honeymoon. She said wedding holiday, explaining that wedding meant a solemn pledge or promise and holiday was really holy day and that marriage was a sacrament and that children were a gift from God.

All the children in the picture were loving Jesus and staring up at Him, holding on to His arms and legs. One of them was hanging round His neck. She could see that He was loving them. He was kissing the hair of one child's head, the little one on His knee.

In the margin of the framing at the top it said, 'Suffer the little children to come unto Me.'

Three years ago, when she was five, Uncle Felix had given her that for a birthday present. He was a priest in a monastery near Enniskillen, 'not a *passionate* priest', her mother had corrected her. 'It's Passionist, dear, as in the passion of Jesus,' and Iggy would join their mother and say, 'It's not the grand monastery either, it's the Graan monastery, and while we're at it, hospital is not hostipple, tomatoes are not bebomatos, they're tomatoes as in your big toe.' That made her think of Iggy's big tommytoe and she wanted to keep that out of her head because it made her sick to think about it, and about him.

Yesterday Uncle Felix had given a one-day retreat for the boys in the Louis Convent primary. Today it was the girls' turn; midday Mass and sermon, confession and then another sermon, followed by Benediction of the Blessed Sacrament.

In the bottom margin of the picture there were three lines:

Oh Jesus who for love of me
Didst bear Thy cross to Calvary
Grant to me to suffer and to die with Thee.

More than once her mother said, 'That child on the Saviour's knee has golden hair like yours, Marion, and the same sky-blue eyes,' but Uncle Felix said, 'No, Marion's hair is more silver-blonde, more like white gold.' That was hard to imagine. Gold was yellow, like a wedding ring. White was like the snowdrops all over the grounds and near the avenue gates, more like the white of her confirmation blouse with its blue shamrocks stitched on to the collar. She had said, 'Blue is wrong, Mammy, shamrocks are green,' but her mother said, 'Blue, dear, is the colour of Our Lady's mantle, of the sea and of heaven; it wards off evil and impurity.' When she thought about this, she asked, 'How can you be certain if something you think or something you've done is bad?'

'For one thing, you're dedicated to Our Lady, you share her name as I do, and she'd never mislead you; also you've got a guardian angel and he *never* sleeps, and that is one example of the proper use of the word *never* . . . it's a word people overuse all the time . . . *He* tells you what's right and wrong . . . your conscience really.'

'In my dreams even?'

'Yes, even in your dreams, dear. Yes.'

Some dreams were so real and so shameful she could cry now or any time thinking about them. Was it dreaming or not when

Iggy came those nights when her mother was in Dublin for a fortnight's retreat at the Marie Reparatrix convent or Enniskillen for a weekend seminar with Uncle Felix at the Graan, and only Bridie in the maid's room at the back of the house with the separate staircase? He came and he did those things and it wasn't dreaming because each time when she wondered if it was a dream she found soiled knickers in the bedside cupboard next morning though she could not remember putting them there the night before. Two pairs she flung into the river below the grotto and the third she burned in the range when Bridie was up ironing in the old nursery. That time she wanted to go up and tell her but she didn't know how. She had a chance another time when Bridie asked about the blood on the sheets and she lied in fright, saying she'd cut herself.

"Deed and you didn't cut yourself, love, blood is nothing to be afeared of, or ashamed of, it could be the start of your monthlies.' As Bridie went on to explain, she kept thinking, I'll tell, I'll tell, I'll tell, but didn't, and heard Bridie say, 'Don't let on I told you. Your mammy mightn't care about me tellin' before herself.' And if she couldn't tell Bridie about Iggy, how could she ever tell her mother about how when she was very small he'd hold her up against his tommytoe till all the grey stuff came out, or the time in the bath he'd put the toothbrush into her bottom and then washed off the twotwos from the handle and from the little hole at the end and said with his Iggy smile, 'Good as new.' Or the other awful time he put it right up between her legs and it was so sore she screamed and bled and all he said was, 'Crybaby, what's up with you?' and she'd said, 'I hate this game, Iggy, and I'm going to tell Mammy when she gets back!'

'You will not – or you'll have us both in trouble. It's your fault as much as mine and *you* know that. *You* know that well.'

He always said *we* and *us* till she shouted once, 'It was *you*, Iggy, just *you* every time 'cause I was fast asleep.'

'Go on,' he'd said, 'don't pretend. You like it as much as I do,' and she'd said, 'I hate it and I hate you.'

All he did then was shrug and walk away.

Where was her guardian angel then? Did Iggy have a guardian angel? Who told him to do those things with the toothbrush and his finger and his tongue to make her head go all swimmy? Was it the Devil did that?

When those things came into her head she felt so soiled, so unhappy, she wanted to shout aloud all the ugly words she'd ever heard at school. Those feelings only came when they were kneeling at the Rosary in winter or down at the grotto in summer, or during the quiet belltime of the Mass when the church was silent and full, and the priest was turning the bread and wine into the body and blood of Christ and her head was so full of the foulness she longed to shout out, that to stop herself from doing so made her tremble and sweat and feel sickish. She had to leave the church once, and another time bite her top lip so hard it all swoll up. Afterwards Bridie asked, 'What happened to your lip, love?'

She had stared at Iggy eating his breakfast and he'd stared back at her as if he half knew what was in her head, daring her to speak, to say: 'It's because of *him*, my brother of sixteen, who put his hand over my mouth the first time and the pain was terrible, a white burning pain and I was raw and bleeding after . . . *him*, Bridie, with the green eyes like Mammy and the reddish wavy hair, him always showing off his teeth, Captain of the Junior House at Mungret whose last report said, "An exemplar to the whole school," and Mammy reading it out so proud and telling everyone.' How could she ever be told . . . ? She'd die of shame . . . So it's me has to die . . . every day and night, ashamed, ashamed, ashamed . . . and the secret hid, but how could you hide such things from God and His mother and all the angels and saints and the millions of dead souls looking down . . . seeing everything? Iggy didn't seem to care about any of that. Was his guardian angel a bad one pretending to be a good one? If she couldn't tell Bridie, she couldn't ever tell anyone except L, her teddy bear. And that was something else she didn't want to think about. So she thought, I'll think of Knockmacarooney in July. That was where Bridie lived in a mountainy area of Fermanagh under Carn rock. She always got those first two weeks off to help her mother and father at hay and in the bog. Last year Marion was allowed to go with her. They were the fourteen happiest days of her life so far, the hearth, and the bog and a horse pulling tumblers of hay in a steep meadow and neighbours being awful nice, 'Who is this princess, Bridie?' and the ass and trap to Mass on Sunday. Not a single word about novenas and daily Masses and pilgrimages, and St Joseph's Young Priests' Society and Lourdes and miracles and Uncle Ambrose in Rome and Uncle Felix in Enniskillen and special prayers for darkest Africa and the conversion of communist Russia and Iggy Iggy Iggy, Munster Captain of the junior tennis team and how the *Cork Examiner* said he was almost certain to be a member of the Davis Cup team before long, like his father before him, the late Philip Cantwell, MRCVS. One night when she asked Bridie's father why he called the boar he kept 'de Valera', he laughed and spat in the fire and said, 'Because he's a very long, very cute auld bollox, that's why.'

Old Mrs Rooney pretended to be cross and said, 'It's not right, Dan, talkin' that way fornenst the child.' Bridie laughed and said, 'She knows far worse than that from school,' to which Marion agreed and then said, 'If he was my boar I wouldn't call him de Valera.'

'Would you not now?'

'No, Mrs Rooney.'

'What name would you put on him so?'

'Iggy.'

Bridie's parents did not understand. Bridie intervened and said, 'She's bold as brass, this lassie. Her brother's name is Iggy . . . Ignatius.'

'And why,' Old Rooney persisted, 'would you call a boar after your brother?'

'Because.'

'Because what?'

'Just because.'

'You wouldn't be that horrid fond of him?'

She had shrugged. Sensing that she would not tell, the talk went on to other things.

Apart from that fortnight with Bridie, daytime at school was the time she liked best. You could read, and learn and play, but not with the Culligan twins or any of the children who lived out the new line in Casement Park. This was not said but it was strongly implied. Her best friend, well, pal of sorts really, and warmly approved by her mother, was Martina Flanagan, who said most of the Casement Park crowd should have their mouths rinsed out with Jeyes Fluid and mustard. Martina's father gave you a pink drink to rinse out your mouth in his surgery. 'All that rough talk,' Martina said, 'is what they hear in their own houses. It's not their fault, they can't help it really.'

That was true, Marion thought, because one evening two years ago at homework she'd blobbed her ecker with a dip pen and said quietly to herself, 'Ah, fuck me.' Her mother was sitting at the fire crocheting the cuff of a surplice for the St Joseph's Young Priests' Society. The crocheting stopped. When Marion looked up, her mother's face had gone very white and her one good eye looked round and staring.

'What did you say just now?'

'Nothing, Mammy.'

'I can't quite believe what I think I heard.'

Silence.

'It's only a word.'

'Where did you hear it?'

'At school.'

Infants!?

'In the playground mostly.'

'What child uttered it?'

'Do I have to tell?'

'Yes.'

'And will you tell Sister Dominic?'

'I don't like telltales but I do like to know.'

Her mother was always saying things like that. How could she find out except from a telltale? But if you said the like of that to her she'd go into a huge huff. Marion went back to recopying her ecker, hoping her mother would forget. She never did.

'You're going to have to tell me, Marion.'

'What do you want me to tell, Mammy?'

'What child or children use that ugly word?'

'Well . . . there's the Culligan twins for starters, and Sadie Caffrey and Josie McGuinness, they're the worst. But there's loads more. They just say it when there's no nuns about and no one passes any remarks on them.'

After a long silence her mother said, 'I don't ever want to hear that word on your tongue again . . . in my life. It's unspeakably coarse and those poor children who use it in common talk have no notion how much they're offending God and Our Lady. Do you understand me, Marion?'

'Yes, mammy.'

'Never in my life again . . . never on your tongue.'

That was two nevers, and for the rest of that evening she worked out that you had to use your tongue for luck, tuck, duck and stuck, but fuck was just your top teeth on your lower lip and maybe the tiniest bit of your tongue away in the back of your mouth. And all the way up the thirty steps of the staircase to the landing she said fuck to herself at every step because it was nowhere near her tongue. When she knelt to say her prayers that night she asked God to forgive her for being bold. She knew well it was far from being bad.

Yesterday during the boys' retreat the Culligan twins were smoking cigarette butts behind the handball alleys and everyone said their skit was the best ever . . . or worst, all laughing, and laughing, and laughing, Martina Flanagan the loudest. They gave out the skit, every second line making big eyes and pursing their mouths up and making big eyes like Sister Emmanuel in pretended disapproval.

> *Joseph and Mary went into the dariy*
> *Where Joseph showed Mary his hairy canary.*

It went on, getting ruder, coarser and more detailed with every line. It took her breath away because it was exactly what Iggy had done to her, and the last two lines made her wonder with sudden fear:

> *Oh Mary Macushla tell us quick and don't tease us,*
> *I was thinkin', says she, of callin' him Jesus.*

Could a baby grow inside her from what Iggy did?

After the skit Martina said that if either of the Culligans died that night they'd go straight to Hell, straight down, definitely; and for certain sure. '*We'll* have to confess it, Marion, because we stayed and listened and laughed.' Marion hadn't laughed once but didn't tell Martina that.

'It's spitting in God's face, you know, and that's blasphemy and nobody can forgive a person blasphemy bar the Pope himself, and he'd need to be in real good humour, and if he was in a pussy humour he'd put you straight out of his big confession box in St Peter's.'

'Why would he do that?'

'Because he's infallible, silly, and if he said no to the Culligans they'd go straight to Hell, straight down definitely, because it's a worse sin than . . . you know . . . the other!'

'What other, Martina?'

'Oh, sins of the flesh, Marion! Any old cod of a PP could forgive you those. Haven't you an uncle out in Rome?'

'Ambrose. My father's brother.'

'A Jesuit, isn't he? They're ten times brainier than other priests. Our crowd here are "poor types", Daddy says, "mostly bogmen in dog collars" . . . and listen, tell me, this uncle of yours, does he ever *see* the Pope in his white frock?'

'Every day walking in his garden.'

'Ah, go to God, Marion, he does not.'

'He does, Martina. He told me.'

'And what does he *do* all day, your uncle?'

'He works in the radio.'

'Vatican Radio . . . gaudy hymns and stuff like that?'

'No. He's in the news section.'

'Posh just the same . . . Rome and the Pope's garden and all.'

That was yesterday, a day like any other. It seemed now that she was half awake all night dreading this coming day, this last morning she would ever be with L, the teddy bear she got for her third birthday. Soon *he* would be six years old. As her mother had given him to her on that day, she'd said, 'This is your

Teddy, love, your own special little boy,' and within hours she
was calling him loveboy. For a day or two her mother had
smiled and then said, 'I don't think, dear, that loveboy is all that
suitable a name. Just call him L . . . would that be nice?'

And so he was called L and all those years he was by far her
best friend. She could tell him anything and he'd listen. He was
a bit of a stupoe at sums but if you gave him time, he could work
things out, but mainly he was kind and patient and you could
kiss him and kiss him and kiss him and not feel shy because he
was a bit shy himself and no matter what, he always told
the truth, not because he was a saint, but because, like her, he
was no good at telling lies. If you thought about it, he was a kind
of brown bear angel completely on your side, you could tell him
very private things and be certain sure he'd never breathe a
word to a living soul. He hated Iggy. Her mother had removed
his black and yellow glass eyes. The hook things at the back
could be, she said, dangerous. In their place she'd darned in
pale blue woollen eyes that gave him a purblind look. Any sort
of hitting or punching terrified him and if you wanted to be
unkind you could call him a coward, but she knew that, like
herself, he was timid but brave.

One evening last week when her mother was reading a life of
the Little Flower, she suddenly said, out of nowhere, 'I've been
thinking, dear, about L, your little teddy friend, and wondering
if perhaps it's time he went.'

Went!!! She'd been unable to think at first, too startled and
disbelieving to grasp what her mother was suggesting.

'But I'll never see him again.'

'You exaggerate, dear . . . and I'm tired of telling you about
the word *never*. If he goes to some deserving child, most likely
you'll see him from time to time . . . if you want.'

Now sick with shock and anger she asked, 'Why should he go?'

'Because you're almost nine, big for your age. You put him sitting on that table and whisper to him during your homework . . . and that's all right because your marks are good enough . . . but taking him to school in your school-bag and talking to him in the school toilets is another matter.'

'I don't . . . '

'Now *don't* lie to me. You've been overheard . . . it's too much . . . it's not healthy.'

Martina Flanagan, she thought. Her mother most likely: telltales.

'Why is it not healthy?'

'Because it's unnatural, that's why.'

'How?'

'Don't get clever, Marion. Don't argue with me. It's unhealthy and it's unnatural, believe me.'

Mary Cantwell did not hear her daughter mutter, 'If it was Iggy's he'd be let keep it.'

'I didn't hear that but I wish you wouldn't call your brother Iggy. You know I dislike it.'

Marion did not respond. She'd heard her mother say another time, 'It's better than Naasi, with its hint of nasty and Nazi. But only just. Your brother's name is Ignatius Loyola, like the founder of the Jesuits.'

And she thought, I know what his name is. I know too much about him. Aloud she said, 'I think it's a horrible name.'

Mary Cantwell put down the biography of the Little Flower, anger growing, and looked intently at her daughter.

'It's sad to think of you as an ungiving child, Marion.'

'I'm not giving you L.'

'Are you not? Then I'm confiscating him.'

During the silence that followed Marion thought she would

cry, managed not to, and said quietly, 'If Ignatius died I'd *never* see him again, would I?'

After a startled silence Mary Cantwell said, 'That's a very odd example. But . . . yes and no, because we're only on this earth a brief while and when we go to Heaven, please God, we'll see your daddy and my mama and papa and Ignatius *if*, God forbid, God should decide to call him . . . but . . . '

I'll just tell her now, Marion thought, and her breathing became suddenly so shallow she knew she would hardly be able to utter, so she said, in a sort of choked whisper, 'I wouldn't care if he was dead . . . '

Her mother's good eye began to pulsate.

'You don't mean that, Marion. You can't.'

'I do . . . and I hope he goes to Hell.'

For a moment it seemed as though Mary Cantwell might strike her daughter.

'That is the most vicious thing I've ever heard any sister wish on any brother, let alone her only brother. How could you utter such a monstrous wish?'

'Because.'

'Because what, child?'

'Because.'

'Is it because you've become jealous of the only boy ever in the Junior House in the history of Mungret to get the Best All-rounder medal . . . and don't smirk in that silly, vixenish way. I'm ashamed any child of mine could be so begrudging, so *mean*-spirited. What *is* wrong with you, child? You've become so unkind and remote, and Bridie thinks the same and so does Sister Dominic.'

Marion looked away and said nothing. Neither broke a protracted silence till her mother spoke . . . slowly and carefully.

'I'm not trying to spite you, dear. I'm doing this for your own good because I love you and because the carry-on with L has become . . . '

'*What* carry-on?'

'The make-believe in the school toilet . . . it's too much . . . it's . . . '

'Is Santa Claus unhealthy, unnatural?'

Silence.

'Is God a bit like Santa Claus?'

'Go to your bed, Marion. You've gone too far!'

That night she made a mound of her knees and sat L in the hollow of her lap and looked at him and told him that most likely he would be going away forever but not to be lonely or afraid because most likely he would be well looked after. She was, she said, almost certain of that. But then he asked in a very small voice could she not hide him somewhere? There were dozens of places. There was a huge attic, three lofted yards, there was the little play cave at the back of the grotto which they called Heaven, a secret place where they had often played for hours long ago and told each other secrets. There was underneath the floor of the tennis house, the willow house beside the river . . . or even up one of the lime trees that lined the haggard field . . . you couldn't see into lime trees even in the middle of winter . . .

It broke her heart to say, 'L, they'd see me going to visit you, no matter where, and there would be a terrible row. I could drown you in the river but I couldn't watch you sinking. I'd want to be with you . . . but I'd rather drown you than think of you with some cruel child who didn't care.' And he said, 'I'd rather be drownded, gone and forgotten than be abused, and that's a fact.'

'And you'd be right,' she said. 'Don't you worry, L. I'll be with you.'

*

Driving back that morning from her weekly voluntary one-hour vigil and six o'clock Mass at the Convent of the Marie Reparatrix, Mary Cantwell drove with extreme caution. The smooth tarmac looked dangerous and she could see that the grass verge was frozen, a thing unusual eight miles inland.

The radio weatherman did mention a cold snap and the possibility of snow later.

She had valid reasons for that caution.

Almost nine years ago, on the second of February, a skid outside Dundalk had altered her life unimaginably. She was eight months pregnant, Ignatius was six, and she and her husband, Philip Cantwell, had left the hotel and the annual veterinary dinner earlier than most. Philip was driving fast. During dinner, across the table Jack Moriarty, three-quarters drunk, had asked Philip if PV stood for paper vet. Through the laughter she had seen the cruelty of the question strike home. She knew from the way he blinked and the way he drank thereafter. Working out of Salmon in a busy, well-established practice, he had inoculated fifty-seven cattle on one day on eight or nine farms within a radius of thirty miles – all from one veterinary-size pack of inoculant. The following day they were all dead, a lethal accident in every sense. Tests proved that the blackleg virus was live. The Swiss pharmaceutical company blamed storage, and although the Veterinary Association fought on his side, it was three years before the farmers got compensation. Meantime most of them shook their heads and said, 'A bad mistake, surely.' They tended to use the word mistake in place of accident, implying a degree of incompetence, more damaging even – they were wary about employing anyone with an aura of ill luck. He had been forced to join the Department, where in fact he seemed to be working quite happily as a 'paper vet', but clearly regarded himself as a failure. And what she knew must be especially galling for him was that he came first or second all the way through college to his finals. Moriarty boozed, womanized, repeated, cogged and scraped his way through, but now ran one of the most successful veterinary practices in the whole country, north or south.

She had thought Philip was driving safely but a little fast, and was about to suggest a decrease in speed, when suddenly there it was, an ass plodding down the centre of the road, head down, blinded by the headlights. He jerked the wheel suddenly, missed the ass and went into a fast spin, a sense of tumbling, then impact, and she knew as she went through the windscreen that her face was torn terribly, and she thought, my baby's dead. Eight days later she woke up to find herself a widow, blind in one eye, with eighty-four stitches in her face and a baby girl of four pounds in an incubator.

Unconscious when Philip was buried, many colleagues came for the month's mind, including Moriarty. When he put his hand towards her outside the church, she ignored it. Drunk before the meal had started that night, he was talking in the bar about 'the blight of grotty grottoes all over the country, all from the hallucinations of a pubic girl. I've been to Lourdes . . . thousands of crutches in that cave and not one wooden leg. It's another God Almighty rotten Roman racket . . . Popes, saints and Mafia all tied up with Hairy Ned!' A lot of his colleagues and their wives seemed to think he was hilarious. She had asked, quietly but firmly, 'What about the terminally ill, Jack, the suicidally depressed, the maimed, the blind, the crippled in wheelchairs . . . what would you say to them?'

'I'd say, "Stay at home and get drunk." Or better still, "Go to the sun and get drunk." Do them far more good.'

She did not reveal at the inquest that Philip had swerved to

avoid an ass. It seemed a ludicrous, almost farcical way for a
young man to lose his life. As time passed she began to think
about his death, and all the obvious things that people tended to
say seemed nonetheless true. There is 'a divinity that shapes
our ends'. God does have His own agenda, His divine plan
which must have included the time and manner of Philip's
death, the loss of her eye and Marion's birth. All were threads
woven into the great weave of Christ's loom. Time would
unravel their meaning, their truth and their beauty. Meantime,
like St Peter, she in a sense had denied Christ by omitting to
mention the ass at the inquest. An ass had carried Mary to
Bethelehem, an ass had carried Christ in triumph into
Jerusalem. There were those very beautiful lines of Chesterton's
that caused pins and needles from her neck to her spine every
time she read them or heard them – 'There was a shout about
my ears, and palms before my feet.'

She bought books and articles about bereavement, attended
retreats and lectures dealing with loss and resignation. Every
now and then she dreamt about those few seconds before that
swerve and the sick, fast spin on that dark road northwards, the
ass always in the dream, plodding, Christ astride, or the
pregnant Virgin, both in a splendour of light, and sometimes
she herself was the Virgin and sometimes Christ was poor Philip
with death in his eyes.

Her rule on arriving home after her Wednesday vigil was to
drink a glass of water, go to bed and then breakfast about ten.
She did not see Marion leave for school on the vigil mornings,
which was why she chose this morning to subtract the
contentious teddy. Less fuss and unpleasantness. Confiscate –
far too strong a word . . . but she must do what she said she
would do. For such a quiet child Marion had become obdurate
and cheeky, seriously cheeky.

She looked down at the floodlit grotto built by her mother in 1922 to celebrate the foundation of the state. It lay half-way between the front of the house and the river, encircled by a birch copse more striking now in winter, the white Carrara marble beautiful against the black limestone, the Virgin ever smiling down, Bernadette Soubirous ever kneeling and staring up in open-mouthed wonder. There were a number of raised sandstone slabs facing the grotto where people could kneel or sit and pray. In good weather there was always somebody there and that was wonderful too, the aura of sanctity.

Was it sometime last May, that Kensington couple, heading for Connemara, said they were related? Descendants? I didn't bother listening . . . something to Richard Atkinson, they said, who'd built Salmon House in the eighteenth century. It was continuously occupied, they said, by their family till 1883. Was Thomas Love, the Newry cattle-dealer, by any chance any connection? Yes. He was my grandfather. 'How very fascinating . . . ' Could they see around grounds and garden? They looked to be in good order.

'Yes,' she'd said, 'there was money in pigs. My father, Laurence Love, started a bacon factory here near the town. It's still in the family.'

'Ah!'

'And he bought back the land sold off bit by bit by your people, but the salmon fishing rights were of course still more valuable than the land on either side of the river.'

'And you *do* charge for that?'

'It's expensive to fish here but costly to have it watched night and day. Poaching is a way of life.'

But the grounds were no longer private. They were open to the public all the year round, free of charge.

'You couldn't very well levy people who wanted to pray, could you?' she'd said.

'Not nowadays,' he smiled. Meaning what? Given half a chance would they still be Paddy-whacking and priest-hunting?

She had walked with them as far as the grotto, catching what she imagined to be a look or half-smile flit between them, nothing as ill-bred as a smirk, but it was something. About the grotto itself they said not a single word. Just looked impassive. Then both exclaimed at the back, 'Oh! Ah!' and 'How very charming.'

Sometime in the thirties Harry Greenan, an architect friend, had designed a children's play area incorporating the back of the grotto, slotting in sandstone shelves, a small hide-and-seek play cave, stone troughs and concealed soil pockets spilling Our Lady's colours – white and blue aubretia. There was a sandpit, a seesaw and a swing, all set in the circle of birch.

'If you don't mind my saying so, I prefer the backside of your grotto to the front.'

And before she could think of a reply, his wife or mistress said, 'It's very imaginative . . . must be a children's paradise.' Pagans. They missed the whole point. Supposing she'd said, 'Yes, I do mind what you've implied and would you both please leave now.' But of course it's afterwards in an access of anger you think of these things to do and say. Deliberately insulting, the almost blasphemous use of the word 'backside' . . . more subtle of course than old Dixon in the gatelodge who snarled 'Rubbish' every time he heard the Angelus on Radio Eireann. *They'd* no children. He'd be the last of the old 'occupiers' anywhere near the place. Protestants. Lower or upper class, they seemed contemptuous both of the Virgin as God's mother and of virginity itself. They would pay for their contempt hereafter. God's mother is not easily sneered at.

She unpinned the black Clones lace mantilla she sometimes wore to Mass, the same mantilla she had worn for the semi-private audience with Pope Pius XII. There was a silver-framed photograph of this moment on the desk in the window. She was on her knees kissing his hand. Philip's brother, Ambrose, had arranged that. It was beyond all doubt the greatest moment of her life, like being in the presence of God, like kissing the hand of God Himself . . . and every time she looked at the photograph, something of the overwhelming emotion of the moment came back to her.

She took off her day clothes, put on a nightdress, dressing gown and slippers, and as she bathed her glass eye in a saline solution, the optician's waiting room at Enniskillen last November came back to her like a coarse shout on a quiet, beautiful night.

She had picked up the feature section of a London quality Sunday showing a large, full-length photograph of Pius XII, with the headline THE SILENT CRIMINAL? Underneath it said, 'Not the evil he did, the evil he did nothing about.' Inside she read and half read, skipping and rejecting and then going back to see if she'd misread, headings and sentences so startling that she put the paper down with shocked disbelief, then picked it up again. The words jumped off the page:

'If there was any justice in the world they should be talking about his criminalization, not his beatification . . .

' . . . the man should be dug up, strung up and burned as a Nazi collaborator.

'His knowledge total, his silence absolute, his crime unforgivable.

' . . . this cold-hearted Roman aristo watching and praying a long way from Gethsemane . . . '

Too dazed to read on steadily, she went to the last sentence.

'. . . past masters at ignoring the brutality of truth, at washing their blood-stained linen in secrecy and silence . . . '

After the opticians she'd gone straight out to Felix at the Graan. He read the feature, frowning: 'It's . . . very biased.'

'Is it true?'

'It's garbage. Garbage sells.'

'It doesn't read like garbage.'

'What could any journalist know about a man like Pius? Ignore it.'

Was it because he was her younger brother or because she knew too much about him that she seldom found his answers satisfactory?

Two months later, collecting Ignatius from Mungret for the Christmas holiday, her brother-in-law, Ambrose, had brought them both into the book-lined library. Like Philip, but six inches taller – 'It's the Norman blood,' he said, 'we Kilkenny Cantwells came here with Richard the Second' – he was in charge of the English-speaking section of Vatican Radio. He had an accent-less voice, narrow, fine-skinned face, gold-rimmed glasses and a gold-filled eyetooth when he smiled. He was here on a break of sorts. He had homework, a bulky file about the Catholic Croats bulldozing orthodox Christian Serbs into Catholicism *or* into mass graves during the war, some hundreds of thousands of them! Accusations too absurd, too monstrous to answer.

When she'd mentioned Pius XII and the Holocaust, he said, 'Every day in every part of the world the Church is vilified. If it's filth or lies, we ignore it; like Christ we remain silent because truth will out in God's own time . . . and yes, the Holocaust was an *appalling* crime, but to vilify Christ's representative on earth is to mock at Christ Himself . . . and God, as we well know, will not be mocked.'

He went on to talk about 'the new man', John XXIII, 'not very

well equipped intellectually,' he thought, 'and clearly fond of
his food and drink. The late Pius spoke twelve languages
beautifully . . . he had such grace, such elegant manners. This
new man has Italian only, but a good man nonetheless, and
after all, St Peter had only one language. And we must
remember that God had a hand in his election and God does not
make mistakes. When we think He does, there is a purpose.'
Restrained, balanced, persuasive, a clerical scholar with six
modern languages.

Ignatius had asked a couple of shrewd questions – you could
see they liked and respected each other, uncle and nephew,
men's men both, good scholars and sportsmen. She was not all
that surprised on the way home in the car to hear him talk of
joining the Order . . . make a good Jesuit, something fastidious
about him, secretive almost. Ignatius Cantwell SJ. Would he
end up like Ambrose, regarded by his peers as one of the
cleverest men in the world? You could see from his report that
he was especially gifted at languages. She'd mentioned this to
Felix. He ignored the possibility of Ignatius joining the Society of
Jesus and just said, 'You can have a hundred languages and be
a bloody bore in every one of them. So Shaw says, and he's
right.'

Levitical jealousy? Certainly Marion is intensely jealous of
Ignatius. Do I talk about him as much as I think about him?
Maybe girls are more emotional, more spiteful than boys?
Bitchy really is the word . . . vixenish I called her, and jealous,
but dear God, to wish him dead and in Hell and not care . . . and
not allude to it or withdraw one word of it in over a week . . .
and Felix poooh-poohing it last night with talk of phases and
the moon and changes . . . and utter nonsense . . . and going on
to ask about the fishing season.

'Felix,' I said, 'I think this is serious,' and he said, 'I wanted to

kill you often as a child, Mary. You used to punch hell out of me
if you didn't get your own way.'

'Did I?'

'You did, and you know you did.'

'That was different.'

'Why?'

'You didn't mean it.'

'I probably did.'

'Felix, if you'd heard her, if you'd seen her face . . . '

'Her face is about the loveliest face I've ever seen on any
child . . . and some lucky beggar is going to get her all to
himself. It's a phase, Mary . . . she's growing up.'

Was he implying, like Bridie the other morning: 'Could it be
the start of her monthlies, ma'am?' in a loud voice, and Dermy
Dolan polishing shoes in the scullery? The best-hearted girl in
the world, but no tact, no sense of decorum whatsoever. I didn't
answer her. I must get that pamphlet in Veritas by Sister Ita
Magdalen . . . Ita handles the whole thing with great delicacy.

She switched off the grotto light and made her way towards
Marion's room. She would send Dermy Dolan with the teddy to
the dry cleaners, collect it later herself before she got back from
school. The trouble is she's refusing to grow up, so growing up
will have to be imposed on her. Yes, she'll be moody for a week
or two but that will pass. Loss and grief were two emotions
Mary Cantwell understood. No need to tiptoe down the landing
to avoid creaking boards. The child was always deep asleep . . .
sometimes almost impossible to waken. The bedside lamp did
indeed show her in profound sleep, mouth slightly ajar. She *was*
an extraordinarily beautiful child, as everyone kept saying, but
even sleeping beauties can seem far from ideal when you see
them open-mouthed, frowning, and lying all crunched up with
that lump again in the middle of the bed. Mary Cantwell felt

slightly embarrassed as she pulled back the bedclothes because there it was, the wretched teddy, pushed and held down between her daughter's legs, innocently of course in her sleep . . . but so unseemly.

As she began to remove the teddy, Marion's grip tightened. She pushed harder against her crotch, her eyes opening and staring up in something akin to terror.

'It's all right, dear, it's all right. Let go.'

Not yet awake, Marion still clutched tightly.

'Let it go, Marion! It's all right. Don't fight me, like a good girl. Let it go!'

Suddenly, awake and abashed, she relaxed her grip and sat up, pulling her nightdress down, aware with a hollow feeling of what was taking place. Her mother was 'confiscating' L, making him into an orphan, giving him away 'to some deserving child'. She heard her own voice wheedling like a three-year-old's.

'No, Mammy, no! Oh, please, Mammy.'

'We've been through this, dear. Don't argue with me.'

'But I love him. He's my only friend and you're giving him away to someone who might hate him.'

'If you could hear yourself. Crying like a baby.'

And although she knew she was doing the right thing, it was with a heavy heart and tears in her eyes that Mary Cantwell left her daughter's room and went back to her own room to try and sleep. She put the teddy bear in a drawer.

Bridie had the main lights and wall-lights on in the basement kitchen. Outside the sky was dark with sleet or snow. She was riddling the woodstove when Marion came into the kitchen.

'Would you look at the sour puss on the lovely girl. What's wrong now?'

When Bridie saw that Marion was too choked up to answer, she closed the draught of the woodstove and went over. Bridie was a big-bottomed woman in her thirties, with a soft, freckled face and a softer Fermanagh accent.

'What is it, love?'

When Marion covered her face and cried inwardly, Bridie put her arms around her.

'Gawdy, gawdy, gawdy . . . whisht, lassie . . . it can't be all that bad,' and as a sob escaped, she said, 'You'll wake the mistress and her up half the night praying for us sinners.'

'She's giving L away, Bridie.'

'I know.'

'Confiscating him.'

'Ah now, you made that up, Marion.'

'I did not.'

'You made her say it so. You back-answered her.'

Silence.

'Only a small bit.'

'What did you say?'

'I've forgotten.'

'You've no wit, love. You don't argy with the like of your mother. You'll not best her . . . and maybe she knows best anyway.'

'Who'd want him, Bridie? It's cruel. She hates him.'

'Where did you get *that* notion?'

'She only loves God and Our Lady and Iggy.'

'Now quit that wild class of talk.'

'But I love him more than anything in the world. He's my best friend.'

'Oh is he now!'

'Don't tease, Bridie. You know you are too. Oh God, what am I going to do? I think I'll die.'

'Well before you do that, would you think of a word with your Uncle Felix . . . '

'Do you think?'

'Nothin' bates tryin'.'

Suddenly Bridie put her hand on her breastbone and uttered, 'Jesus Christ!'

Standing outside in the recess of the basement window a tall, capped figure stared out of brown spaniel eyes, smiling through yellowed gapped teeth, a week's stubble on his gaunt face.

Marion waved out at him and laughed and said, 'It's Wishy Harte.'

'Thanks be to God somethin' can make you laugh.'

'Oh, let him in. Bridie, he looks famished.'

'Are you mad in the head? He'll have the whole house hoppin' with fleas.'

'The scullery so.'

Lifting her plate of porridge and mug of tea, Marion followed Bridie out to the scullery and to the back door, where she was letting Wishy in and half giving out, half greeting him warmly.

'Wishy Harte, you put the heart crossways in me, staring in that way like a ghost. Why don't you knock or ring like any other Christian body?'

The answers, when they came at all, were twenty or thirty seconds after the query, monosyllabic, apologetic, accompanied by a smile or nod.

'Sit down there and eat that porridge and we'll get you a wedge of soda. Where have you been all summer and half the winter?'

'Here and there, Bridie.'

'Where mostly?'

'The west.'

'At what? Still the horses, is it?'

'Aye.'

'Fair to fair . . . ten horses trotting behind you . . . forty miles a day for next to nothin', for what wouldn't get you a bed for the night! Bad rogues them dealers and knackers. You'll catch your death, so you will, out in all weathers.'

'We'll all catch that, Bridie.'

'That's for sure.'

Marion watched him eat, fascinated by his scarecrow gauntness, his oddness, his slowness, his disconnection from ordinary life, his extraordinary gentleness.

Cycling home one evening through Casement Park she had come across a screeching gang of brats, chanting again and again as he passed, smiling uncertainly:

> Wishy Harte
> Let a fart
> That cracked the roof
> Of the butter mart.

Enraged by the smiling, they began throwing a bric-à-brac of rubbish, tins, sticks, turnips, bottles and stones, till something sharp cut his neck. She could tell from the way his head jerked and saw blood come through his fingers. He looked at his bloody hand and then at the children, without anger, his eyes dazed and hurt. The taunting stopped. In the silence she heard herself shout as loud as she could, 'Ye striggs of Felon . . . ye rotten, rotten cowards!'

'Striggs of Felon' was how Bridie's father described the foul pus that came out of a cow's infected quarter. She had memorized it for future use. Going over she tugged the cuff of his jacket and led him out on the road to Salmon, where Mary washed the wound, called a GP for stitches, and took him over – not only cutting his fingernails but bathing his feet in hot water and Dettol, cutting his toenails and giving him a pair of Philip's good working boots. Again and again she said, 'He could be Christ.' To herself she said, 'In a sense he *is* Christ.'

Marion delayed cycling to school without L in her schoolbag. She watched Wishy eating so slowly, delicately, almost absent-mindedly. She found it hard to believe that anything about him could be the same as Iggy. Like L he probably had no tommytoe.

'What do you think of all day long, Wishy?'

'Things.'

'What things?'

For a couple of minutes she thought he wouldn't or couldn't answer. Then he said, 'If I was a bird, I'd fly.'

'Where to?'

'Heaven.'

'So would I, Wishy.'

Bridie called from the kitchen, 'Marion, you'll be late. Go.'

She was glad it was retreat day. Every year they had a different Order of priests – Franciscans from Rossnowla, Passionists from Enniskillen, White Fathers from Cootehill, Oblate Fathers and Dominicans from Dublin, none of Uncle Ambrose's Order, Jesuits. They only gave retreats to the Marie Reparatrix nuns or Louis nuns, and her mother thought it unsuitable for a priest to be staying in a convent, and of course there was no hotel 'remotely civilized enough to cater for such men'. So they all stayed at Salmon, where they loved the tennis and the croquet and the bridge and the musical evenings and every one of them blessed the house. 'The most blessed house in Ireland,' Mary Cantwell often said. 'The Atkinsons by now are well exorcized, thanks be to God and the Jesuits.'

This was the first time Marion would hear her Uncle Felix on his home ground. From yesterday the boys reported him to be 'great craic and lots of scary bits'. The morning session was mostly stories, a few jokes, some questions and answers followed by Mass. Afternoon was very different. He seemed like somebody else, staring up at the stained-glass window of St Patrick banishing the snakes from Ireland. When there was utter silence, he began:

'St Matthew tells us, "It were better for that man, that woman, that boy or that girl, that a millstone be placed around their necks and that they be cast into the depths of the sea."'

He paused and lowered his voice.

'Down down down as deep as the sky is high. Down down down to that undiscovered underworld where sightless monsters of the deep cruise in everlasting darkness and loneliness. And who are these tragic creatures plummeting to perdition? And why!? I will tell you girls what St Matthew tells us. "They are those who lead astray these my little ones." And what does he mean by "astray"? I will tell you what he means.'

Felix continued in this manner, giving examples of what to do, how to be aware of the wiles and guiles of the Devil. 'Girls, put on the armour of Jesus Christ, and for God's sake and your own, guard your tongue and your soul night and day against the snares of Satan.'

As he continued, one of the Culligan twins whispered to the other, 'Your bum and your hole.'

From where she was sitting Marion could see the Culligans and a group around them giggling.

Felix stopped and stared down at the group. All stopped except the Culligans, who were now out of control. She could see their shoulders going like jelly. Felix waited and waited, looked up at St Patrick, then down at the Donegal altar carpet specially commissioned and presented by his mother, Helen, to celebrate the Eucharistic Congress of 1932, gold chalice and white Eucharist set on a beech-green base edged by an intertwining Celtic pattern.

Slowly he raised, pointed and held his left arm in the direction of the Culligans and said so slowly it could scarcely be heard: 'There are two girls on the outside of the sixth row who look like twins, and those two girls are . . . '

He paused and uttered a great shout: ' . . . sniggering and giggling in the presence of Almighty God.' The Culligans for all their bravado got quite a fright. Josie went white and Breede went red. Outside, recovered, they said to Marion, 'A noisy auld shite, that uncle of yours.' They refused to confess to him despite Sister Louis Mary's threats and urgings. As the other girls queued obediently, Louis Mary came over.

'If you don't want to confess to Father Felix, Marion, that's perfectly understandable.'

'I don't mind,' Marion said.

She didn't. She was fond of her Uncle Felix . . . more than fond . . . loved.

Lying reading behind a couch one night she overheard her mother telling Iggy, 'He hasn't caught one salmon on our stretch or any other for thirty years.'

'You're not serious!'

'I am. A duffer at golf, worse at tennis or croquet, but as a fisherman – hopeless.' She dropped her voice. 'A few years back the Prior of the Graan phoned to thank me for the two beautiful salmon Felix had caught and presented to the community from our stretch. "We're all grateful and impressed, Mary," he said.'

'You mean . . . '

'Bought them up the town in McElwee's fish shop.'

'Good God! Did you tell the Prior?'

'Of course not.'

'You should have, Mother. That's not sport – it's cheating. He's a chancer, old Felix.'

'But harmless, Ignatius, surely.'

'I'm not so sure.'

She missed what they said next. Heard only laughing, and remembered thinking, 'I hate them, both of them.' She had gone fishing the previous summer with Felix. He seemed to fumble, get overexcited and lose a lot of baits in trees and river weeds, while other men on that same day on the other side of the river caught good fish. Clearly it upset him. He talked to her about the light, and being on the wrong bank, and being out of casting practice. 'My casting is gone to hell. It really is damnable.' In his room in the Graan she had noticed a whole shelf of fishing books, well used, and knowing what she knew, she felt terribly sorry for him for being so unlucky and loved him all the more for it, unlike Iggy and Ambrose who almost always caught something, and praised each other's skill as fishermen, all-rounders, exemplars.

In the confession box immediately after, she'd said, 'Bless me, Father, for I have sinned.' Felix looked through the grid at her and said, 'Marion, sweetheart, how are you?' He was the only person who called her 'sweetheart' quite naturally.

'I'm fine, Uncle.'

'Are you going to frighten me with your terrible sins?'

For about ten seconds she didn't know how to answer and then heard him say, 'No place for banter, eh. On you go. How long since your last confession?'

She told him, and then trotted out disobedience, laziness and lies about her eckers being done when they weren't.

'Anything else?'

She took a deep breath and said, 'Sometimes very bad words come into my head.'

'Yes?'

'At Mass and at the Rosary, and I want to shout them out.'

'Words like what?'

She knew fuck, shite, bugger, prick, cunt, bollox, arsehole, and hoor. Tommytoe she knew was only a pet word for a boy's thing and fanny for a girl's. They weren't really bad words. She heard herself say, 'Hoor.'

Felix repeated the word and made it sound like door.

'Do you know what it means?'

'Yes, Uncle.'

'And why do you feel you have to shout out such words?'

'Because I hate Iggy.'

'You do?'

'Yes, Uncle.'

'And why is that now?'

'Because . . . '

'Hate is a much stronger word than whore or any of the other words that come into your head, far stronger. It is a terrible word, and a terrible thing. I don't think you hate Ignatius, Marion. I won't believe it.'

'I do.'

'Why?'

She began and told him everything. When she stopped, she wondered if he'd gone to sleep, so long was the silence.

'Are you asleep, Uncle Felix?'

'Very far from sleep, very far.' Then he asked her, 'Did he penetrate you?'

Not quite certain of the word, she hesitated. He clarified, 'Put his organ into your body.'

'Yes, Uncle.'

She could see him put both hands up to his head. His voice had become odd.

'And did you not cry out?'

'Mammy was always away . . . and he put his hand over my mouth.'

She heard Felix mutter, 'Jesus God. So no one knows.'

'No.'

'Or guesses.'

'Well . . . Bridie was on a night off and Mammy'd gone to a Vincent de Paul meeting. She'd forgot something halfway down the avenue and walked back. There was no car noise. Iggy was in my bed and when he heard the front door he got out and sat on the side of the bed and said, "If you open your mouth, I'll kill you. You're no innocent." When Mammy came in I thought, "I'm all right. She'll know. She'll guess. She'll save me," and she said to Iggy, "What are you doing, Ignatius, in Marion's room?" and he stared back at her and said, "*Talking. What* did you think I was doing?" and she got all flustered and left. But I think she guessed.'

'You must tell her.'

'I can't.'

'You must.'

'She won't believe me, Uncle.'

'Of course she'll believe you.'

'She won't.'

'I believe you, sweetheart. Of course she'll believe you.'

'She won't. I know she won't. Can't you tell her for me, Uncle? She'll believe you.'

'Not from confession I can't. Tell me again at Salmon – this evening – and then I'll tell her.'

He gave her absolution and then for a penance: 'A few Hail Marys for the very troubled Marys in our family. Stay brave, Marion, stay brave,' and blessed her.

Parking her bicycle in the coach house she could see her

mother across the yard. The duckhouse door was open and Wishy Harte was sitting on a stool, looking down at the top of her head. She was on her knees, bathing his feet and cutting his toenails. Her face was very close to his feet because of her single eye.

Wishy looked over and responded to Marion with a slow uplift of his left hand, something between a salute and a blessing.

In the warm kitchen she knew from Bridie's face.

'I don't know, love . . . honestly.'

'You do, Bridie.'

'True as God. All I know is Dermy took him to the dry cleaners.'

'The what!'

'The dry cleaners . . . and your mother was to pick him up later. That's all I know. I didn't ask.'

'Oh God, Bridie . . . the dry cleaners.'

'I know. I know, love.'

'Where *is* he . . . '

'You'll have to ask her yourself.'

From the kitchen window Marion watched her mother crossing the cobbled yard, a towel over her forearm, soap, Dettol, nailclippers and nailscrubber in a copper basin. Like a one-eyed altar server.

As Mary Cantwell approached the outside basement door she could read unmistakable hatred in her daughter's face. She did not want a scene in the kitchen in front of Bridie, sensing her tendency to softness and to side with the child. Without looking at Marion she said, 'Go up to the living room, Marion. I'll be up in a minute.'

When she heard Marion's footsteps going up the sandstone staircase, Bridie said, 'She's not just in a quare state, ma'am, she's in a fury, so she is. I never seen her as wicked cross.'

'I can sense that, Bridie . . . It'll be all right.'

'God and I hope you're right, ma'am.'

As Mary Cantwell followed her daughter up the staircase, Bridie sat heavily in a kitchen chair, fumbling for her Gold Flake cigarettes and matches. She closed the kitchen door, not wanting to hear the altercation.

Marion was looking out the living room window, watching a heron gliding downriver towards the sea, when she heard her mother's voice.

'It's rude to talk with your back to somebody.'

'It's cruel to give things away that don't belong to you and are precious to *other* people. Cruel.'

'You think I'm cruel, Marion? Turn round, child. Answer me.'

Marion turned and looked down at her mother's rubber overshoes. They were standing very close together. She wanted to say, 'I hate your old galoshes and I hate you.'

She said nothing.

'Look at me, dear.'

Mary Cantwell mollified her voice to a pleading note.

'I love you, Marion, as much as any mother can love a daughter. I did what I thought was right and I did it for your sake. Do you believe me?'

'Yes.'

'Well then, can we just get back to normality and . . . '

'I've something to tell you.'

'Very well.'

'It's very bad . . . it's about Iggy. Ignatius. He did things to me in the bath when I was small . . . and times when you were away. He penetrated me between my legs . . . and . . . '

She did not see the open-handed slap, so hard it not only

knocked her down to the parquetry surround but blinded her with pain and tears and took her breath away, blood spilling down on to the blouse of her uniform. She could not see or make sense of the falsetto scream of words, like separate smarting blows, spitting from her mother's mouth till they settled into a trembling voice saying, 'How dare you utter such filth about Ignatius when I know and you know it's a monstrous lie.'

Then all she could half see was the raging mouth because of a blur in her eyes, a nightmare mouth. It must be a nightmare mouth because her mother had never in her life struck her in the face before, and as the ringing in her ears began to ease, she could now see her mother's face twisting in anguish, tears pouring out of the good eye, and then she was kneeling on the floor with her arms around her, sobbing and saying, 'Oh, my lovely lovely daughter, you must be unwell to say such things. Jealousy is bad enough, but to lie like that is a grievous . . . grievous mortal sin. Do you not understand that?'

Marion managed to nod.

'Tell me you're lying, dear, and we won't ever mention it again in our lives. You *were* lying, weren't you? Tell me the truth now, Marion, you were lying just now about your brother, weren't you? Don't be afraid. Tell the truth.'

Marion could feel her head nodding again.

'Oh, I knew it. I knew it absolutely. Thank God and His Virgin Mother you came out clean with the truth. That's all that counts, dear, the truth. Oh my God, my poor child. Let me wipe your poor nose. Oh, look at that dreadful welt on your face. Did I do that to you? Can you forgive me, Marion, my beautiful, beautiful daughter? Can you forgive me?'

And again Marion nodded and thought: 'I will never talk to her in my life again, never . . . ever . . .'

'Oh, thank God, thank God, thank God.' Mary Cantwell had stopped sobbing and was now hugging and kissing and saying, 'A little cup of cocoa, dear, would that be nice? A little cup each. Just the two of us and we'll forget the whole thing. Every last bit of it. It never happened, clean slate, new beginnings. But silly me, what did I do but give all our milk to Wishy Harte . . . poor Wishy, he loves milk. I can send Bridie . . . no, Bridie has ironing to catch up on. I'll . . . '

Mary's face was very close to Marion's. They were almost nose to nose.

'I know. We'll send you out for a drop to Mahoneys. They'll be started evening milking by now. Slip on your coat . . . the two-pint can, your bicycle lamp and you'll be back here in two shakes. Won't you, dear?'

Marion nodded again, got into her school uniform coat, put the small copper can on the spring carrier of the bicycle, her mother following, talking talking talking, touching, hugging, crying, laughing, blowing her nose, and to every direct question her daughter answered with a nod, until finally she got on to her bicycle and set out for Mahoneys of Longfield on the other side of the town. It was the first farm beyond Casement Park. Cantwells had been getting milk from John and Vera Mahoney for over a quarter of a century. Mary Cantwell did not trust pasteurized milk.

There was a hasky wind blowing off the sea as she cycled, her mind unable to cope with what had happened. Or what might yet happen. She would never again speak to her mother – that much was simple and certain. The sky was a darker grey than the grey of the Louis Convent. Even the snowdrops all over God's acre looked cold. The streetlights came on as she approached Casement Park, very few people about.

John and Vera Mahoney were brother and sister in their

fifties. Vera kept homemade fudge for children callers in a
cupboard in the dairy. From August on there were apples as
well. Both were hand-milking when she arrived, shorthorn
cows in a clean whitewashed byre, lit by two long neon lights.
Both greeted her warmly. As Vera dipped with a porringer into
a ten-gallon churn, she said, 'What happened to your face,
Marion?' Unready for the question, she had no answer. Vera
suggested, 'Trouble at school?'

She nodded.

'That big Dominic nun, was it?'

Marion agreed, unthinking.

From under a cow John Mahoney was peering out, a bucket
between his knees. 'Boys adear, if she done that to you, she
should be horsewhipped, so she should.'

And Marion was thinking, why do the answers and the
questions seem so – nothing?

'Do you know what I'm goin' to tell you, John?'

'What is that, Vera?'

'This child is in shock. She's not fit to talk. You'll take the van
out now and you'll run her home, so you will.'

'I will, I will man surely.'

'You'll leave your bike here, Marion. John'll run you home.'

As in a dream she heard herself say emphatically, 'No, no,
no. You're awful good. But no, no. I'll cycle home. I want to
cycle home.'

'You're sure?'

'I'm sure.'

As they watched her leave, John Mahoney said, 'Thon's a
holy fright, whoever done it. We should've kept her, Vera, till
she was at herself.'

'Agin her will? We couldn't. God help her . . . cratur . . .
growin' up can be hard too.'

'Hard as growin' old, Vera.'

'Harder, John, harder.'

There was a flurry or two of snow as she cycled back. Uncle Felix would be there. Would he see her face and know what had happened? 'I can tell him in private, then he would tell her and she wouldn't hit him and scream her head off or howl lies lies at him the way she did at me and she won't say sorry to me 'cause I won't be there to hear her . . . I'll be gone somewhere and she can make cocoa and talk to Iggy for the rest of her life.'

Halfway through Casement Park she saw a familiar shape lying face down in the gutter. With a heart-twist of grief and disbelief, she got off her bicycle, milk spilling from the can on the carrier as she ran towards the shape.

Before she picked him up she knew unmistakably, and when she saw that he was now blind, his woollen eyes cut out, his stomach ripped open spilling fibre, an arm and a leg torn off, it was like a terrible punch in the stomach, so winding her she felt unable to scream out her sorrow and rage. It was directly outside Culligans and Caffreys. There was a dark entry between the two houses. She wanted to knock on Culligans' door and tear their eyes out and shout, 'Give me back his eyes, his arm, his leg.' But she knew they would look at her and at each other and shrug. That would be worse.

There was nobody anywhere about on the street. She went to the dark of the entry and sobbed there till she could sob no longer, talking and whispering to him all the time, kissing his blind sockets, poking back the fibre into his stomach and putting him carefully under her cardigan and then buttoning up her coat, his face resting against her breast so that he would know again that he was loved deeply and truly, and that no one would ever confiscate him again and that no mad dog foul-mouthed Culligans would ever rip and tear at him again . . .

never . . . never . . . because he was the only one in the world who knew what happened that terrible third time when he had been so brave and tried to save her when she was fast asleep. She had held him down then between her legs and Iggy just said, 'What are you at? Let go . . . ' and when she wouldn't, the side of his hand came down on the back of her fingers with such sudden force that she could remember afterwards only the way he was chucked and the sad look on his face as he tumbled and tumbled through the air to land upside down on her dressing table.

One thing was certain, she would not go home. She could go on down this entry to the wicket gate that gave on to a lane that led to an old coach road, grown in now, that would bring her out on this side of the river to the cattleyard and stables that lay outside the grounds and garden of Salmon House.

It was growing darker and colder, the snow had settled and was now falling continuously, lightly, on the street and rooftops and all over the adjoining countryside. Snow made no difference. They could go on blindfolded to where they were going. We'll be happy there, just you and me. Wishy might be sleeping on a hayloft. She might talk to him. She might not. There would be shelter and time to think, to make plans.

The phone rang from the six o'clock news item until midnight; old friends, new friends, forgotten friends and acquaintances, the factory manager and factory employees, people from all over the Island, and almost non-stop the media and gardai. Both Mahoneys had arrived, almost incoherent with worry and guilt. Felix talked to them all. Mary and Bridie were too distraught to talk. It was on every news bulletin till closedown and then again at 6.30 a.m. They knew it off by heart . . . name, age, appearance, last seen, how dressed, the abandoned bicycle and the spilled milk, the green Vauxhall car that a child was seen getting into, Leitrim registration. It turned out to be a Ballyshannon man collecting his daughter from a music lesson. The gardai were no longer following 'a definite line of enquiry'.

All night they prayed, mostly in the bay window of the bedroom looking down on the floodlit grotto; mostly the Rosary. At 5.30 Mary asked Felix to celebrate Mass.

'I will say Mass, Mary, for all of us.' His voice sounded distant, his manner unlike himself. Was he so overwhelmed that he seemed unlistening every time she began to talk? Even more extraordinary, when grief took hold of herself and Bridie, the comfort of his arm went round the maidservant's shoulders. And have I lost that too, no brother comfort, the only pure and perfect love, brother for sister, sister for brother? And then she thought again how she'd told . . . no . . . said, half said I suppose, how I'd lost my head and struck with sudden temper for the first and last time in my life, but deservedly, if you'd been here, Felix, known her moods, her cheek, her lies and this nonsense of a teddy bear in the school toilets and lies about Ignatius, too shameful to repeat. And all that time he was looking past my face, his head nodding or shaking, saying *nothing*, not one single, solitary word of comfort, and when he did look into my poor eye his two were full of accusation, or is that the doubt and terror in my own heart? Is there no comfort so? Here on earth? Or in Heaven? And she prayed in a whisper, Oh God you have left me half-blind and husbandless, will You now take my beautiful, my only daughter from me . . . I don't know what to think or how to pray . . . and Felix is cold and so unlike himself, and God must hate me too, but if He takes her He's hateful and I'll hate Him. Oh, God in Heaven, protect the child, let me die . . . don't take her, she's innocent, I'm the guilty one. Take my body and soul, not my daughter.

Aloud she began to pray, 'Remember, oh most glorious and loving Virgin Mary, that never was it known that anyone who implored Thy assistance, fled to Thy protection or sought Thy intercession was left unaided. Remember, remember, remember.'

The snow had piled high against the back of the grotto, leaving the front almost snowfree. When Felix heard about the Ballyshannon man he phoned the local Superintendent, who came to the house immediately. Alone with him downstairs, Felix said he was fairly certain his niece was in shock. He was not at liberty to say why, but perhaps they should start thinking along other lines.

'Not an abduction?'

'I think not.'

'You're talking about garda divers, Father? Dragging equipment?'

'Yes.'

As light broke slowly they saw Wishy Harte walking like a scarecrow Christ towards the grotto. He sat on a stone seat, took a crust out of his pocket and began to eat. The gardai had questioned him at great length and, Felix thought, with unusual tact. Yes, he had seen her for 'a small time. Then she left.' Again and again they asked what she had said. 'Going home,' he said. 'Going home.' They had searched and double-searched every outbuilding, loft and shed . . . no trace of her whatsoever. There seemed nothing else they could do till daylight, when local volunteer search parties, extra gardai and troops promised from Finner Camp would widen and intensify the search.

'Poor Wishy,' Bridie said.

'You should bring him down something hot,' Mary said.

'We should all go out for air,' Felix said.

They arrived together at the grotto, Bridie carrying a tray with porridge, bread and tea. It was Wishy who spoke first.

'No . . . word . . . of . . . Marion?'

'No, Wishy, no word.'

All three watched him eating his porridge very slowly till he looked up to answer Bridie's question.

'How long was she with you, Wishy?'

'A small time.'

'But how long. A minute? Two? Three? Four?'

He looked away, thinking, and said again, 'A small time, Bridie.'

'And what did she say?'

'Goin' home.'

'That's all?'

'Aye. "Goin' home" she said.'

None of the three dared look at each other or at the blackness of the river flowing between the white banks, aware that Marion could be somewhere down there on her way to the sea. It was too terrible an image to contemplate. Then Mary picked up on something Wishy muttered that sounded like 'Heaven'.

'What did you say?' she asked with such intensity that it startled him.

'I mind now,' he said very slowly. '"I'm goin' home," she said, "to Heaven."'

At first Felix could not understand why his sister and Bridie looked at each other and began screaming and running to the back of the grotto, both scooping armfuls of snow frenziedly from the area directly in front of the playcave. Both saw at the same time the buckled shoes and white stockings. It was Bridie who pulled her out to reveal the reality of rigor mortis, L in a vice grip against her breast like a blind infant. Felix could see at once that nothing looked so utterly dead as his dead niece, nor had he ever heard a cry so inhuman as the cry that seemed to come savagely from his sister's lungs.

Wishy Harte had come round, and was standing, holding his mug of tea, when Mary slapped it suddenly from his hand and began to pummel his shoulders and chest, shrieking, 'Christ, oh Christ, if you said "Heaven" last night, we could have saved her. Fool . . . we could have saved her. Fool . . . fool . . . idiot. Half-wit. You let her die. Oh, Jesus Christ.'

Felix pulled her away roughly, saying loudly, 'Stop that, Mary. He's a simpleton.'

Wishy stood blinking, frightened, his arms up protectively, watching as Mary in frenzy snatched Marion from Bridie, kissing her and whimpering and stumbling with grief to the front of the grotto, where she staggered and slipped against the statue of Bernadette Soubirous. It tipped over, struck a stone seat, and as the head snapped off Mary held her child up to Our Lady of Lourdes and howled: 'How could you let your Son do that to her? Let her die like that. How? How? How? Were you deaf, dumb, blind to her sorrow? Oh, my Marion, Marion, my only beautiful beloved daughter, Marion,' and it was then that Felix covered his face for the first time, his other arm around Bridie. Wishy Harte, arms still outstretched, stared unsmiling from desolate, uncomprehending eyes. The marble face of the Virgin Mary did not respond to Mary Cantwell's anguish. It continued to look down, smiling.

BIOGRAPHICAL NOTES

SHEILA BARRETT was born in Dallas, Texas, and has lived in Co. Dublin since 1969 after moving there with her Irish husband. Some of her short stories have been anthologized and two novels published by Poolbeg.

MICHAEL COLLINS was born in Limerick in 1964. He was educated in Ireland and the USA, and now teaches at the University of Notre Dame in Indiana. He has published a novel and two short story collections, the most recent being *The Feminists Go Swimming* (Phoenix House).

MAXIM CROWLEY is a Dutch-born Irishman, born 1945, with Galway connections. He was educated in England and now lives in Belgium where he works as a writer and translator. He has published some poetry, but 'Writing Cookbooks', his prose début, is the first story of a collection he is working on.

LEO CULLEN was born in Co. Tipperary in 1948 and now lives and works in Dublin. His first stories appeared in the *Irish Press* 'New Irish Writing' page and Blackstaff Press published his first, highly praised collection, *Clocking Ninety on the Road to Cloughjordan.*

JOHN DUNNE lives and teaches in Portlaoise, Co. Laois. He has published short stories and a novel, *Purtock* (Anna Livia Press) and is principal fiction reviewer for *Books Ireland*. His story, 'Eel', won last year's Writers' Week Powers Gold Label Short Story Award.

ANTHONY GLAVIN was born in Boston in 1946. He lived in Co. Donegal from 1974 to 1982, then returned to the USA, and is now back in Ireland where he is Literary Editor of New Island

Books. All his early stories appeared in the *Irish Press* 'New Irish Writing' page, and he has published a collection, *One for Sorrow* (Poolbeg Press).

SHEILA GORMAN was born in Dublin in 1949. She has a Master's Degree in the History of Art and is engaged in a series of art book collaborations with her brother, a painter and printmaker. She has had short stories broadcast by the BBC World Service and RTE.

CLAIRE KEEGAN was born in 1968 and raised on a small farm in Wexford. She studied English Literature and Political Science in New Orleans, and graduated from the University of Wales with a Master's Degree in The Teaching and Practice of Creative Writing. A winner of the William Allingham Short Story Competition, the BBC 'First Bite' Competition for young writers and 1997's inaugural William Trevor Short Story Award, her stories have been broadcast by the BBC and RTE.

EUGENE McCABE was born in Glasgow in 1930 and educated in Dublin and at University College, Cork. His play, *King of the Castle*, won the first Irish Life Drama Award, and his first work of fiction, *Victims*, won the Royal Society of Literature Award. He has also published a collection of short stories, *Heritage*, and a novel, *Death and Nightingales* (Secker & Warburg).

COLUM McCANN was born in Dublin in 1967. In 1990 he won the Sunday Tribune/Hennessy Literary Award, and in 1994 his first short story collection, *Fishing the Sloe-Black River*, was published by Phoenix House to wide critical acclaim. He has also published a novel, *Songdogs*.

MIKE McCORMACK was born in the west of Ireland in 1965 and lives in Galway. His début short story collection, *Getting It in the Head* (Cape) won him the 1996 Rooney Award.

BRYAN MACMAHON was born in Listowel, Co. Kerry, in 1909. Novelist, poet, playwright, short story writer, he has for many years been one of Ireland's most eminent men of letters. In 1972 he was awarded an LL.D. by the National University of Ireland for his services to Irish writing.

PETER McNIFF was born in Manchester in 1937. He had many jobs before coming to Ireland almost forty years ago, where he has worked in journalism and as a producer in RTE. His first stories were published in the *Irish Press* 'New Irish Writing' page and he won a Hennessy Literary Award in 1986.

PADRAIG ROONEY was born in Co. Monaghan in 1956. His first stories appeared in the *Irish Press* 'New Irish Writing' page and in 1982 Poolbeg published his novel, *Oasis*. For many years he has been teaching English in a number of countries, including Algeria, France and Japan.

DERMOT RYAN was born in Dublin in 1970 and studied Natural Science at Trinity College. He has recently worked in the Department of Chemistry, University of California, Irvine. 'The Last Laugh' is his first story to be published.

UNA WOODS was born in Belfast in 1948. Her first work appeared in the *Irish Press* 'New Irish Writing' page and a short story collection, *The Dark Hole Days*, was published by Blackstaff Press. She has contributed poetry and stories to magazines and anthologies in Ireland and the USA.

Unpublished short stories are invited for consideration for future volumes of *Phoenix: Irish Short Stories*. MSS will not be returned unless a stamped, addressed envelope is enclosed. Writers outside the Republic of Ireland are reminded that, in the absence of Irish stamps, return postage must be covered by International Reply Coupons: two coupons for packages up to 100g, three coupons for packages 101g to 250g. All MSS should be addressed to David Marcus, PO Box 4937, Rathmines, Dublin 6, Ireland.